The

*Three sisters find rugged husbands
in the wild Wild West*

Beautiful heiresses Charlotte, Miranda and
Annabel Fairfax have only ever known a life of
luxury in Boston. Now orphaned and in danger,
they are forced to flee, penniless and alone, into
the lawless West. There they discover that people
will risk all for gold and land—but when the sisters
make three very different marriages to
three enigmatic men, they will each find
the most precious treasure of all!

Read Charlotte and Thomas's story in

His Mail-Order Bride

Already available

Miranda and James's story in

The Bride Lottery

Available now

and

Annabel and Clay's story

coming soon!

Author Note

When I wrote *His Mail-Order Bride*, the story of Charlotte Fairfax, who assumes another woman's identity and ends up married to an Arizona Territory homesteader, I did not intend to write three books. However, it seemed natural to follow with the stories of Charlotte's sisters, Miranda and Annabel, and it became a trilogy, The Fairfax Brides.

I wanted the heroines to have distinct personalities, and I wanted to write three different heroes, yet there are common elements throughout the books. All three sisters have to flee from their embittered cousin Gareth, who seeks to control the Fairfax fortune. All three heroes are loners, but in his own way each of them longs for a woman to love, someone to call his own, someone who will make him complete.

The Bride Lottery is the story of the middle sister, Miranda, and James Blackburn, a part-Cheyenne bounty hunter. Brave and bold, Miranda thirsts for adventure and meets new challenges head-on. James has lost everyone he has ever loved and lives in a dark world of death and danger. When fate throws them together, James finds a chance for redemption in Miranda, but the violence of his profession stands in their way.

I hope you'll enjoy reading about Miranda and James. Annabel's story will complete the trilogy. The youngest, clever but emotionally volatile, Annabel has some growing up to do before she can stand up to her older sisters and find her place in the world.

TATIANA MARCH

The Bride Lottery

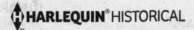

Recycling programs
for this product may
not exist in your area.

ISBN-13: 978-0-373-29927-0

The Bride Lottery

Copyright © 2017 by Tatiana March

This edition published by arrangement with Harlequin Books S.A.

For questions and comments about the quality of this book,
please contact us at CustomerService@Harlequin.com.

Printed in U.S.A.

www.Harlequin.com

Before becoming a novelist, **Tatiana March** tried out various occupations, including being an accountant. Now she loves writing Western historical romance. In the course of her research, Tatiana has been detained by US border guards, had a skirmish with the Mexican army and stumbled upon a rattlesnake. This has not diminished her determination to create authentic settings for her stories.

Books by Tatiana March

Harlequin Historical

The Fairfax Brides
His Mail-Order Bride
The Bride Lottery

Harlequin Historical *Undone!* eBooks
The Virgin's Debt
Submit to the Warrior
Surrender to the Knight
The Drifter's Bride

Visit the Author Profile page at Harlequin.com.

Chapter One

Boston, Massachusetts, July 1889

The night had fallen. In the darkness of her bedroom at Merlin's Leap, Miranda Fairfax held up a single candle. The flickering light fell on the pale features of her younger sister, Annabel. "I don't like leaving you behind, Scrappy." Miranda used the childhood nickname reserved for moments of tenderness. "Cousin Gareth could set his sights on you next."

"No." Annabel spoke calmly, even though fear lurked in her amber eyes. "He might have gotten away with declaring Charlotte dead but to do the same with you would raise suspicion. One dead sister is feasible. Two dead sisters would trigger an alarm. I'll be safe, even after you've gone."

Miranda agreed, and yet the thought of leaving Annabel alone at Merlin's Leap filled her with dread. The gray stone mansion by the ocean just north of Boston had been a happy home, until four years ago, when their parents died in a boating accident. Since then, the sisters had been at the mercy of their Cousin Gareth, who had come to live with them and was determined to get his hands on the Fairfax fortune.

Charlotte had been the heiress, and Cousin Gareth had attempted to force her into marriage. After Charlotte ran away two months ago, Cousin Gareth had claimed the body of some unknown woman as her. With Charlotte officially dead, Miranda stood to inherit, and now Gareth's efforts to bring about a marriage were focused on her, forcing her to flee.

"Write to Charlotte and post the letter as soon as you can," Miranda reminded Annabel. "She needs to understand what Gareth has done. When she turns twenty-five next May and gains access to Papa's money, she'll need to prove she is alive before she can claim her inheritance."

"I'll write and find some way to mail the letter." Annabel's voice quivered. "Just think…if we hadn't agreed on a code word for Charlotte to get a message to us, we might believe she is dead, instead of hiding in the Arizona Territory, pretending to be some homesteader's mail-order bride."

Miranda lifted the candle higher. "We would have known she's alive from the telegram you retrieved after Cousin Gareth tossed it in the fireplace. The way the constables described the dead woman found on the train made it clear it couldn't be Charlotte."

"But without Charlotte's message we would have feared the worst," Annabel suggested.

"I know." Miranda's tone was bleak. "We'll keep the same code word. Once I'm safe, I'll write to Merlin's Leap as Emily Bickerstaff. Cousin Gareth will intercept the letter, but with any luck he'll share the contents with you."

"Make it a letter of condolence," Annabel suggested. "Emily was Charlotte's friend. One could assume she might have heard about Charlotte's passing and would write to the surviving sisters, to express her sympathies."

Miranda forced a smile. "Good idea."

Despite being sensitive and prone to weeping, Annabel was the cleverest of them. The best way to calm her nerves was to get her focused on some practical dilemma. The middle sister at twenty-two, Miranda knew she was considered the brave one. She suspected the others had no idea how much her feisty front was bravado.

In the parlor, the clock chimed midnight.

"It's time." Miranda blew out the candle and set it down on the rosewood bureau. Solid darkness fell over the room. She would have to make her way downstairs without the benefit of light, for even at this hour the servants might be spying on them.

"Good luck." Annabel's tearful voice rose in the darkness. Slim arms closed around Miranda in a trembling hug. Miranda returned the embrace. One more gesture of sisterly love. One more moment of comfort before she faced the unknown. She wanted to cry but suppressed the need. She was the strong one. She had to be.

Gently, Miranda eased away from her sister's clinging hold. "Check the escape route."

Annabel fumbled over to the window, parted the thick velvet drapes. A thin ray of silvery light spilled into the room. Craning her neck, Annabel studied the sky through the glass. "The clouds are thinning. There'll be moonlight."

"Damn," Miranda muttered. Normally she avoided swearwords, but tonight she'd employ any means to bolster her courage. Anger might hasten her footsteps as she raced down the gravel path and across the lawns into the shelter of the forest.

She wore a black gown and bonnet, a mourning outfit from when their parents died. The dark clothes would blend into the shadows. And if she pretended to be a widow, it might make things easier during the journey. Men might be less likely to bother a woman grieving for a recently departed husband.

For men *would* bother her, Miranda knew. She had beauty that attracted them. Her sisters had complained about it often enough, saying it was unfair how she had inherited the best features in the family—their father's fair hair and blue eyes, their mother's slender height and patrician elegance.

Miranda had never cared about her looks before. But now she did. They would be a nuisance for a lone female traveling out to the lawless West. To rebuff unwanted advances, she would have to rely on the rest of her heritage, for she had also inherited Papa's fiery temper that flared up like a firecracker and fizzled out again just as quickly, leaving her to regret things said or done in a moment of anger.

"Hold the curtains ajar to let in the moonlight," Miranda instructed her sister.

"Promise you'll write the instant you get there," Annabel pleaded. "And send money."

"I'll write." Miranda sighed in the shadows. "And I'll try to send money."

Promises were cheap, and that's all she could afford right now. To help Charlotte escape, she'd been able to steal a gold coin, but twenty dollars could not have taken Charlotte very far. To have ended up in the Arizona Territory she must have traveled without a ticket on the train.

After discovering the theft, Cousin Gareth had taken care not to leave money lying around in his pockets. Miranda only had two dollars and a quarter, and their mother's ruby-and-diamond brooch she'd managed to stash away. Like Charlotte, she would have to take her chances, travel on the train without paying her fare.

Annabel claimed to be too timid for such brazen acts and had chosen to stay behind. When Miranda reached Gold Crossing, she'd find Charlotte, and together they would come up with a way to send money for their youngest sister to join them.

One more time, Miranda went over the plan with Annabel. "Keep a lookout as I go downstairs. Remember, if lights come on in the house, you'll need to create a diversion. Start screaming. Pretend there is an intruder. Get the servants to search the rooms. Keep them indoors, to minimize the chances they might spot me as I make my dash for freedom."

Annabel nodded, long dark hair gleaming in the moonlight. "I'm not totally useless." Irritation sharpened her tone. "Screaming is my specialty."

"That's the spirit, Scrappy," Miranda said and took a deep breath. "Here I go."

She pulled the door open, slipped out without a sound. Like a silent wraith, she moved through the house. She'd been practicing, taking the stairs with her eyes closed while the servants were busy with their chores. Now her diligence paid rewards. One, two, three...

Miranda counted out the twenty-seven steps down to the hall, sliding her hand along the polished mahogany balustrade. She kept her eyes open, letting them become adjusted to the lack of light. It would be impossible to see anything in the house, but it might help her when she stepped out into the moonlight.

In the hall, Miranda dragged her feet, in case there was a boot or an umbrella carelessly flung about. She fumbled at the air until her fingers tangled in the fronds of the big potted palm. Three steps to the right. Her outreached hand met the carved timber panel of the front door, homed in on the iron lock.

Slowly, slowly, she twisted it open. *Click.*

The sound broke the silence, as loud as a gunshot in her ears. Miranda flinched, waited a few seconds. When the house remained quiet, she eased the door open, stepped across the threshold, pushed the door shut behind her and leaned back against it, applying pressure until the lock clicked again.

Ahead of her, the arrow-straight gravel drive and the lawns flanking it loomed dark in the moonlight, the colors flattened to black and gray. Night air enveloped her, soft and warm. It was a small consolation she was making her escape in July instead of the winter.

Gravel crunched beneath her feet as she set off at a cautious run along the drive. After a dozen paces, she turned left, across the lawn. Scents of lavender and roses drifted over from the flowerbeds. Beyond the gardens, Miranda could hear the dull roar of the ocean. Nothing else disturbed the quiet. No sounds of alarm from the house.

But what was that? Another crunch of gravel? Was someone following her?

Like a hunted animal, Miranda froze on the lawn, halfway between the drive and the shelter of the forest. *Listen! Listen!* She swallowed, a labored movement of her fear-dry throat. For a few seconds, she waited, poised in utter stillness.

Nothing but the steady crashing of the ocean against the cliffs. She must have been mistaken about the sound of footsteps. Bursting back into motion, Miranda darted into the cover of the trees. She had hidden a bag there, smuggling out the contents bit by bit, pretending to be coming out to admire a goldfinch that nested in the big maple by the edge of the forest.

First step completed. She was clear of the house. Next, she'd have to walk four miles to the railroad station in Boston, where she'd sell her mother's ruby-and-diamond brooch and use the proceeds to buy a train ticket to New York City. From there on she would have to find her way to Gold Crossing, Arizona Territory. Without money. Without the protection of an escort.

But Charlotte had managed it, and so could she.

Her bag was a soft canvas pouch, sewn in secret from a piece of sailcloth. Miranda hoisted it from its hiding place, dusted off the moss and dried leaves and flung the bag over her shoulder.

The thick forest canopy blocked out the moonlight, and she fumbled her way through the oaks and maples, arms held out, feeling her way forward like a blind man. Branches swiped across her face. Twigs snapped beneath her feet.

Her footsteps seemed to have an echo. Twice, Miranda paused, suspecting she might have heard the stealthy sounds of someone following. Both times, the crashing and thudding and the snapping of twigs ceased as soon as she stopped moving.

It must be her imagination, Miranda decided. She had made her escape. She was on her way to join Charlotte in the rough, uncivilized West.

To her surprise, new sensations stirred inside her. A wildness. A sense of adventure. All her life, she'd felt stifled by the constraints that fell upon a young woman in polite society. Now those constraints were gone. She could be whatever she wanted to be.

Dawn came. Woken by birdsong, Miranda got up from the grassy knoll where she had settled for a few hours of sleep, so she could walk to Boston in daylight. By now, her escape might have been noticed. The footmen and grooms might be looking for her, and it remained imperative to avoid capture.

She brushed twigs and bits of grass from her hair and clothing, then set off walking along the forest path, her body stiff from the rough night, her stomach growling with hunger, her skin itchy beneath the dew-damp gown of black bombazine. As the sun climbed higher, the air grew cloying with heat.

A loud crash sounded ahead, followed by alarmed voices. A public road skirted the edge of the forest. Miranda crept closer and peered between the trees.

A fine carriage, drawn by a matching team of four, had come to a halt. Silver gleamed on the harnesses. A burly coachman in green livery sat high up on the bench. Miranda craned forward for a better view. The coach was listing to one side, a wheel loose from its bearings.

The coachman climbed down from his perch. "Mrs. Summerton?" he bellowed. "Are ye all right?"

"I am fine, Atkins." The reply came in a calm, refined voice.

Miranda waited. Atkins went to the coach door, yanked it open. He held out not one hand, but both. Puzzled by the boldness of the gesture, Miranda watched, got an explanation as the coachman lifted out a little girl with blond ringlets and a frilly dress.

He repeated the action. Again. And again. Four little girls, as alike as peas in a pod. Next, a beautiful woman emerged. She was fair-haired, dressed in an elegant blue gown tailored to accommodate her rounded belly. She looked no more than twenty-five.

"Thank you, Atkins." The woman glanced around. "Where is Jason?"

"The footman ran ahead for help."

Frowning, the woman surveyed the listing conveyance. "How long before we can get going again?"

"Depends on how long it takes to round up help. Once we have enough men to lift up the carriage, it will only take a moment to secure the wheel."

One of the little girls tugged at the woman's skirts.

"Can we play, Mama?" The little imp, perhaps seven or eight, gestured at the mud on the roadside.

"But darling, you'll get dirty, and we are going to a birthday party in Boston." The woman glanced up at the rising sun and wiped her brow with a lace handkerchief.

The four little girls swarmed around her. "Can we play, Mama? Can we play?"

Atkins lifted a wooden stool out of the carriage and propped it on the ground. Mrs. Summerton sank gratefully onto it and gave her forehead another pat with the cloth. Miranda could feel exhaustion coming off the woman in waves.

The little girls darted around their mother, giggling and shoving, as bouncy as rubber balls. The woman closed her eyes. Her body swooned on the stool. The coachman put out a hand to steady her.

Taking pity on the pregnant mother, Miranda stepped out from the cover of the forest. She picked up a smooth pebble from the ground, wiped it clean against her canvas bag and walked up to the group.

"I'm a magician," she said. "The fairies in the forest sent me to amuse you."

Miranda held out both palms, tossed the pebble between them and fluttered her hands about, the way Cousin Gareth had taught her long ago, before he went to seed and became an enemy. She closed both fists and held them out. "Which hand is the stone in?"

"That one! That one!"

Mrs. Summerton opened her eyes and observed the scene in silence. Glancing over to Atkins, she appeared reassured by the man's presence. Big and burly, he had the means to restrain any threat from a lunatic.

Miranda spoke, allowing her education to show. "My name is…" her eyes strayed toward the trees from which she had emerged "…Mrs. Woods." She disliked lying, but it made no sense to leave a trail for Cousin Gareth to follow.

"I was taking a stroll in the forest," she went on. "I needed a moment of privacy after my husband's funeral. I am on my way to back to New York City, but the train can wait. I thought you might benefit from assistance to entertain your young ones."

Miranda opened her right fist. Empty. The left fist. Empty. She tugged at the nearest blond pigtail, shook the pebble out of it. The little girls jumped up and down, screaming in delight.

Mrs. Summerton broke into a smile of relief. "Thank you. If there ever was an angel sent from heaven, you must be it." She pointed at the little girls. "Two sets of twins. Can you believe it?" She rubbed her belly. "This one will be a boy. My husband is convinced."

While they waited for help to arrive, Miranda kept the four little girls occupied, allowing their mother a moment of peace. Soon a young freckle-faced footman brought a crowd from the public house down the road and they hoisted up the carriage for the coachman to secure the wheel.

"Would you like to ride to Boston with us?" Mrs. Summerton asked.

It would save time and keep her out of sight. And she could hear the plea in the woman's voice. Miranda accepted the offer. By the time they reached the city, Miranda had adjusted her ideas about the joys of motherhood. She alighted at the railroad station, with another four dollars in her pocket and an offer of a position as a governess if she ever needed one. The mere thought made Miranda shudder. She hurried away, the voices of the four little hoydens ringing in her ears.

Chapter Two

The money Miranda had earned entertaining the boisterous Summerton children allowed her to buy a ticket on the train to New York City, which avoided having to sell Mama's brooch in Boston where someone might have recognized her.

On the train, she kept her face averted, her bonnet pulled low. An express service covered the journey in six hours, but to save money Miranda took a slow train that made frequent stops. By the time they arrived in New York City, darkness had fallen.

Once the passengers had dispersed in their carriages and hansom cabs, only creatures of the night remained—gaudily dressed women past their prime, accosted by men willing to benefit from their favors. The evening cool did little to clear the sultry air thick with coal smoke.

Appalled at the squalor, Miranda found a hidden corner behind an empty newspaper stand and huddled there for the night. All thoughts of finding a jeweler to sell Mama's brooch vanished. She hated the city and could not wait to leave. In the morning, as the station grew busy again, she snuck on board the first westbound train.

Traveling without a ticket proved easier than Miranda had expected. Days turned into nights and nights into days. The train made frequent stops, in small towns and at water towers, and she used them to move from car to car, to minimize the chances of getting caught.

Twice, she charmed a conductor into believing she'd misplaced her ticket. Another conductor proved immune to feminine allure, and Miranda burst into tears, pretending to be too distraught by the loss of her husband to produce her documents.

Despite her success in evading exposure, an uneasy feeling prickled at the back of her neck. A sensation of being watched. Miranda told herself it was only natural. She had become a lawbreaker, and the guilty conscience put her nerves on edge.

Through the window, fields and meadows gave way to run-down tenements and warehouses. The glass-paneled door at the end of the car swung open. The conductor—the small, potbellied man who had been immune to her charms—strutted up the aisle.

"Chicago!" he yelled. "Next stop Chicago. Everyone change. Southern Pacific Railroad to St. Louis and all towns south. Union Pacific Railroad to all towns west."

Miranda gathered up her sailcloth bag. To economize, she'd avoided the dining car, instead taking the opportunity to buy bread and cheese and stuffed pies from platform vendors. Even then, she had less than a dollar left.

She followed the stream of passengers down the metal steps. The platform teemed with life. Between a farmer with a pushcart full of potatoes and a donkey with two heaped panniers, Miranda glimpsed a man—and felt a blow in her gut.

Her frantic eyes took in the fawn trousers, the peacock blue coat. The tall hat, the silver-topped walking stick. Light brown hair and long sideburns. Pale skin and the sullen features of a man who drank too much, gambled too much and seemed to harbor a bitter grudge against life.

It couldn't be. But it was. Cousin Gareth.

He must be following her. And whatever she did, she must not lead him to Charlotte. Miranda spun around and set off running in the opposite direction. She knocked into the pushcart, sent a flurry of potatoes rolling over the platform. The farmer burst into an angry bellow. Passengers tripped over the spill, crying out complaints. Miranda dipped and darted through the throng, bumping into people as she hurtled along.

A train was pulling away. With an extra spurt of speed, Miranda raced after it, her boot heels clicking a frantic beat against the concrete platform. The whistle blew. A cloud of steam billowed from the engine. The train left the station but Miranda kept up her chase, leaping down to the tracks. Her canvas pouch fell off her shoulder. Not pausing to pick it up, she forced her legs to move faster.

Lungs bursting, arms pumping at her sides, skirts flapping around her feet, she hurtled along. She was gaining on the train, the gap shrinking. Five yards. Four. Three. Another merry whistle, and the train clattered onto another set of rails, slowing down for an instant while the wheels negotiated the junction.

With a desperate burst of effort, Miranda threw herself forward and grabbed the handrail around the small platform at the end of the last car. Her feet lost contact with the ground. Grimly, she hung on, the toes of her button-up boots bouncing against the timber sleepers, her fingers locked in a death grip around the iron handrail.

The train increased its speed. Pain tore at Miranda's arms. Inch by inch, she dragged herself upward, her body like a coiled spring, her muscles vibrating with the effort. A violent shaking seized her. She almost lost her grip but managed to swing one foot up on the iron steps. Another foot. With a final jerk of her arms and shoulders, Miranda flung herself onto the platform and collapsed there, panting for breath, exhaustion and relief coursing through her.

When finally her senses sprang back to life, Miranda looked up. She could see the Chicago skyline disappearing off into the distance. Beneath her, the train rocked with a steady motion. The sun baked down on her black clothing, adding to the perspiration that coated her skin. She reached up one hand, found her bonnet dangling by its ribbons.

Slowly, she scrambled to her feet, her fingers clutching the handrail. She tried the handle on the door at the end of the car. Unlocked. Miranda went through. It was the mail car, with boxes and parcels stacked on both sides of the narrow passageway. A thin man in a white shirt with sleeve garters was sorting letters into slots on a wooden rack.

He stared at her. "Where did you come from?"

Miranda gave him a shaky smile. "I almost missed the train."

He puffed out his narrow chest with an air of authority common to petty bureaucrats all over the world. "You can't stay here," he said. "This car is for authorized personnel only."

Miranda sank onto a wooden crate. She could see the man wanted to tell her sitting on mail items was against the rules. She peered up at him from between her lashes. "May I rest here for a moment?" she pleaded. "I promise to move into another car at the first stop."

The man bristled but appeared mollified. He resumed sorting letters into the wooden pigeonholes mounted on the wall. "How far are you going?" he asked. "Are you going all the way to San Francisco?"

"No. I'm going to the Arizona Territory."

The man grinned with the smug satisfaction of someone who possesses superior knowledge and intends to gloat with it. "In that case, you're on the wrong train," he replied with thinly disguised glee. "This is a Union Pacific Railroad express service to San Francisco and all towns west."

Miranda had never known hunger could cause such pain, as if tiny teeth were gnawing at her insides. She had lost the last of her money with her bag, and for three days she had eaten nothing but leftovers from meal trays waiting for collection outside the compartments in the first-class Pullman car.

At least she was safe from Cousin Gareth, for it would be impossible for him to catch up the express service. If she continued to San Francisco, she could take a south-bound train to the Arizona Territory. The roundabout journey added to the distance, but she would eventually get to Gold Crossing—if she didn't die of starvation first.

Already, the train had chugged through Iowa and Nebraska, where the endless prairie landscape could almost make one believe the world might be flat after all. So far, Miranda had been successful in dodging conductors, but the most recent one—a big, rawboned man with a bushy moustache—had his eye on her, she could tell.

At the next stop, Miranda switched to a second-class car and spent a moment inside the convenience, unstitching the ruby-and-diamond brooch sewn into her petticoats. Then she walked up and down the aisle, assessing the female passengers.

She chose a buxom woman who sat by herself, dressed in tight corsets and a gaudy purple gown. No respectable woman would buy anything from a stranger on a train, but this female possessed the right mix of expensive clothing and a common touch.

Miranda slipped into the empty seat on the padded

bench beside her quarry. She clamped down on her scruples and opened her fist to display the lure of the jewel. "Excuse me for approaching you so boldly, but I am in urgent need of funds. I have a family heirloom I wish to sell. I thought perhaps you might be interested." She gestured at the woman's purple gown. "The rubies would match your dress."

The woman peered down at the brooch, then returned her attention to Miranda. There was no mistaking the greed that flashed in her eyes. "What's your name, darling?" The words came in a coarse accent, the voice raspy with whiskey and tobacco. The heavy scent of perfume failed to mask the stale, unwashed smell.

"I am Miss Fai— Mrs. Woods."

Plump fingers fumbled at Miranda's palm as the woman picked up the brooch. She inspected the jewel carefully. "It is real gold," Miranda hurried to reassure her. "And the stones are genuine diamonds and rubies."

"It says Fairfax here. I thought you said your name's Woods." The woman pointed at the engraving. *To my darling wife. H. Fairfax.*

Miranda swallowed. She was leaving a trail, but it could not be helped. "The brooch belonged to my mother," she explained. "Woods is my married name."

"I see." The woman spent another moment examining the brooch. Then, as if losing interest, she dropped the jewel back in Miranda's palm. "No, thank you." She made a flapping motion with her hand, ushering the intrusion away.

Baffled, Miranda rose to her feet. She could see the shine of covetousness in the woman's eyes, could see all her chins wobble with the eagerness to possess, and yet the matron had not even asked for the price.

"Thirty dollars," Miranda said. "It's worth three times as much."

Ignoring her, the woman turned to look out the window. Miranda walked away, blinking back tears of defeat. She settled on an empty bench and rested her head against the wall, in the hope that sleep might offer a moment of respite from the gnawing hunger.

It seemed only seconds later the conductor was shaking her awake. It was the big, rawboned man with a bushy moustache, and he was scowling down at her. Behind him, the woman in a purple gown was standing in the aisle, gripping the seatbacks for support, her ample frame wobbling with the motion of the train.

"Search her," the matron demanded. "She stole my brooch."

The conductor's large hand clamped around Miranda's arm. "Stand up."

"She came and sat beside me," the woman went on. "All friendly like. Just plopped down next to me and started talking. I knew something was wrong right away. A respectable person does not approach strangers like that. It took me no time to realize she'd walked off with my ruby-and-diamond brooch."

"Empty your pockets," the conductor told her.

Not a request, with a polite *miss* or *ma'am* at the end of it. An order, harshly spoken, the sharp tone already classifying her as a criminal.

Anger flared in Miranda, fizzled out again. Hunger, fatigue, the hopelessness of her situation, all succeeded in curbing an outburst of temper where common sense might have failed in the past. She could see the lecherous glint in the man's eyes. With a shudder Miranda realized that if she resisted the order, he might use her refusal as an opportunity to insist on a bodily search.

Not voicing a single word of protest, Miranda reached into the pocket on her gown, pulled out her mother's brooch and displayed it in her palm.

"It has an engraving," the matron said. "'To my darling wife. H. Fairfax.' Fairfax was my mother's name. Nearly a hundred dollars it is worth. Real diamonds and rubies."

The conductor put his hand out. "Let's see your ticket."

Miranda could hear the note of triumph in his voice. The man knew she didn't have a ticket. Instinct told her he'd been harboring his own plans to benefit from her plight. If the woman hadn't come up with her brazen scheme to acquire the brooch without paying for it, the conductor would have cornered her into an empty compartment, demanding intimate favors in exchange for a free passage.

The flare of anger finally won. "Here," Miranda said. "Take it."

She flung the brooch at the matron, hitting her squarely on the nose. The woman screamed, pretended to collapse into a swoon, but the real purpose of her fainting fit was to duck down and snatch up the brooch. She managed the motion with surprising agility for someone so amply built. The jewel safely clasped in her fist, she scurried back down the aisle to her own seat.

The conductor pulled out a pair of handcuffs from a pocket on his uniform. Forcing Miranda's wrists together, he slapped the irons on her. "Next stop is Fort Rock, Wyoming. I'll hand you over to the town marshal. He'll hold you until you've paid the fine. One hundred dollars."

One hundred dollars. Miranda closed her eyes as she felt the cold steel bite into her skin. There was no way she could raise such a sum. The man might as well be asking her for the Crown Jewels of the British monarchy, and the treasure of the Spanish Crown on top of it.

Chapter Three

The marshal's office was in the small concrete jailhouse next to the station. Miranda didn't resist when the conductor escorted her over during the fifteen-minute stop. She could feel people staring at her, on the platform, from the train windows. She didn't care. She was too hungry. Too tired. Too defeated. Let them lock her up. At least they'd have to feed her, unless they wanted a dead woman in their jail.

"Marshal! Bringing in a prisoner!" the conductor bellowed, relishing his role as a lawman. He was holding on to the chain that linked the cuffs, leading her behind him like a dog.

Her temper rising once more, Miranda jerked free from his grasp. The conductor grinned. He fell back a step and gave her a shove on the buttocks, nothing but a poorly disguised grope. Miranda tried to kick him on the shins but almost stumbled and ended up lurching headlong across the jailhouse threshold.

Cool air greeted her. Built like a square block with thick concrete walls, the jail only had one tiny window high up in the rear of the single cell. The front office contained a desk and two chairs, both of them occupied.

The cell behind the iron bars was twice as big and empty. Miranda eyed the narrow cot with longing.

"What is this?" The marshal straightened in the wooden chair behind the desk. He was young, barely in his thirties. Dressed in a dark suit, with neatly cut sandy hair and even features, he looked more like a merchant than a man who spent his life fighting crime. If it hadn't been for the tin star on his chest and a gun in a holster at his hip, Miranda would never have guessed his profession.

"Caught her stealing on the train and traveling without a ticket."

Miranda listened in silence as the conductor enumerated her transgressions. She didn't even try to argue her case. She *was* guilty of traveling without a ticket, and no one would believe her if she protested her innocence to the theft of the brooch.

The marshal pulled open a desk drawer, counted out a hundred dollars and demanded a receipt. The conductor pocketed the money and removed the handcuffs. He raked one more lascivious look over Miranda before hurrying back to the train.

Miranda rubbed her wrists. Her ears perked up when the marshal turned to his teenage deputy, who was loitering in the second chair, balancing on two legs against the unpainted cement wall.

"Fetch Lucille," the marshal said. "Tell her I have one for her."

The chair crashed down to four legs. The innocent blue eyes of the fresh-faced deputy snapped wide. "Lucille?" His gaze shuttled to Miranda. "But this one looks like a lady…"

"She's a lawbreaker who owes the town a hundred dollars." The marshal made a shooing motion with one hand while using his other hand to lock the receipt in the desk drawer.

The young deputy—in Miranda's opinion his posterior should still be wearing out a school desk—loped off. The marshal turned to face her. He eyed her up and down. Now that she thought of it, his short, straight nose and wide mouth resembled those of his teenage deputy. Father and son, Miranda guessed, which made the lawman older than she'd assumed at first glance.

The marshal lifted his brows at her. "Hungry?"

Miranda nodded. He gestured for her to sit down in the chair his son had vacated and reached for a parcel in a linen napkin on the desk. Unwrapping a slice of crusty pie, he dumped it on a tin plate and carried the plate over to her. Perched on the edge of the chair, Miranda closed her eyes and took a deep inhale. Oh, the heavenly smell of it!

"My wife bakes the best pies in town," the marshal said.

Miranda blinked her eyes open and gave the food one more appraising glance before she took a big bite. Remembering her manners, she muttered a thank-you through the mouthful. She crammed in another bite. The marshal reached over and tried to take the plate away from her. Miranda craned forward in the seat and nearly toppled over, her fingers clinging to the plate, as if glued to it. The marshal tore the plate free from her grasp.

"If you've been starving, you got to eat slowly."

He stood in front of her and waited for her to chew and swallow before he allowed her another bite. Miranda had barely finished devouring every morsel when two sets of footsteps rang outside. A shadow blocked the sunlight through the open doorway.

Miranda squinted. Lucille—for it could be none other—evidently shared the fashion sense of the lady who had stolen her brooch. Scarlet gown, tight corset, rouged cheeks, red hair in an elaborate twist, all topped with a frilly pink parasol.

Lucille moved inside, taking up most of the space. She snapped her parasol shut, ran an assessing gaze over Miranda, then glanced over her shoulder at the marshal.

"How much?"

"A hundred."

"I can do that." Lucille pointed with her parasol, almost poking Miranda in the gut. "Let's go, sweetheart."

Miranda shrank back in the hard wooden seat. "I can't—"

The marshal cut her short with an ushering motion. "Go," he told her. "I have a bounty hunter with four bank robbers arriving before nightfall. If you stay, you'll have to share the cell with them. Wouldn't wager much for your chances."

Lucille smiled and pointed to the open doorway with her parasol.

"I'm not a prostitute," Miranda said through gritted teeth, but she followed the woman, blinking when they emerged into the bright sunlight.

The train was just leaving, the whistle blowing, steam rising in the air. In the window, the matron in purple was watching. Miranda's hands fisted. The cow! She was wearing Mama's brooch on her bulky chest! Miranda looked about for something to throw, but there was nothing suitable in sight. A cart full of potatoes would have served her well now.

The tip of the parasol poked into her ribs. "Come along, darling."

Miranda turned back to Lucille. "I am not going to work for you."

Lucille's eyes narrowed. "Until I've made a hundred dollars from you, you'll do exactly what I tell you. If I tell you to jump, you ask how high. If I tell you to run, you ask how fast. If I tell you to take your clothes off, you ask if I want it quick or slow. Do you understand?"

The parasol plunged into Miranda's ribs, hard enough to bruise. Miranda nodded. She was getting the impression that Lucille's parasol had no more to do with blocking out the sun than Cousin Gareth's silver-topped cane had to do with assisting walking. They were weapons, pure and simple.

She followed Lucille down the street. Fort Rock was a decent-size town, with a central row of timber buildings with false fronts that made them look taller. There were two side streets, both flanked with unpainted log cabins. They were in Wyoming now, Miranda recalled. A cool breeze stirred the air and a line of snowcapped mountains rose on the horizon.

They entered a saloon through the swinging doors. Four young women in various stages of undress lolled about on padded chairs. Two were smoking and playing cards. A petite blonde was knitting what appeared to be an endless scarf, and a dark-skinned girl was reading aloud from a book that sounded like a penny dreadful.

The sting of smoke sent Miranda into a coughing fit. She flapped a hand in front of her face to disperse the thick cloud that saturated the air.

"Oh, we have a delicate one here," one of the smoking girls said. Tall and thin, with dark hair and a sullen expression, she blew out another plume of smoke.

"Not fresh meat again," another one drawled. "Business is slow as it is."

"She's not competition." Lucille used her parasol to prod Miranda into the center of the room. "Girls, what do we do when business is slack?"

The black girl who'd been reading grinned. "We run a promotion."

Lucille nodded, pointed at Miranda with her parasol.

"This one owes me a hundred dollars. But with business so slow, it's not worth the effort to break in a new girl. We'll do something to bring in the decent men. The ones who might drink and gamble but won't pay for a woman unless they get to keep her."

Two of the girls burst into a loud cheer. A shiver ran over Miranda. It sounded like they were talking about selling her into slavery. She gathered her courage. Papa had defeated a mutiny on one of his ships and he'd drilled it into his daughters never to show fear.

She feigned a bored tone. "May I ask, what is this *promotion* you're planning?"

"Well, a bride lottery, of course," Lucille replied.

"And you'll be the prize," added the knitting blonde.

Miranda had to admit Lucille was an astute businesswoman. The madam instructed the girls to set up a low platform by the window near the entrance. A hooked rug and a rocking chair went on the platform, and Miranda's task was to sit in the rocking chair.

All day. All evening.

Instead of her black mourning gown, she wore a soft wool dress in pale blue, modest in cut, with lace ruffles at the collar and cuffs. Her hair was twisted into an elegant upsweep, the formal look softened by a few strands left loose to flutter around her face.

During the day, sunshine through the window gilded her, like an impressionist painting. In the evenings, an oil lamp burned on the small table beside her. She was allowed to pass the time sewing or reading. Sometimes, the tabby cat that lived on kitchen scraps would come in and sit on her lap, and she'd stroke the animal, drawing comfort from the gentle vibration of its contented purring.

Next to this scene of domestic harmony, separated

with a hemp rope from the saloon floor, the way a valuable exhibit might be guarded in a museum, stood a sign.

Bride Lottery
Tickets $10
One ticket per person only

The rule to limit the number of entries had been subject to much debate among Lucille's girls. In the end they had agreed that the banker, Stuart Hooperman, was known to be eager to acquire a wife. If he bought a dozen tickets, it would reduce the odds for anyone else, which might dampen wider interest.

During the day, most of the men who came into the saloon were polite enough not to stare. Instead, they stole covert glances at her while they sipped their drinks or ate their meals. At night, when the whiskey flowed, some grew bolder and crowded by the rope, ogling at her, whispering comments to each other.

Miranda blocked them all out of her mind. Growing up with servants, she had developed the skill of ignoring their obtrusive presence, and now she put that skill to use. Mostly, her thoughts dwelled on her sisters, and on Cousin Gareth.

Was he still pursuing her, or had he given up and returned to Merlin's Leap? Or had he figured out the message in Charlotte's letter and was on his way to Gold Crossing? How was Annabel faring alone at Merlin's Leap? Had she managed to write to Charlotte, alerting their eldest sister that she was presumed dead?

"Who do you want to win?" asked Shanna, the black girl, as she drained whiskey from the barrels behind the counter, getting ready for the evening. She was the most talkative of the girls, the most eager to find out about Miranda's past.

Miranda lowered the canvas fabric she was sewing. In truth, she had not allowed her thoughts to dwell on the prospect of marriage. When she was not thinking of her sisters, her mind was occupied with escape plans. Lucille, of course, had seen right through her, had pointed out the marshal kept an eye on the trains, Miranda would die in the wilderness if she tried to flee on foot, and anyone who stole a horse was hanged, female or not.

"Makes no difference to me who wins," Miranda replied.

Shanna straightened behind the counter. She was solidly built, with big breasts and wide hips, yet she moved with grace. Her face was a perfect oval, her eyes large and almond shaped. She would have been a beauty, had it not been for the jagged scar at the corner of her mouth and two missing front teeth.

"Trust me, it makes a difference." Shanna touched her scar. "Some husbands are worse than others." For a second, she stilled, in the grip of some unpleasant memories. Then, with a brusque, efficient gesture, she slammed the bottles of watered-down whiskey on the counter and hurried off into the kitchen.

Miranda stared after her. For a moment, the cloak of numbness she'd wrapped around herself flared open, allowing fear to flood in. Quickly, Miranda emptied her mind and filled it with thoughts of her sisters. If Charlotte was managing to survive pretending to be some man's wife, so would she.

Chapter Four

Today she'd know her fate. Miranda sat in the rocking chair, reading the Psalms. Her choice of reading matter was limited to the Bible and a stack of penny dreadfuls. Her feet pushed in a frantic rhythm against the platform beneath her, sending the rocker into a wild swing. She kept reading the same lines over and over again, not taking in the words.

"Watch out," Nellie cried. "You'll do a cartwheel in that chair."

Nellie was the petite blonde with a passion for knitting. She didn't know how to make shapes, only straight to and fro, so she knitted long woolen scarves with brightly colored stripes. The girls already had at least two each. Nellie tried to give them away to her customers, but some had a wife at home which created a problem.

There were four girls in the saloon. Nellie and Shanna, and two brunettes—the quiet, brooding Trixie and the plump, good-humored Desiree. To Miranda, the girls did not seem unhappy, except perhaps Trixie, who was the plainest and the least popular with customers.

Many of the men who paid for their services were regulars, and the girls saw them as friends. Fort Rock was a mining town, and sometimes, when a prospector had a lucky strike, he would take on a girl as his exclusive sweetheart.

And all the girls dreamed.

They dreamed that one day some man would love them enough to give them the shiny badge of respectability. Take them away from the saloon life, to someplace where no one knew of their past and they could become one of the women who greeted each other on the boardwalk outside the mercantile and went to church on Sundays.

"Showtime, girls!" Lucille called from the top of the stairs.

She announced her entrance with the same words every night and she always wore shades of red. Scarlet, purple, magenta, pink—gowns decorated with ruffles and bows and teamed up with elaborate headdresses. Tonight, ostrich feathers bobbed over her auburn upsweep as she made her regal descent.

Downstairs, Lucille picked up a big glass jar from the end of the bar counter and walked over to the rocking chair where Miranda was seated. She banged the jar down on the small table beside Miranda. "You can do the honors tonight."

Inside the jar were folded tickets. The men who wanted to participate in the lottery handed over their money and Lucille wrote down their names on bits of paper torn from a receipt pad. Each ticket was folded into a square and dropped into the jar.

Nellie shook her head in dismay. "Only ten suitors."

"It's enough," Lucille replied. "I'm breaking even on the bride. And I've sold an extra fifty dollars' worth of whiskey to the men who came in to inspect her." She made an airy gesture toward the working girls. "And have you not been twice as busy as usual?"

Desiree tittered. "Staring at the bride put the men in the mood."

The batwing doors clattered. Miranda glanced over. Oh, no. Not *him*.

Slater, a huge, swarthy man with a drooping moustache, had been the first to lay his money down for the lottery. Miranda had been on display for six days, but only in the last two days, after Shanna's grim warning that not all husbands would be the same, had the carefully built barrier around her emotions cracked. From that moment on, she had felt the men's eyes on her, like insects crawling on her skin.

Some were reverent and worshipful, some greedy and lecherous, and after tonight she would become the property of one of them. He might be gentle, he might be rough, he might be cruel, and there was nothing she could do about it.

The terror Miranda had kept at bay broke free, making her hands damp and her heartbeat swift. She kept her eyes on the Bible that lay open in her lap and pretended to read. She was the brave one. She refused to let anyone see her fear.

Slater sat down, big and bony, the long duster like a tent around him, spurs jangling on his boots. He ordered a steak, as he did every night. He had a narrow, hollow-cheeked face and long yellowing teeth, which he liked to pick clean with the tip of his knife after he finished eating.

Little by little, customers drifted into the saloon. It was Saturday night, the busiest in the week. Lucille would have liked to keep the lottery going for a month, but she knew the men lacked patience and would start wrecking the place if they had to wait any longer.

Saturday had been chosen, partly because it was the payday at the mine, and partly because the preacher came over on Sundays and could conduct the wedding.

By eight o'clock, a sweaty, unkempt crowd filled the

saloon. The piano plinked, the whiskey flowed and the greasy smells of frying onions and meat floated in the air. Thick clouds of cigar smoke hung over the tables where men gambled away their weekly pay. Shrieks of feminine laughter mingled with rowdy, masculine voices.

Two more miners bought a ticket and stood transfixed by the rope barrier, staring at Miranda as if she were about to sprout wings and fly. And yet she understood their reverence would do her no good at all. They lived in a tent, survived hand to mouth, and the way they pushed and shoved at each other hinted at a violent nature. She'd starve, she'd freeze, and she'd very likely be beaten once the novelty of a having an educated wife wore off.

The marshal walked in accompanied by a man Miranda had not seen before. Lean, medium height, in his late twenties, he had straight black hair that fell to his shoulders, and sharply angled cheekbones. His skin was smooth and bronzed. From the dark coloring and the long hair, Miranda assumed he might have some native heritage, but when he got closer, she could see that his eyes were pale gray, almost like chips of ice, and just as cold.

The two newcomers settled side by side at the bar, both with one boot propped on the brass rail. The stranger jerked his chin in her direction and said something to the marshal. The marshal replied, grinning. Lucille ducked beneath the counter, poured whiskey into two glasses— the good stuff, not the watered-down swill—and smiled at the men.

The stranger listened to the marshal, knocked back his drink, slammed down the empty glass and ambled over to Miranda. He stepped over the rope and came to a halt in front of her. Miranda's kid slippers hit the floor. The chair stilled its rocking. The man might only be medium height, but it made his presence no less threatening.

"Read," he ordered.

"Wh-what?" she stammered.

He leaned forward. With him came the scent of soap and leather and the aroma of good coffee and expensive whiskey. His eyebrows were straight, his pale eyes deep set, and they seemed to glitter, as if a flame flickered somewhere deep within. He tapped one lean finger on the book she was clutching in her trembling hands.

"Read," he said. "Aloud."

She opened a page at random. Psalms. Number eighty-eight.

Her eyes strayed to a verse in the middle, and she read: "'I am confined and cannot escape; my eyes are dim with grief. I call to you, Lord, every day...'"

The man held up one hand. "Enough."

Miranda fell silent. She noticed a scar on his palm, a star-shaped, puckered mark. Without another word, the man turned away and walked back to the bar. Miranda watched as he reached into his pocket and tossed a gold coin on the counter.

Lucille tore a page from the receipt pad, printed down a name, folded the ticket and came to drop it into the glass jar on the small table beside Miranda. The dark man with the icy eyes picked up his refilled whiskey glass and resumed his conversation with the marshal. He never once glanced in Miranda's direction again, unlike the other ticket holders, who were jostling by the rope, craning forward and staring at her with the eagerness of thirsty men denied access to a spring.

Lucille banged a pewter mug against the counter. "Silence," she yelled. "Bride lottery will begin. Marshal Holm will officiate. His decision will be final. Anyone who complains will spend the night in jail with the four bank robbers brought in today."

Four bank robbers. Miranda recalled the marshal saying something about them a week ago. A bounty hunter was supposed to bring them in. They must have been delayed, and the dark man with the marshal must be the bounty hunter. Why on earth would a man like that, a transient without a permanent home, be interested in a wife?

Marshal Holm walked up to the rope and smiled. Miranda's temper flared. She was being offered up like a sacrificial lamb and he behaved as if a smile would smooth things over. She cleared her throat and put her plan in motion—not as good as escaping but better than accepting the vagaries of luck.

"A dying man is usually granted a final request," she announced tartly. "May I have one?"

"You ain't dying if I win you, sweetheart," one of the drunken miners yelled. "You'll learn your life has only just begun." Swaying on his feet, he waved at the prostitutes. "These ladies can vouch for me."

Nellie and Desiree shouted back obscenities that made Miranda's ears burn.

"Your last wish as a single woman?" the marshal prompted.

Miranda picked up the glass jar and shook it, making the tickets rustle inside. "Not a random draw," she explained. "I'd like a chance to ensure that I end up with a man who possesses the qualities required for a successful marriage. I want to ask these men questions. Set conditions. Those who fail to give satisfactory replies to my questions or refuse to meet my conditions will be eliminated, until we have a winner. Does that suit you?"

"That's a splendid idea," Lucille called out.

Of course Lucille would think it a splendid idea, Miranda thought with a trace of bitterness. It would stretch out the suspense, keep the whiskey flowing and the cash register ringing.

Marshal Holm nodded. "I guess I can go along with that."

Miranda closed her eyes and fought the wave of gratitude. She didn't really care, had formed scant impression of the men who had entered the draw, but she was desperate to avoid Slater, the big hulk who picked his teeth clean with the tip of his knife.

She rose from the rocking chair and turned toward the room, like an actress on the stage. "Only clean shaven men. No beards, no moustaches. Day-old stubble is acceptable."

Right there, in front of her horrified eyes, Slater took out his knife. He held it in his right hand and picked up the whiskey bottle from the table with his left hand and poured a stream of whiskey over the blade to clean it.

He set the bottle down again, raised the knife, pinched his nose with his thumb and forefinger and sliced off one side of his moustache. Then the other side. The sandy wedges fell on the tabletop and lay there like a pair of dead baby squirrels.

Nausea churned in Miranda's belly. Slater was determined, she granted him that. She suspected that if he won her, he'd be just as determined to make the most of having a wife. He'd have no mercy. She'd cook and clean and carry and fetch all day, and continue her toil in bed at night. Even though Miranda's isolated spot in the bridal display had prevented her from engaging in many conversations with Lucille's girls, she had been able to listen and observe. Any romantic notions about a wedding night had vanished.

"Only men who can read and write," she called out.

"How will you verify the skill?" asked Hooperman, the trim, neat banker in his early forties. He was a widower, with two children. He would have been the obvious choice, if it hadn't been for Miranda's experience with the boisterous Summerton girls in Boston. In two hours, the little monsters had driven her to the brink of insanity.

"Easy to check," Lucille declared. She tore off pages from the receipt pad and handed them out to the lottery participants. "Read something aloud," she told Miranda. "These gentlemen will write it down."

Miranda leafed through her Bible, picked the trickiest passage she could find. After the men had found pencils, she dictated a sentence and the candidates scratched down the words. Lucille collected the pages and inspected them. Once those with too many spelling mistakes had been disqualified, only three candidates remained.

Hooperman the banker.

The dark bounty hunter.

And, horror of horrors, Slater, who was grinning with victory. Blood beaded on his upper lip where he'd sliced too deep while shaving off his moustache. His tongue kept poking out to lick away the droplets.

Miranda could feel her legs shaking. A knot tightened in her belly. She sank on the rocking chair. It would have to be the banker. An educated, well-bred man. Maybe his children would be nice, and there were only two of them.

"The next question is to test a man's education," she announced. Her brain went blank as she tried to come up with the right task to eliminate Slater. She could remember the Lord's Prayer, but Slater might have been brought up in a devout home, or in a church orphanage, and there was a possibility he might know the words.

In a flash of inspiration, Miranda recalled her father's favorite poem. She took a deep breath and called out, "'Yet all things must die.'" Blank stares met her. Good. That's exactly what she wanted. "It's from a poem, by Alfred Tennyson," she added. "What is the next verse?"

The banker put up his hand. "What happens if no one knows?"

The marshal considered. "The lady can make her choice."

The banker broke into a smile of triumph. "I have to confess I don't recall the words, even though I greatly admire the romantic poets. Tennyson. Keats. Shelley."

Slater did not give up so easily. His narrow features puckered into a frown. "'Because we were all born to die?'" he ventured.

Miranda exhaled a sigh of relief. "No."

Slater got to his feet, as big as a mountain in his grimy duster. He scowled at her. "How do I know it's not right? You could say that about anything."

"Because it goes, 'The stream will cease to flow, the wind will cease to blow, the clouds will cease to fleet.'"

The verses came in a deep, husky voice. It was the first time Miranda had heard the bounty hunter speak more than one word at a time. A shiver rippled along her skin as his eyes swept over her, cool and indifferent, unlike the hot, hungry glare of Slater, or the admiring glances of Hooperman.

Miranda swallowed. Honesty remained her only choice. "Yes," she said. "That's how it goes."

The bounty hunter got to his feet. He raked a glance over the girls, nodded at Nellie and headed toward the staircase. Appearing confused, Nellie hovered on her toes, then trotted after the man. A paying customer was a paying customer.

At the top of the stairs, the bounty hunter paused to let Nellie pass. He turned back to survey the crowded room below. His eyes settled on Miranda. "Be ready to ride out in the morning." He spoke in a deep, emotionless tone that made even everyday words sound threatening. "We'll leave right after breakfast."

Chapter Five

Miranda tossed and turned on the narrow cot in the storeroom where she slept at night. She could hear the music booming downstairs, could feel the walls vibrating with the merriment. The stairs creaked with footsteps as the girls brought their clients upstairs. A few doors down the hall, her bridegroom was busy enjoying the favors of Nellie.

Did the man have no shame? It was the eve of their wedding. Miranda groaned into the darkness at her misplaced indignation. Surely, for all she cared, the bounty hunter could line up every one of Lucille's girls and take his turn with each of them.

How had she let it happen?

How had she ended up as a lottery prize?

For a week, she had sat on display, spinning her empty dreams of an escape. She had done nothing to help her situation. She could have tried to send a telegram to Charlotte in Gold Crossing. She could have asked the marshal to track down Cousin Gareth. Anything would be better than an unknown future with an icy-eyed bounty hunter.

But no, she'd been like one of those big birds Papa had seen on his travels. Ostriches, he'd called them. When some danger threatened, they dipped down their long necks and dug their heads into the sand, pretending the enemy didn't exist. That's what she had done.

Pretended her problem didn't exist.

Hoping it would go away.

But it had not.

It was down the hall with Nellie.

When morning came, Miranda awoke bleary-eyed. The storeroom had no windows, but she could hear the wind howling outside, could feel the gusts that buffeted the timber building. Summer weather in Wyoming seemed as unpredictable as the ocean storms that crashed and roared at Merlin's Leap.

She got up and considered her dress choices. Surely, the bounty hunter would respect a widow's grief? No, Miranda decided. The black mourning gown would remind him she was supposed to be experienced with men. She'd wear the pale blue.

Hastily, Miranda washed, dressed and packed her things into a canvas pouch she'd sewn while sitting on display. She surveyed the shelves of the storeroom, added candles, matches, canned meats, dried vegetables to her bag. After starving on the train, she wouldn't risk having to flee without supplies again.

Even as her mind dwelled on an escape, Miranda knew it would be the last resort. She had no money, no means of transport. The frontier region offered few opportunities for a woman to earn her living. Unless the bounty hunter turned out cruel, a position as his wife had to be better than entertaining an endless stream of strangers in a saloon.

On the landing, Miranda peeked down over the balustrade. Lucille and the girls sat around one of the gambling tables, dressed in their most conservative gowns. It surprised Miranda to see them up so early, for they rarely rose before midday.

When they spotted her, Shanna started belting out the notes of Mendelssohn's "Wedding March." Miranda walked down the stairs. The bounty hunter pushed away from the counter where he'd been hunched over a cup of coffee. He was wearing his tall boots and a long duster. His hat lay by his elbow and his saddlebags by his feet, ready for riding.

"Stop that noise," he ordered.

Shanna ceased her singing. Silence settled over the room, as heavy and sudden as the fall of an ax. The bounty hunter strode up to meet Miranda at the bottom of the stairs. He curled one hand around her elbow and ushered her across the floor to a compact, brown-haired man who sat at a table, eating porridge from a china bowl.

By the look of him, he was the circuit preacher—black suit, pious expression and a prayer book open on the table in front of him.

"I want no ceremony," the bounty hunter said. "Just a piece of paper to sign."

The preacher lifted the napkin tucked into his collar and touched a corner to his lips. "Before I am able to issue a marriage certificate, you have to express your consent to the union."

"I do." The bounty hunter tightened his grip on Miranda's arm and turned to glare at her. His head dipped in a single, sharp nod. When Miranda didn't respond, he gave her a light rattle, as if to shake the words out of her, the way one might shake apples from a tree. "Let's hear it," he said.

"I do *not*," she muttered.

His chin jerked. The twin slashes of his black eyebrows edged upward. His inscrutable expression cracked a little. It appeared to Miranda that the corners of his mouth were fighting not to curl up in a smile.

"Yes, you do," he told her. Turning to the preacher, he said, "She does. Where do we sign?"

"I need to hear the lady give her consent."

"And hear it you shall," the bounty hunter replied. He bent closer to Miranda and whispered into her ear. "It's me, or a jail cell with four bank robbers who don't care about adding rape to their sins. Which do you prefer?"

Miranda pursed her lips. Always stubborn, she hated to give in to blackmail. But on this occasion resistance might be ill-advised.

"I do." She spoke through gritted teeth.

"Good," the bounty hunter said. "She does. Where do we sign?"

The preacher looked pained. Behind Miranda, Lucille and her girls were muttering complaints about the lack of romance. The bounty hunter turned his head and scowled at them over Miranda's shoulder. "You worry about your own weddings and leave this one alone."

Before Miranda could think, one of her booted feet rose and slammed down on the man's instep. He flinched. Although no sound passed his lips, Miranda knew she'd caused him pain. Good. He deserved it. It had been a cruel comment. He must be aware of how little chance the saloon girls had of ever getting a wedding of their own.

"That was nasty and uncalled for and lacking in chivalry," she lectured.

The bounty hunter's mouth fell open. For a second, he stared at her, speechless. Miranda could see something flicker in his eyes. Anger. Perhaps even respect. Then it changed to a flash of amusement, and his mouth curved into a rueful smile.

"If you expect chivalry from me, you're sorely mistaken." He turned back to the preacher, one hand still clutching her arm. His other hand settled over one of the big revolvers in the twin holsters at his hips.

"Now, where do we sign?"

"Name?" the preacher asked, looking at her.

"Miranda Fairfax." She had thought about it carefully. Cousin Gareth was less dangerous than the bounty hunter. She was not afraid of leaving a trail. She *wanted* to leave a trail.

The bounty hunter's eyes narrowed. "I heard your name is Woods."

She gave him a strained smile, cherishing the tiny triumph of telling him a lie, one he might suspect but had no way of proving. "That was my married name."

"Name?" the preacher said, addressing the question to the bounty hunter. It was clear to Miranda the brown-haired pastor had chosen to cut his losses over the ceremony and wanted to get back to his cooling porridge.

"James Fast Elk Blackburn," the bounty hunter replied.

The preacher frowned. "You sure you want the Fast Elk in there?"

The bounty hunter hesitated a moment. "You can leave it out."

They took turns signing the marriage certificate. The preacher copied the details into his record book and handed the certificate to Miranda. The bounty hunter leaned over her, snatched the document from her fingers and slipped it into a pocket on the buckskin coat he wore beneath his long duster. "I paid good money for you and I'll keep this for now."

"Ten dollars," Miranda muttered tartly. "A fortune indeed."

"Maybe that's all you're worth."

Miranda bit her lip to stop an angry retort. *You walked right into that one,* she told herself. *And now, shut up, before you'll make it even worse.* She had her provisions. Now was the time to gather her wits and start making plans for an escape.

This is a mistake, Jamie thought as he ushered the blonde beauty out of the saloon. He'd acted on impulse. He should have known better. In his profession a man needed cool judgment to stay alive. He had a premonition that hauling the little Eastern princess along with him for four days, until he could get rid of her, would not inspire cool judgment.

He'd have to get her a horse of her own. Last night, he had tried to bury his lust in the saloon tart, but his mind had given the girl beneath him the flawless features and the proud carriage of the woman he was now towing in his wake.

If he rode four days with her arms around his waist, her breasts pressing to his back, he might start thinking with the wrong parts of his anatomy and end up hitched to her for good—an idea that did not suit his plans.

"Can you ride?" he asked.

"Yes. Faster than you, I'll bet."

Jamie smirked. "That depends on the horse, not you."

Although she was tall, the girl had to break into a run to keep up with him as he strode down the street. Clouds whipped about in the sky overhead, but it wouldn't rain today. The weather was clearing, and tomorrow it would be sunny. He could tell.

He could always tell. Sensing the weather and reading signs were what he got from the quarter of his blood that was Cheyenne. The rest of the Indian mumbo jumbo he could do without. All of that mysticism junk his sister, Louise, had embraced with such fervor before her untimely death.

Jamie paused to let his wife catch up. "I thought you said you're faster than me."

"On four legs. Not on two."

Smart mouth she had, his little Eastern princess. Four days in her company would be filled with temptation. Jamie led her past the storefronts, mostly closed for Sunday. A few men loitered on the boardwalk, smoking, talking, watching them with envy in their eyes.

Maybe he could auction the little princess when he was done with her, Jamie thought. He suppressed a smile. No, he'd be a good boy, cut her loose and give her enough money for the train fare to wherever she'd been trying to get, with no ticket and no money to buy food.

Before parting with his ten dollars, Jamie had got the facts from Marshal Holm. According to the railroad conductor who'd arrested the girl, she'd been caught stealing. Jamie suspected the accusation might be false. She seemed too proud to steal, but Jamie knew from personal experience that sometimes an empty belly ruled stronger than pride.

They came to a halt by the pole corral where the four horses of the bank robbers stood idle, tails flicking at flies. "Take your pick," Jamie said and gestured at the horses. "Don't go for the paint. He's going lame."

She spent a moment studying the animals and spoke with her gaze intent on them. "The buckskin has sores on his flanks from the cruel use of spurs. The bay has mean, shifty eyes. The black is a stallion. I don't like to ride stallions. They start to misbehave the minute there's a mare within a mile."

"Aren't you a picky one?" Jamie grumbled. "Good thing you had to take a husband in a draw. If you were left to choose, no one would have been good enough for you."

"How astute," she replied, and pursed her mouth into a prim circle of disdain. Her eyes raked him up and down in a look that plainly dismissed his worth. Then she turned back to the four horses in the corral and said, "Can you take the bank robbers' horses before they've even been convicted? Is it part of the bounty?"

"It is, if you bring them in dead."

"Dead?" Her pretty blue eyes snapped wide, then narrowed into angry slits. "You said… You threatened me with them…"

"I never said they weren't dead. I merely said they didn't care about adding rape to their sins. Considering they are dead, I'm sure that's correct."

"You…you…oaf…"

"Oaf?" He smirked at the little princess. "Is that the best you can do?"

"I'll work on it," she said tartly. "I'm sure that a few weeks in your company will expand my vocabulary."

Not weeks, sweetheart, Jamie thought. *Four days, and that's four too many.*

"Which will it be?" he asked. "The buckskin that's been mistreated and is looking to take his revenge, or the shifty-eyed bay, or the uncontrollable black stallion?"

"How about one of those?" She pointed to the next corral where half a dozen horses from the livery stable jostled at the water trough "Can't you sell these four and buy me something better? A horse suitable for a lady?"

Jamie sighed in resignation. "Let's go and take a look."

He hung back as his little Eastern princess, Miranda— what a fitting name for a woman who was bound to drive him crazy with complaints during the next four days— leaned over the corral fence and inspected the horses.

A gust of breeze molded her skirts against her legs. Strands of golden hair fluttered around her face. She wedged one boot on the lowest rung and climbed up for a better look, agile and slender. Like a blonde version of an Indian princess. Jamie hurried to quash the thought.

"That one." Her arm shot out to point at a gray Appaloosa with an evenly spotted coat.

Jamie groaned. Indian princess indeed. He should have guessed she'd pick the most expensive horse at the stable.

Ten minutes later, he had traded all four of the bank robbers' horses against the Appaloosa, and had been forced to haggle not to owe a balance. He'd been crazy to think marrying her was going to save him money.

He ushered the little princess into the cool, shady interior of the livery stable. Once they were inside, he nudged the toe of his boot at the bank robbers' saddles and bridles that lay in a heap on the floor.

"Pick your saddle and tack."

"My saddle?" She looked down at the pile by their feet, then back up at him. "But I can't… I've never ridden astride… I'll need a side saddle…"

The moment of payback had arrived. Jamie felt a twinge of shame, but he brushed it aside. It was best to make the little princess hate him, in case he wasn't as good at resisting temptation as he ought to be.

He lowered his voice, bent to speak into her ear. "Considering you're female, it shouldn't be too difficult to learn to spread your legs."

Chapter Six

It took a few seconds for the bounty hunter's lewd comment to penetrate Miranda's brain. How dare he speak to her like that? Her hands fisted in impotent range. *The... the...oaf!* She longed for stronger words—ones she hoped to add to her vocabulary very soon.

In an effort to overcome her fury, she focused her attention on the equipment carelessly stacked on the floor. It was clear which set held the most appeal. Saddle and bridle in black leather, shiny and supple, carefully maintained. She could see a pair of matching saddlebags, too. The metal studs that decorated each piece might be silver.

Miranda was about to point out her choice when her gaze strayed to the bounty hunter. The oaf—*James Fast Elk Blackburn*. He was leaning against the timber wall, arms crossed over his chest, watching her from under the brim of his hat. She might not be able to match him in dirty talk, but she could gain some measure of petty revenge by vexing him.

"I want to try out the saddles," she declared.

He pushed away from the wall. "All of them?"

"That will be the only way to know which one fits the best."

The long canvas duster flared wide as Blackburn

moved toward her. Halting toe-to-toe with her, he pointed at the gray Appaloosa tied to the hitching post outside the livery stable. "There's your horse." He gestured at the heap of equipment by their feet. "There's your saddles and bridles. Try them out to your little heart's content."

Oh, yes, Miranda thought. *This is going to be very satisfactory indeed.*

She turned to survey her new horse. The black saddle with silver studs would look beautiful on the gray. She pointed at a worn saddle in cracked tan leather. "Let's start with that one. It looks a bit smaller than the others."

When Blackburn didn't move, she directed an impatient frown at him. "Well, what are you waiting for?"

"I'm waiting for you to get on with it."

"Do you expect me to know how to saddle a horse?"

A worried notch appeared between Blackburn's straight dark brows. "You told me you can ride. If I recall right, you boasted that you'll ride faster than me."

"And I'm sure I do. However, I never told you that I know how to saddle a horse, or brush one down, or feed one, or clean up after one. I've always had grooms for that."

She ran her eyes over the bounty hunter, making it clear that she expected him to take on the duties of a groom. "Well?" she said, mirroring his brusque command a moment earlier. "I'm waiting for you to get on with it."

Blackburn jerked his head in the gesture she'd noticed before, a bit like a stubborn mule tossing its mane. It made the thick strands of black hair swing about his shoulders. He had an expressive face, when he forgot to hide his thoughts, but the range of his expressions seemed mostly limited to anger, irritation and disbelief.

The bounty hunter heaved out a sigh but sprang into action. A secret thrill of victory rippled over Miranda as she watched him crouch down, pick up the worn saddle, walk out to the hitching post, lift the saddle onto the Appaloosa, adjust the position and tighten the cinch.

She hurried after him and came to an abrupt halt beside the horse. The animal's gray flanks rose in front of her, like the brow of an ocean liner. How was she going to get up there, without the aid of a mounting block, or a groom to give her a boost? And she'd rather die than admit to her failure and ask Blackburn for help.

"Well," the deep, husky voice said behind her. "The saddle is on the horse. I'm waiting for you to get on with trying it out."

Miranda circled to the horse's head. They had already made friends while the bounty hunter went inside to negotiate the purchase with the livery stable owner. She held out her hand. The horse nuzzled her palm, its nose cool and damp against her skin.

"I have a name for you," she whispered to the Appaloosa. "Alfie. For Alfred Tennyson. A very famous poet, and a nobleman. That is what I'll expect from you. Noble behavior. Please don't let me down. See that man behind me? He is a rogue, with no manners. He is just waiting for me to fall flat on my face."

After stroking Alfie's long nose to emphasize her plea, Miranda circled back to his side. She grabbed hold of a stirrup, kicked up one foot. Her skirts got in the way and she almost toppled over backward. Determined, Miranda yanked her skirts up over her knees and tried again. She managed to wedge the toe of her button-up boot into the stirrup. With tiny hops, she moved closer to the horse and grabbed the saddle horn with one hand, the cantle of the saddle with the other, and bounced up.

And bounced back down again.

Peering backward beneath her arm, Miranda stole a glance at the bounty hunter. He was standing still, watching her, his long duster blowing in the breeze. The repertoire of his facial expressions seemed to be growing, but instead of the smug smile she had expected, he was staring at her, spellbound, as if witnessing a complicated circus act.

She'd show him! Miranda pushed the toe of her left foot deeper into the stirrup, bent her right knee, tensed every muscle and bounced up again. Her hands clung to the saddle. Her left foot wobbled in the stirrup as she hung poised in the air. Little by little, she managed to shift her center of gravity forward, until she found her balance and could fling her right leg over the horse's back.

She was up! She was sitting astride the horse. Alfie beat one hoof against the ground and craned his head backward, as if to look at her and say, *How is that for noble behavior?* Miranda sank deeper into the saddle. She'd done it. She'd mounted on her own. She gave a tiny whoop of victory and flashed a smile at Blackburn, forgetting his arrogance, even forgetting his crude comment about her riding position.

"How's the saddle?" he asked.

She wiggled her rump to test the fit. "It's not comfortable."

Dismounting was a lot easier, Miranda discovered, with gravity helping instead of hindering. She tried all four saddles, and then she claimed she couldn't be certain of her choice and insisted on trying two of them again.

The bounty hunter kept swapping over the saddles. She could see a muscle tugging at the side of his jaw. His shoulders were rigid, his face set in stone. His gaze remained locked somewhere on the horse's flanks, refusing to rise up to her as she sat up on Alfie and gloated over her success, both in mounting without aid and in vexing him.

"The black saddle," Miranda said in the end, when

Alfie started to get bored with the constant fussing. "I like that one best. Take off this one and put that one back on."

Jamie gritted his teeth. He had to get her some new clothes. Did the little blonde princess not understand what she was doing? Blithely, she'd yanked up her skirts, exposing dainty leather half boots and a pair of shapely legs.

Then, when she'd hopped around on one foot, the other foot stuck in the stirrup, knee pointing skyward, her skirts had bunched up in her lap, giving him a tantalizing glimpse all the way up to a bare, milky-white thigh and the garter that held up her stocking.

Things had gotten a little easier when she swung astride and the skirts settled around her, but even then he could see a part of her leg. He was covered in sweat, and it wasn't just from the effort of heaving the saddles on and off the horse. He'd barely had the presence of mind to keep an eye on the entrance to the livery stable, to make sure the owner wasn't lurking in the shadows, enjoying the spectacle.

"You'll need a pair of trousers for riding astride," he informed his wife.

She was crouching on the ground, admiring the black saddlebags with a fascination that made Jamie suspect she had wanted the silver-studded set all along.

She frowned at him. "Surely I can't wear trousers. It's not decent."

Not decent. He made a strangled sound, something between a groan and a laugh. "It will be a damn sight more decent than the way you need to pull up your skirts when you climb into the saddle."

She stared at him. Her blue eyes kept widening until he could see rims of white all around the irises. Hot color washed up to her cheeks. "Heavens," she breathed. "I didn't realize." She peered into the saddlebag, as if wanting to crawl into it. "I didn't mean to…"

"It's all right," Blackburn said grudgingly. "No one was watching."

"No one but you."

"I don't count, do I?"

She pursed her lips. "I guess you don't. We *are* married, after all."

The answer took him by surprise. He'd meant he didn't count because she had made it clear he was so far beneath her in social status he barely qualified as a member of the human race. Moreover, her embarrassment confirmed she hadn't been tormenting him on purpose. Mollified, Jamie squatted beside his little Eastern princess and joined her in examining the saddlebags.

"These are Mexican," he said. "Silver-studded. They'll look good on the gray."

She glanced up from beneath her lashes and flashed him a smile that made his breath catch. "That's what I thought when I first saw them." She met his gaze, earnest and eager now, and spoke without a trace of hostility. "I do want to learn how to look after a horse. I always did, but it upset the grooms when I asked. They feared for their jobs."

"That's good." Jamie pushed up to his feet. "Let's put the bridle and the saddlebags on the horse. Then we'll go over to the mercantile. We'll get them to open up even though it's Sunday, and we'll kit you out."

"These are wonderful. Can I try them on for size?" Jamie watched his little Eastern princess clutch a pair of denim trousers in her hands, as if they were a gown made by a Paris fashion house. He was starting to suspect he might have been too harsh in judging her. The thought gave him pause. It would be better to remain enemies.

The shopkeeper, a small dark man with clipped speech and an oddly precise way of moving, pressed his finger-tips into a steeple, as if praying for a sale. "Let me show you some boots and coats. And you'll need a couple of shirts, and a hat, and a rain slicker."

An hour later, Jamie was sitting on a wooden stool by the counter, drinking coffee while Miranda kept darting in and out of the small fitting booth at the back of the store. He shook his head as he watched her parade up and down the aisle. How did she do it? She never once looked at the price tags, but she unerringly selected the most expensive of everything.

"I like this hat best," she informed him.

"Of course you do," Jamie muttered.

"What?" She stilled, hands raised to adjust the tilt of the brim as she admired her reflection in the mirror. She frowned at him through the glass. "Is it wrong?"

"It's about ten dollars wrong."

"Ten dollars?" Her face fell with comprehension. She took down the black leather hat, fingered the band of silver beads around the crown. Her voice was very small. "I thought it would go nicely with the saddle."

She turned toward him. Her eyes seemed very bright. "I'm sorry," she said softly. "I wasn't thinking… My parents died four years ago, and I haven't had anything new since, and I've never bought any ready-made clothing before. It's been so much fun, I got carried away." Putting on a brave smile, she turned to the storekeeper. "Let's start again. Point me to the cheapest hats and coats."

Jamie let his eyes drift over her. She'd picked a pair of black knee-high boots and a short coat in black deerskin, cropped at the waist, Mexican style. The hat had straight sides and a short, flat-topped crown. She looked as if she had ridden up from south of the border. If it hadn't been for the fair hair, everyone who saw her would expect her to talk in Spanish.

"Ring it up," Jamie said to the storekeeper.

"But…" Miranda studied the price tag on the hat. "You can't…"

"We've spent enough time in here. I'm not going to sit through you picking out something else," Jamie said gruffly, even though he knew it was a bad idea to let her keep the clothes. The whole idea of marrying her had been to save money. And now his little Eastern princess had become a little bandit princess, a transformation that made her even harder to resist.

Jamie closed his mind to the misgivings and turned to the counter. He pulled up his shirt to reach his money belt and handed over his hard-earned cash. He almost jumped when he felt the light touch of fingertips on the back of his hand.

"Thank you," the girl said. "It is very kind of you."

If you expect chivalry from me, you're sorely mistaken, he'd told her a few hours ago. A nasty suspicion niggled in Jamie's mind that Miranda Fairfax—his wife—had the ability to turn everything in his life upside down before he could get rid of her.

Chapter Seven

This marriage business might not be such a bad idea after all, Miranda thought as she rode out of town behind James Fast Elk Blackburn. She had acquired an excellent horse, a fancy saddle with silver studs and a lovely set of new clothes.

It appeared a husband had a duty to look after his wife, and the bounty hunter took that duty seriously. She doubted he'd ever let her go hungry. If only she knew what price he would extract for his protection, her nerves might not be quite so jumpy.

Overhead, the sky was clearing. Swallows dipped and soared over the grassy meadows, the way seagulls swooped over the ocean waves at Merlin's Leap. The air smelled clean and fresh. In the distance, sunlight glittered on the mountaintops.

For an hour, Miranda rode in meek silence, and then she could no longer tolerate the uncertainty. She had to know what he wanted from her. She urged Alfie forward, until she was riding alongside the bounty hunter's bay gelding.

"Where are we going?" she called out to him.

He kept his eyes straight ahead. "You'll find out."

"Why can't you tell me now?"

He shot her a sharp glance. "Shut up and ride."

"I can ride and talk at the same time. Can't you?"

"Be quiet. You're annoying me."

It was not a playful retort. It was a surly, brooding complaint. Perhaps he regretted spending all that money on her. Ten dollars might have seemed cheap for a wife, but she had quickly turned into a bottomless pit of additional expense.

The path narrowed and Miranda fell back behind the bounty hunter's horse. For the rest of the day, they rode across the grassy plateau at a steady lope, pausing frequently to stretch their legs and to let their mounts rest. The bounty hunter ignored her, except to issue an order or to warn her to keep out of the way. Tension ratcheted up inside Miranda. When they stopped for the night, the bounty hunter set a soot-covered coffeepot to boil on a fire he had built from dead branches in a circle of stones on the ground.

Miranda gathered her courage and perched beside him on the fallen log where he had sat down. "Why won't you talk to me?"

"I don't like to talk."

"Why did you marry me?"

"You'll find out."

"You'll find out, you'll find out," she mimicked. "You sound like a parrot in a cage."

"And you talk too much." He shot her a frowning glance. "Can't you do something useful? Like cook supper, or groom the horses, or build a fire, or clear a place on the ground to sleep, instead of hovering around and annoying me?"

Miranda spoke quietly. "It is not my fault that I'm gently bred. Unlike you, I'm not nasty and surly by nature. I'm asking because I want to know. If I prepare myself for whatever it is you want from me, I might be able to perform the task better."

She had never heard anyone heave out such a loud sigh. It made the air vibrate with frustration and irritation and exasperation and aggravation and impatience. James Fast Elk Blackburn might not like to talk, but it seemed he had no trouble communicating his bad temper without words.

Miranda walked away, but she was not giving up.

She was merely regrouping for another attack.

A fire crackled in a circle of stones, casting shadows in the darkness. The soft night breeze whispered in the trees. The horses, hobbled to stop them from straying, grazed on the long grass by the brook. The aroma of roast turkey, already eaten, lingered in the air.

Jamie drank the last of his coffee and studied his little bandit princess. She sat beside him, staring into the flames. He could sense her fear. During the evening, she had drawn tighter and tighter into a ball, shoulders hunched, knees pressed together, as if she wanted to disappear into herself.

He should have been gentler with her, but the emotions she stirred up in him had made him morose. It grated that she looked down on him, the way his mother's family had looked down on his father. The physical reactions she sparked in him didn't help, either. It was best to keep his distance. Healthier for them both. The worst of his feelings was guilt, though. It was clear she was on the run, perhaps from being tied to a man twice her age, and now she had ended up married to a savage who killed people for a living.

The right thing would be to explain what he wanted from her, but Jamie couldn't talk about it. Death might be his trade, but when it came to the death of his mother and his sister and his niece, his mind locked up. He didn't know if it was because they were women, or because they were family, or because they were the only people he had ever loved.

"Who is Woods?" he asked. When the girl didn't reply, he added, "Your husband. Are you a widow or not? Is he still living?"

As Jamie considered the question, it occurred to him that if Woods still lived, it would simplify things. The marriage would be bigamous, invalid as such, and he would avoid the trouble of seeking an annulment when the time came.

The little princess kept picking bits of bark loose from the log they sat upon, her eyes intent on the task, the way a hungry sparrow might concentrate on the search for a worm.

"He doesn't exist," she muttered.

"He doesn't exist?"

"That's right. He is a figment of my imagination." She shot him a glance. "I thought it might make it easier for a woman traveling alone to be assumed a widow."

"Where are you from?"

"I thought you didn't like to talk."

"I changed my mind."

"Boston."

The flickering flames sent shadows dancing over her face and hair. She looked frightened, but also fierce, strangely untamed. She'd probably fight back if he tried to bed her. Scratch and claw and bite. The thought reassured Jamie.

"I was out East once," he told her. "Baltimore. It was a long way there and an even longer way back."

She contemplated him and gave a slow nod. Jamie got an odd feeling she understood what he meant—that the journey back had felt longer because it had been without hope.

Her gaze returned to the fire. "I live in a place called Merlin's Leap. It's a big old house by the ocean. I have two sisters. I'm the middle one."

Jamie knew he needed to put her fears to rest. On purpose, he had waited for nightfall to have the conversation. He talked better in the darkness. "I'm not going to hurt you. There's something I need you to do for me. A job. It will only take a few months. When it's done, you can go."

"Will anyone else hurt me?"

Right to the point. She was smart. Perceptive.

"No," he said. "It's not that kind of job."

"Will I have to harm anyone?"

"No."

"Will I have to break the law?"

"No."

"What will I have to do?"

"Clean in a saloon. Just sweep and scrub and dust."

"Sweep and scrub and dust for a few months? And then I can go?"

"That's about it. There's a bit more to it. You'll find out." He got up, tossed another branch into the fire, pointed at a big rock a few yards away. "Sleep next to the stone. It's better not to leave your back exposed. I've put a bedroll and a blanket down for you."

"You didn't buy a bedroll for me."

"I gave you mine. I'll sleep with a blanket."

"Thank you," she said. "That is kind of you."

That is kind of you. Jamie suppressed another twinge of guilt. If he were kind, he'd put her on the next train back to Boston and take care of his problems without her help.

"I'll see you in the morning," he told her. "If you need to wake me up at night, call out from a distance. Whatever you do, don't creep up on me and touch me. I'll most likely slit your throat."

He saw her shrink into that tight ball again. *Idiot,* Jamie berated himself. He'd planned to reassure her, not to scare her out of her wits. He'd best shut up before he made things even worse.

He walked off into the darkness and stretched out beside another rock. After setting his pair of guns and the knife he carried in his belt down on the ground within easy reach, he wrapped up in a blanket and closed his eyes.

Years ago, he'd learned to go to sleep at will, or at least fall into the half-awake doze that served him for sleep. But tonight the restful slumber didn't come. His ears attuned to a soft feminine voice singing some kind of a song in the darkness, so faintly it sounded almost like the wind whispering. When he finally dozed off, he dreamed of an angel choir, complete with halos and wings and shimmering robes.

It had been unwise to boast about her skills as a rider, Miranda thought as she cantered behind James Fast Elk Blackburn, following the course of a wide, shallow river. He had decided to make the journey in three days instead of four, and after bragging about her horsemanship she felt unable to complain about fatigue and sore muscles.

So far, the weather had favored them. Dry, crisp days, with dewy mornings and starlit nights. They had crossed hills and valleys, followed creeks and streams, but however far they rode, the snowcapped mountains on the horizon never seemed to get any closer.

Since their talk by the firelight on the first night, they had barely exchanged a word. The bounty hunter didn't expect her to help with the chores, so she didn't even try. She ate what he put in front of her, rode when he told her to ride and slept the minute she'd finished chewing and swallowing whatever he had shot and cooked each night.

Ahead of her, Blackburn lifted his arm in a signal and halted his horse. His bay gelding was called Sirius. If Miranda had known, she might have called the gray Appaloosa Orion instead of Alfie, but she'd gotten used to the name and didn't wish to change it now.

"It's over the next hill," Blackburn told her when she caught up.

"What's the town called?"

"Devil's Hall."

Devil's Hall. Miranda hoped the place didn't live up to the name but she decided not to ask. Blackburn probably would ignore her question anyway. As they set off again, at a slower pace now, to allow the horses to catch their breaths, a sudden boom shook the ground, followed by a muffled rumble, like the sound of distant thunder.

"What's that noise?" Miranda asked.

"They're blasting at the mine."

A second later, the acrid odors of an explosion blotted out the smells of parched grass and drying buffalo chips. Unlike the eastern end of the prairie, where the buffalo had been hunted to extinction, in Wyoming the herds still roamed. Miranda had seen several groups of the huge, bulky beasts in the distance.

When they crested the ridge, a long valley spread before them. A river flowed through the middle. The town seemed quite a big place. There was a main street, with two-story buildings on both sides. The rest of the houses were scattered about in random clusters. On the opposite slope of the valley, the mine workings cut an ugly black crater in the earth.

As they drew closer, Miranda could pick out at least two saloons. "Carousel" boasted a brightly colored banner with the name on it in big letters and a balcony over the porch. "Purgatory" had no porch or balcony, and the name was daubed directly onto the timber wall. Miranda said a silent prayer that she'd end up at the Carousel instead of the Purgatory.

They had made good time, and it was only the afternoon. Miranda saw several people in the street, all men, dressed in drab clothing and bowler hats. She'd discovered that the kind of wide-brimmed hat she had chosen was useful in the south to keep out the sun, but this far north the winds were fierce, and people preferred hats not so easily blown off their heads.

Blackburn drew up outside a small, two-story, timber-frame house. He dismounted, tied Sirius to a post, far enough from the flowerbeds that decorated the front yard to protect them from the appetite of the horse, and then he turned around to hold Alfie by the bit.

"Get down," he ordered.

"I thought you said the saloon."

"We'll stop here first."

His manner was terse. Instinct told Miranda she was about to find out what Blackburn had meant when he told her there would be "a bit more" to her task than cleaning. Whatever it was, it was bad enough for him to have refused to talk about it.

She jumped down. Blackburn tied Alfie to the hitching post, marched to the front door and pounded the iron knocker. A woman opened. Tall and thin, with graying hair pulled back into a tight bun, she had the kind of pinched, sour expression that reminded Miranda of Mrs. Matheson, the least favorite of their governesses at Merlin's Leap.

"Afternoon, Mrs. Van Cleef," Blackburn said. "I've come for Nora."

The woman dried her hands on her apron and gave a nod. "I'll get her."

Who is Nora? Miranda wanted to ask, but something in Blackburn's manner warned her into silence. They waited. She heard the clip of Mrs. Van Cleef's footsteps and a lighter tapping sound, and then a little girl shot forward from the woman's shadow. She was perhaps eight or nine, fragile of build, with sallow skin, dark eyes and shoulder-length black hair in a blunt cut, with a straight fringe across her forehead.

"Uncle Jamie," the child cried and ran out, skirts flapping around her feet.

So intent had Miranda been on staring into the hallway that she had failed to notice Blackburn had dropped to his knees. He spread his arms wide and the little girl barreled into him, babbling in a voice that rang with joy.

"Uncle Jamie, I missed you so much. I missed you more than the moon and the sun. I missed you more than all the planets and the stars."

Bittersweet memories flooded into Miranda's mind. She and her sisters had played that game with their parents, too, competing over who loved whom the most, but it had been the sea for Papa and arts and music for Mama. *I love you more than the ocean. I love you more than the east wind. I love you more than Mozart, more than Michelangelo.*

"Easy, Skylark," Blackburn said. "You mustn't run. You'll wear yourself out." He pushed up to his feet, took the little girl's hand in his and turned toward Miranda. "Look what I got for you, Skylark. A new mama. What do you think of her?"

Chapter Eight

A new mama? The words went off like a gunpowder explosion in Miranda's head, destroying all rational thought. She stared down at the little girl, who was staring back at her.

Slowly, the joy in the little girl's face faded. She darted a glance at Blackburn and whispered, "She doesn't like me…" Then the child twisted around to glance back at Mrs. Van Cleef with a nervous expression that spelled *Any more than this one does.*

Without releasing the little girl's hand, Blackburn lifted his other hand. His fingers closed around Miranda's arm. He applied the same silent warning he'd used when they stood in front of the preacher and he'd dragged the consent of marriage out of her.

"Of course she does." Steely fingers bit into Miranda's arm. "She's always wanted a little girl of her own to look after. Haven't you, Miranda?"

Miranda studied the child. She seemed a timid little thing. And there was only one of her. Not four, like the boisterous Summerton girls who had worn her nerves into a tangle in five minutes. When Miranda didn't say anything, the little girl blinked. A solitary tear spilled out from beneath her thick dark lashes and rolled down her cheek.

Seeing that tear, sensing the loneliness and grief the child so valiantly tried to hide, jolted Miranda out of her stunned reticence. *A new mama.* That implied Nora must have lost her mother, and most likely also her father.

Even after four years, Miranda's own grief remained raw, and she'd been on the verge of adulthood when she lost her parents. How much worse must it be to lose a parent while still a child? Moreover, she'd had her sisters for support, but Nora had been left alone in the care of unsympathetic strangers.

Mortified at the thought that Nora believed she didn't like her, Miranda yanked her arm free from the bounty hunter's grip and sank to her knees in front of the child. "Of course I've always wanted a little girl of my own." She coaxed a shaky smile onto her face. "Hello, Nora. Or may I call you Skylark?"

Big brown eyes gave her a wary inspection. A tiny hand reached out to touch the golden strands that fluttered free from her upsweep. "I like your hair."

Miranda's smile gentled. "I hope you'll find a lot more to like about me. I can do magic tricks, and I can sing songs from faraway lands. I can draw pictures, and I know the names of lots of stars, and I can tell how fast the wind blows."

The little girl looked up at Blackburn. The love and trust in the child's gaze tugged at Miranda's heart. "I think she's going to be a good mama," the little girl whispered.

Blackburn released the child's hand and spun her to face the hallway. "You go back upstairs and help Mrs. Van Cleef pack your things. Then you and your new mama will move to your old room at the Carousel."

Miranda waited until Mrs. Van Cleef and the little girl

had vanished up the stairs. Then she turned to Blackburn and spoke in an agitated murmur. "Why didn't you tell me? And what did you mean when you said it's only for a few months? That girl is no more than eight or nine. She is going need someone to look after her for years to come."

"She's sick. She won't live much longer."

"Sick? What with? Who is she?"

"She's my niece. The child of my only sister, Louise. I'm her only living relative. Nora was born with a weak heart. As her body grows, the heart is less and less able to keep up. The doc says she only has a few months left."

Blackburn darted a glance into the shadowed hall where footsteps clattered once more down the stairs. He finished in a rush. "My sister died a few weeks ago. I've been paying for Mrs. Van Cleef to look after Nora."

Miranda had a dozen more questions, but Nora had reappeared and the questions had to wait. The child was moving more slowly now, and her color was poor, with a bluish tinge on her lips.

"Let's go." The little girl spoke in a weak, breathless tone. She slipped her hand, not in Blackburn's, but in Miranda's. The child's skin was cold, the fingers so fragile they might snap.

"Come along," Nora said, looking up at Miranda. "I'll show you where we live. Uncle Jamie can follow us with my bag and the horses."

Miranda held the child's hand gently and clamped her teeth over her bottom lip to contain the mix of emotions—pity, anger at the cruelty of fate, and a hollow sense of helplessness.

And, eclipsing them all, a deep, aching surge of protectiveness. As the brave one, she'd used her courage to shield her sisters whenever she could. Now she would need every bit of that courage to help Nora through her final months.

Courage for Nora, and courage for herself. For, inevitably, a bond would form between them. With her quiet dignity, with her pretty features and big brown eyes, with her sincerity and her thinly disguised need for affection, Nora would be an easy child to love. And her tragic situation, with each passing minute precious, would make that love grow and flourish like weeds after the rain.

With a sigh, Miranda gave Nora's fingers a light squeeze as they set off down the dusty street, leaving behind the unfriendly home of Mrs. Van Cleef.

To see a dying child to her grave.

That's what James Blackburn required from her.

Miranda studied the small room at the end of the upstairs corridor at the Carousel. It contained two narrow beds, one on either side, with little space in between. A window let in northern light and gave a view of the mountains. The beds had been stripped bare. The walls had no pictures. Cooking smells from the kitchen rose through the floorboards.

"Not very cozy," she remarked.

"We'll fix it the way it used to be," Nora said. "I have Mama's things in my bag."

Miranda settled the child to sit on one of the beds and crouched in front of her, ignoring Blackburn, who stood hovering in the doorway. She'd been ignoring him ever since they left Mrs. Van Cleef's house. It hadn't been easy to ignore a man who'd ushered her along with a firm grip on her arm and introduced her to the saloon owner as his wife, but somehow she'd managed the feat.

Mr. Nordgren, the man who owned the saloon, spoke English without an accent but showed his Nordic origins by saying *"jaa"* instead of "yes." He looked her up and down and told her it was five dollars a week plus room and board. He finished the interview by asking her to keep the child quiet and do the cleaning between dawn and afternoon and learn to call him Nordgren, without the prefix of "Mr." in front of it.

That had been all. She was employed.

"Maybe you can call me Miranda," she told the child. "If you call me Mama we'll just get confused. And I'll call you Nora, or Skylark."

The little girl nodded. "I have Mama's pictures in my bag."

"We'll put them up later. I need to talk to your Uncle Jamie first. Then I'll get us something to eat and we can put the pictures up on the wall before we go to bed."

She rose and followed Blackburn, who had retreated into the corridor. He didn't protest when she closed the door so the child wouldn't overhear the conversation. Miranda faced him squarely, finally acknowledging his presence. "I want to make sure there is a clear understanding between us," she told him. "Is Nora the only reason you married me?"

Blackburn shrugged, but the gesture lacked his usual confidence. "You'll save me a lot of money. I was paying Mrs. Van Cleef five dollars a week to look after Nora. I got you for ten. I'll break even on you in two weeks."

"With what you spent on the Appaloosa and on my clothes, it will take you at least a year to break even."

"I'm selling the Appaloosa. You don't need a horse. There's nowhere for you to go and I need the money. I owe for doctor's bills and my sister's burial."

"What did your sister die of?"

"Bullet in the chest. Louise was caught in the gunfire

when the bank was robbed a few weeks ago. The robbers got eleven thousand dollars and it cost my sister's life."

A shiver ran over Miranda. "Those four men you killed?"

Blackburn nodded. "Bounty hunting is my trade, but sometimes I get to mix business with pleasure." He made that jerky motion with his head again, the one that made his raven locks skim his shoulders. "You'd best remember that I track people down for a living. I'll be riding out tomorrow morning but I'll look in on you in about a month. If I discover that you've abandoned Nora while I was gone, I'll find you, and I'll kill you."

"Dear me." Miranda lifted a single eyebrow. "I'm shaking in my boots."

She saw one corner of the bounty hunter's wide mouth tug up in the reluctant smile he sometimes failed to hide. "And very expensive boots they are, too," he replied.

"I'd like two things from you."

He shook his head. "Can't let you keep Alfie. I need the money, and it would cost too much to keep a horse at the livery stable. More than you make cleaning in the saloon."

"Wait to hear what I'm asking before you refuse." Miranda paused, making sure she had Blackburn's full attention before she continued. "I want you to give me a better reason why you married me. You didn't do it just to save money. It is important for me to hear you spell it out."

Blackburn pushed the edges of his long duster apart and curled his hands over the butts of his revolvers. The gesture might have threatened another gunfighter, but it didn't scare Miranda one bit. "Say it," she demanded.

His dark brows gathered into a frown and he spoke in a low, gruff voice. "You saw Mrs. Van Cleef. She's a sour old coot, but she was the only woman in town prepared to

take in a kid who is part Indian. I want something better
for Nora, for her last few weeks. She's lost her mother. I
can't look after her. I need to be out there, making money
for doctor's bills. I saw you in that saloon, in your blue
dress, looking like an angel. I hoped you might give her
love. At least I hoped you might give her more affection
than Mrs. Van Cleef ever could."

"I'll try," Miranda promised. "But I have one condi-
tion."

"Let's hear it."

"As long as I live at the Carousel, I never, ever want to
hear you creep along the corridor into the bed of one of
the saloon girls. We might be married in name only, but
I will not suffer the humiliation of seeing my husband
with another woman, the way you went with Nellie on
the eve of our wedding."

There. She'd said her piece. Now she could go back
to ignoring him. Miranda turned toward the door, curled
her hand over the knob.

"Wait," Blackburn said. Miranda glanced back over
her shoulder. He'd pulled a rolled-up exercise book from
inside his duster and was holding it out to her. "You might
like to read to Nora from this in the evenings."

Miranda took the booklet, flicked through the pages. It
was a collection of poems, hand written, in an educated,
artistic hand. The first page said: "Eleanor Wilkinson.
My favorite poems."

"It belonged to my mother," Blackburn said. "Lucky
you picked Tennyson for your question. That particular
poem is on the second page. My mother wasn't so fond
of Keats."

Something fell into place in Miranda's mind. "Before
you bought a ticket for the bride lottery, you asked me
to read from the Bible… I thought it was because you

wanted to hear my voice…but you were making sure I wasn't just holding the book for show."

"I wanted to check that you could read out for the child." He tugged his hat deeper on his head and made a move to leave. "I'll go and see to the horses." Halfway along the hall, he turned to look back at her. "I'll come by later to say goodbye to Nora."

Chapter Nine

Miranda knelt by the narrow bed. "How are you feeling, Skylark? Ready to have lunch?"

She would have liked to stroke the child's brow, but her hands were wrapped in strips of cotton torn from an old pillowcase. It had turned out her skin couldn't tolerate the lotions to polish the mahogany counters and brass rails in the saloon.

Nora gave her a quivering smile. "I am tired."

"I know, sweetheart. I'll fetch you some broth."

Miranda got to her feet, looked down at the pale face framed by the blunt wedge of black hair. A lump swelled in her chest. Valiant and brave, the child never complained but bore her illness and the loss of her mother with stoicism beyond her years. And every display of affection made her bloom, like a flower bloomed in sunlight.

The slightest praise made her glow. A hug brought out a radiant smile. Magic tricks caused her to laugh with joy. Learning about the wind and the stars filled her with wonder, and a bedtime story made her eyes shine with delight.

How could one resist such a child? In only a week, Miranda had grown to love her with a fervor that hurt. Perhaps it was because her sisters were so far away. All the affection she normally gave them was now poured on Nora.

"I won't be long," Miranda said and set off for the kitchen.

Downstairs, she paused by Nordgren's office, a small, wood-paneled room with a hatch that opened through to the saloon, allowing the owner to keep an eye on the gambling tables. Now, midmorning, the saloon was quiet, with only a few muffled voices drifting through.

"I've come for my pay," Miranda said.

Nordgren, a tall, broad-shouldered man in his forties with red-gold hair, looked up from his ledgers. His eyes narrowed. "What's wrong with your hands?"

"Blisters." Miranda inspected the bandages. "My skin reacts to the soaps."

Frowning, Nordgren bounced a pencil in his fingers. "It will get worse. I had another girl like that once. The skin just peeled off in strips." He gave her one of his penetrating up and down looks. "Can you do anything else? Sing? Dance?"

Sing? Dance? In a saloon?

The suggestion ought to shock her, but instead a flicker of excitement sparked within Miranda. When she fled from Merlin's Leap in the night darkness, she had felt the constraints of society fall away, like shackles from a slave.

I can be anything I want to be.

A slow, wicked smile tugged at her mouth. "I can sing. Opera arias and sea shanties."

Nordgren's pencil stilled. He gave her another perusal. "Don't matter what you sing. Just make sure you give the men something to look at. The stage costumes are in the storage room."

He pulled open a desk drawer, took out a handful

of silver dollars, counted out five and pushed the stack over to her. "This is for last week. We can talk about an increase in pay once I've seen how you perform on the stage."

Her thoughts awhirl, Miranda hurried out of the room. A doubt niggled in her mind that Mama and Papa would have disapproved of one of their daughters singing and dancing on a saloon stage.

She dismissed the concern. Her parents had always taught her to rely on her own judgment, and now it seemed more important to secure gainful employment than to cling to social propriety.

The huge, spotlessly clean kitchen was unoccupied but sweltering with heat. Miranda filled a bowl with chicken broth from the pot bubbling on the stovetop. Then she returned upstairs and fed Nora until the child grew too tired and slumped against the pillows.

"When will Uncle Jamie come back?"

There was such longing in the question, such worship in the child's eyes, anger stirred in Miranda. How could James Fast Elk Blackburn remain absent at a time like this? She hated to admit it, but she missed him, too. She had not realized how much during those silent days of riding she had grown to rely on his quiet strength.

"I'm sure he'll be back soon," Miranda reassured the child.

With a soft sigh, Nora closed her eyes and drifted off to sleep. Miranda used the time to compose a telegram to Charlotte. She had decided to postpone writing to Annabel. If Cousin Gareth had returned to Merlin's Leap, he would intercept the message. The excuse of a letter of condolence could only be used once and she preferred to save it for later.

Jotting down words, striking them out again, pausing

every now and then to check on the sleeping child, Miranda composed her message as the sun crested in the sky.

> Mrs. Maude Greenwood, Gold Crossing, Arizona Territory. Traveling to join you. Delayed with important work. Annabel alone home. Cousin Gareth followed me until Chicago. After that whereabouts unknown. Perhaps back Merlins Leap. Send news. Carousel Saloon, Devils Hall, Wyoming Territory. Love. Miranda.

Satisfied, Miranda counted the number of words. Forty-two. Just as well she had decided to postpone writing to Annabel, for sending the telegram would eat up most of her five dollars.

Lamps in wall brackets with reflectors behind them illuminated the small stage at the rear of the Carousel Saloon. Miranda had turned the wicks right down, to dim the lights for her first performance. She had rejected the skimpy costumes in the storage room, instead altering her pale blue wool gown to be low-cut at the bodice.

Although the saloon was crowded, with men sitting at the tables and standing along the counter, hardly anyone was looking in her direction. Nordgren had not advertised her debut, allowing for the possibility that she might back out at the last minute.

Miranda took a deep breath and stepped out from the shadow of the velvet curtain. She lifted her parasol and twirled it overhead. Her experience with Madam Lucille had served as a valuable lesson. The storage room had provided a frilly parasol and Moses, the elderly black cook, had sharpened the steel point, turning it into a more effective weapon.

The piano players at the Carousel were miners who

played music to their own liking and came and went as
they pleased. Miranda had decided to perform without
accompaniment. Foregoing any introduction, she burst
into a song.

"As I walked out one morning fair
Out there I met Miss Nancy Blair

I shook her up and I shook her down
I shook her all around the town

I run her all night, I run her all day
And I run her until we sailed away

Only one thing grieves me mind
To leave Miss Nancy Blair behind."

Silence fell at the tables. Men turned to watch. Whiskey glasses halted in midair. Vaguely, Miranda was aware
of the attention as she sang and twirled the parasol and
moved about with tiny mincing steps and rolled her eyes
to emphasize the comedy of the words.

She should have been ashamed of making a spectacle
of herself. She should have been afraid of the roomful of
lusty, drunken men. But she was neither. She could sense
a wall of emotion coming toward her, but it was not lust.
It was laughter and friendship and admiration and gratitude. She had sensed the same as a girl when crews from
Papa's ships came to visit Merlin's Leap.

The miners in the saloon, just as the sailors on the
ships, were men far away from home. Lonely men, separated from loved ones. The music would entertain them,
and if they looked at her with longing in their eyes, it
was not *her* they were pining for—she was the symbol

for every sweetheart they had left behind or hoped yet to meet.

Emboldened, Miranda walked to the edge of the stage and halted there. She sang the final verse, smiled at the audience. "Hello, gentlemen."

A few hoots and rowdy protests rose from the crowd. Miranda tilted her head to one side and lifted her brows. "I'm calling you gentlemen, because that is what I expect you to be. I am here to entertain you with my songs. They are called sea shanties. I grew up by the ocean, the daughter of a sea captain. Sea shanties are songs sailors sing on ships to accompany their work."

They were staring raptly at her. Miranda waited a beat, to make sure she had their undivided attention. Then she lowered the parasol and took a step to where a straw-filled flour sack she had prepared for the purpose sat leaning against the wall.

"If anyone should be tempted to try anything ungentlemanly, be warned." She lowered her parasol and struck the point like a rapier into the sack of straw, drawing laughter and cries of mock horror from the audience.

"And if that isn't enough, you should know that my husband is a bounty hunter. He hunts men down for a living, and he is very jealous." She smiled, twirled her parasol, put one hand on her hip and gave a little wiggle. "Now that we have all that cleared up, enjoy the music."

"What do we call you, darling?"

"You can call me Miss Randi."

She turned her back on the men, walked a few steps, peered coquettishly over her shoulder and burst into another song. Oh, she was having such fun. Much better than scrubbing and cleaning. In all honesty, she would be lying if she claimed not to enjoy male admiration, as long as the admiration did not cross a line.

I can be whatever I want to be.

And now that something was a saloon singer. She would make sure to negotiate a higher salary with Nordgren. If her parents were looking down from heaven, Miranda suspected they might be chuckling with amusement, even as they shook their heads in disapproval.

And, if seeing his wife parade in a low-cut gown in front of a crowd of men annoyed the bounty hunter, who had tricked her into marriage and had given her the heartbreaking task of caring for a dying child, Miranda would regard it as a bonus.

However, the best part of her new role was the working hours. Nora was at her strongest in the mornings, and Miranda hated to leave her alone then. Because she would be performing in the evenings, she could spend more time with Nora, take the child on outings, make her final weeks as happy and fulfilling as possible.

Miranda checked her upsweep in the mirror and tugged the bodice of her gown higher over her breasts. For eight days now, she had been singing in the saloon, with great success. If only Charlotte would reply to her telegram!

Downstairs, Miranda made her way to the stage. The crowd parted to give her unfettered passage. Mostly, the men treated her with respect. The few exceptions had tasted the sharp point of her parasol or the fists of the more gentlemanly customers.

As an added precaution, she kept reminding the men about her jealous bounty hunter husband. By now, her frequent comments about James Fast Elk Blackburn had created an illusion of a loyal wife devoted to her absent husband.

She climbed up to the stage, struck a pose. Just as she was about to launch into a song, the post office messenger, a tall, gray-haired war veteran, came through the swinging doors. Miranda's heartbeat quickened. He was coming in her direction! And he was holding a telegram! He came up to the stage, reached up with his good hand.

"For you, Miss Randi."

"Thank you." Her voice trembled. The fear she had tried to keep at bay surged. Why had it taken so long to get a reply from Charlotte? What could be wrong?

"Is it your husband, Miss Randi? Has he been killed?"

Startled, she looked into the crowd. A new fear clenched in her chest. It had never occurred to her that something could happen to the bounty hunter, even though his job involved danger. "I apologize, gentlemen. I need a moment of privacy."

She withdrew into the shadows behind the velvet curtain and unfolded the slip of paper with shaking hands. Why should it matter to her if Jamie Blackburn had met an end fitting to his profession? But it seemed that it did, and not just because it would leave her alone to take care of Nora.

Her eyes refused to focus on the text, postponing the potential bad news. Then she could no longer drag it out. She lifted the text closer to her eyes and read the telegram in the dim light of the lamp in the wall bracket.

Dear Miranda. Married happily. Sorry delay. Have been to San Francisco to claim inheritance. Annabel traveling to Gold Crossing with money for ticket. Aware Cousin Gareth followed you at Merlins Leap but no news since. Take care. Be well. Come soon. Have telegraphed money order one thousand dollars to bank Devils Hall. Inform if need more.

Miranda pressed the telegram to her breast. Both her sisters were safe. Annabel was on the train, secure with money. And Charlotte was married! If Cousin Gareth returned to Merlin's Leap, he would not find Annabel there, and if he had gone after Charlotte in Gold Crossing, she now had a husband to protect her, as a husband should protect his wife. Her mouth pursed in dismay. Where was he? Where was James Fast Elk Blackburn?

The night chill was falling as Jamie rode into Devil's Hall. He'd been on the road for three weeks and two days, earning five hundred dollars by tracking down a pair of men who had robbed a mine payroll across the border in Colorado.

Both outlaws had been wanted dead or alive. Jamie had tried to take them alive, but all too often an outlaw destined for the rope preferred to take his chances in a gunfight. If they didn't win their freedom, at least they gained a clean, quick death.

After he'd hauled the bodies to the nearest sheriff's office, Jamie had gone into a saloon, however he had foregone his usual custom of paying for a woman to celebrate staying alive. It puzzled him how a man could derive pleasure from being told to stop doing things he normally enjoyed doing, but when a little redhead had perched on his knee to whisper suggestions in his ear, he'd gained an odd sense of satisfaction from sending her away, telling her he was a married man.

In town, the grinding and clattering at the mine had ceased for the day. On Main Street, the two saloons shone like beacons to guide weary travelers. Jamie took Sirius to the livery stable and headed for the Carousel.

As he pushed his way in through the batwing doors, the Carousel appeared unusually crowed, yet strangely quiet. Most of the customers had their backs to the door. Careless fools. A man couldn't expect to live long that way. Jamie tried to see what they were all staring at but couldn't get a view of the small stage at the rear of the room.

As he edged closer, he could hear a feminine voice singing a flirty, playful tune, something about a sailor with a girl in every port. It reminded him of how he'd lain awake for three nights, listening to Miranda singing her melodies, her voice so low that he'd had to strain his ears just to hear the faint rustle of sound, never mind the words.

Jamie pushed forward, ignoring the angry glares directed at him as he elbowed his way past the men who had risen to their feet to watch. The singing girl was twirling about, wiggling her hips, her back toward the audience.

My, Jamie thought. This one would be hard to toss off his lap, should she choose to settle upon it. Tall and slender, with a waist no bigger than the span of his hands. Fair hair, piled up on her head in a loose knot that suggested a man could make it tumble down with a single tug. The whole tempting package was squeezed into a pale blue dress that hugged every feminine curve.

The girl turned around and minced toward the edge of the stage. Jamie let his gaze drift upward, curious to see her face, but got distracted by a pair of milky white breasts that rose above the low neckline of her dress. The pale blue fabric of the dress seemed oddly familiar. His gaze slid the final few inches up to the singer's face.

Hellfire and damnation.

Had Jamie not been shocked to immobility, he would have jumped up to the stage and pulled his wife out of the hungry glare of thirty other men. How did she dare? How did she dare to flaunt herself on the stage after she had ordered him to respect his wedding vows?

Emotions twisted within him, each targeting a different part of his body. For a fraction of a second, he took his eyes off Miranda to glance at the men around him.

Close your eyes, he wanted to yell. *She is not yours to look at.* Then his attention returned to her.

She sang. She smiled. Her blue eyes sparkled. Her red lips pouted with air kisses. She sent the men coy looks from beneath her lashes. She twirled on her feet and wiggled her hips and shimmied her shoulders and did a million other things that made Jamie's pulse riot.

When the song came to an end, she struck a few more teasing poses while the crowd of men burst into applause. Some whistled and cheered. "Thank you," she called out, and gave a deep bow that offered an even better view of the milky white tops of her breasts.

Straightening, Mirada surveyed the crowd—and spotted him.

All daintiness left her movements. She marched to the edge of the stage, jumped down to the plank floor and cut a path toward him through the throng. It surprised Jamie how easily the men parted, but when Miranda got closer, he understood.

She was swishing her parasol about and muttering, "Get out of my way, get out of my way," her voice an angry growl that inspired men to obey. She came to a halt in front of him, her lovely features in a scowl. Jamie's already overwrought mind took another tumble, this time with confusion. Why was she furious with him? He hadn't done anything. He'd been away, taking care of business. She was the one behaving unlike a married person should.

He noticed her body tense, saw her mouth flatten into a hard line. Her shoulders twisted as she pulled back one arm. The instinct that had helped Jamie stay alive for eighteen years while he hunted outlaws warned him that she was about to deliver a hard slap across his face.

She didn't.

A small hand clenched into a fist, swung through the air and crashed into his jaw. The lady packed a bigger punch than Jamie would have expected from someone so dainty. He reeled, was forced to stumble backward to restore his balance.

Jamie rubbed his aching jaw. "What was that for?"

Instead of a rational reply, Miranda burst into a stream of insults that proved just how far her vocabulary had progressed beyond *oaf* in three short weeks.

"What's wrong, Miss Randi?" someone shouted.

"Is he bothering you, Miss Randi?"

"Do you want me to shoot him for you, Miss Randi?"

Questions peppered the air around them. Jamie would have laughed, had he not been so alarmed. A bunch of drunken knights in shining armor, offering to protect his wife from him. Icy sweat coated his skin at the prospect of danger. He lifted his hands high, clear of his guns, to make sure no one could claim an excuse to draw on him.

"Don't kill him," Miranda said. "He's my husband."

"Ohs" and "ahs" of surprise rose from the crowd, and then melted into a chuckle. "It's the husband." The words rippled around the room as the men repeated the comment to each other, like some kind of a secret code.

Miranda stepped up to him, so close her frothing skirts brushed the toes of his dusty boots. She craned forward, lined her mouth next to his ear and spoke in a muffled whisper that no one else could hear.

"Kiss me," she said. "Kiss me like you mean it."

Chapter Ten

Kiss me. Kiss me like you mean it.

Jamie froze. He stared down at the exquisite face tipped up toward him. A notch creased Miranda's brow. Through the multiple layers of his duster and coat and shirt, Jamie could feel slim fingers poking at his ribs, prodding him into action. A frown of impatience flickered across the flawless features of his little Eastern princess, whose latest transformation had turned her into the queen of the night.

Slowly, Jamie dipped his head. Every instinct screamed a warning. He knew without a doubt that if he obeyed her command, it would be the most dangerous thing he had ever done. More dangerous than any outlaw. More dangerous than a gun pointed at him. More dangerous than a rattlesnake coiled on a sunlit rock.

But he did it anyway. Just as Miranda parted her lips in a soundless whisper that spelled out *now*, Jamie closed the last of the distance between them and settled his mouth upon hers. Without a conscious thought, he wrapped his arms around her and hauled her to his chest.

At first, Miranda went rigid. Jamie guessed she'd anticipated a gentle peck, not an openmouthed kiss. But that's what she got. He could taste her shock and resistance as his lips slanted across hers. Something bold and powerful flowed through him. He'd never felt such a wild sense of elation at a woman's nearness, not even at the moment of completion in a saloon girl's bed.

Equally frightened and fascinated by the sensation, Jamie kept the kiss going. Because Miranda was so tall, he didn't need to bend, merely to incline his head. He could feel the length of her body molded against his. They seemed a perfect fit, her slender curves against his hard planes, her soft mouth beneath his hungry one.

As the seconds ticked by, Miranda grew responsive. Her hands eased their grip on his shoulders and swept up to the nape of his neck. Jamie could feel her fingers shifting through his hair, a delicate touch that sent another wave of pleasure rippling through him. He inhaled her scent, a fresh, floral soap, different from the cloying perfumes many saloon girls used. He could taste coffee, and the faint residue of tooth powder.

Slowly, Jamie became aware of the rowdy chorus of voices around them. Some of the comments were good-natured, but some were lewd, and Jamie could hear the hard edge of envy mingled with the friendly banter.

He broke the kiss, lifted his head. Miranda tried to follow, rising on tiptoe, eyes closed, lips parted. He withdrew his arms from around her, caught her chin with the edge of his hand and swept his thumb across her lips.

"That's enough for now, Princess."

Her eyelids fluttered up. She blinked a few times, as if emerging from darkness into a bright light. Slowly, the languid look in her eyes faded away. Instead of the fury Jamie had expected, a lost, disoriented expression settled on her features.

He took her hand and ushered her toward the exit. "Let's go, Princess. I appreciate the welcome, but now it's time for you to explain why you're prancing about on the stage seducing men instead of looking after the child I left in your care."

Miranda allowed Blackburn to steer her through the throng. If she were totally honest, she had hit him not just out of anger at his high-handed interference in her life, but out of anger at herself. The surge of delight that had flared inside her when she spotted him in the crowd was the last thing she should have felt at the sight of him. He was the enemy. He was at the root of the bewildering mix of happiness and grief that was tearing her apart.

"Let's hear it," Blackburn prompted.

"I hit you because I hate you. I hate you for marrying me. I hate you for bringing me here and making me love a child who is going to die. I hate you for the helplessness I feel. I hate you for leaving me alone to face the ordeal of watching her grow weaker each day as her time runs out."

Blackburn halted between the crowded tables. Standing rooted, he scowled at her, as if he had no idea what she was talking about. Miranda sailed past him and flounced out through the batwing doors of the Carousel, into the cool darkness of the night.

"Oh, why am I even trying to explain?" she said with an angry flap of her hand when he caught up with her on the boardwalk. "It's enough for you just to know that I hate you."

"You sure showed it in there." Blackburn pointed back inside with that annoying jerk of his head. Trust him to lack the good manners to ignore that small, inconvenient kiss. Perhaps *small* wasn't the right word, Miranda admitted. *Insignificant.* That was better. One insignificant kiss, exchanged out of necessity.

"That was for their benefit." She gestured to take in the Carousel, where the merry tune of a piano was now plinking out. "When I started performing, I needed something to keep the men from pestering me. I threatened them with a jealous husband and they got it into their heads that I..."

"That you what?"

Miranda swore she could hear amusement in that deep, husky voice. The bounty hunter smirked—Jamie, she thought of him as now, because Nora kept talking incessantly about her Uncle Jamie. For nearly a month now, Miranda had been obliged to admire James Fast Elk Blackburn for his noble existence as a crime fighter, a fine specimen of American manhood who in one handsome package combined the native heritage of the Cheyenne Nation, the adventurous spirit of the frontiersmen and the educated mind of an Eastern gentleman.

"A very jealous husband that you what?" Jamie prompted.

Miranda flattened her mouth. He knew what she had been about to say. What she had convinced all those men who came to drink at the Carousel to think, but only as a ruse to keep them from getting improper ideas about her.

That I love my husband very much. It was beastly of James Blackburn to attempt to force her to say it out loud. *Beastly* was her younger sister Annabel's favorite word and it served very well in this instance.

"Whom I...*respect*...very much," Miranda said in the end. "Of course, I'm not talking about you. I'm talking about an imaginary husband, one I married out of my own free will, and you are simply fulfilling that role in the eyes of the saloon crowd."

While they had been talking, they had drifted along the boardwalk, away from the noise of the Carousel and the Purgatory, to the better end of the town.

"Since when have you been singing at the saloon?" Blackburn asked.

"Since my second week. It turned out my skin can't tolerate the soaps for cleaning. My hands came up in blisters. When Nordgren asked me if I can do anything else, I told him I can sing. He offered me a trial. The men liked my act. I get five dollars a night, instead of five dollars a week, and it leaves me free to spend time with Nora during the day."

Jamie gripped her arm, forcing her to a halt. Their footsteps faded into silence. He gave her a tiny jerk that spun her around to face him. It occurred to Miranda that Jamie had an advantage, because he took care to keep his back to the light that spilled out of the saloons, hiding his face in the shadows while the lamp glow fell upon her.

"What happened to the rest of your dress?" he asked.

Automatically, Miranda glanced down. The tops of her breasts shone pale in the faint glimmer of light, like two uncooked buns rising from a baking tin. How inconsiderate of the man to draw attention to the more embarrassing aspects of her musical career.

"Nordgren said that if I wanted the position, I had to give the men something to look at. He offered me a costume that was little more than a corset with a tiny pumpkin-shaped skirt attached to it, and a pair of black fishnet stockings. We compromised."

She glanced up to Jamie's face but the darkness hid his expression.

"Where are we going?" she asked, peering ahead along the boardwalk.

"Huh?"

Miranda repeated her question. Jamie seemed about to nod off, judging by the way his face remained tipped downward, and he appeared to have lost his train of thought. Finally, he gathered himself and looked about him.

"I live at the Carousel," she reminded him. "I don't

know where you're going, but you'll need to escort me back to my room."

How was it possible for her to know he was grinning, even though she couldn't see his face? And how was it possible for her to know exactly what he would say, even before a single word came out of his mouth?

"But of course, I must sleep in your room. I am the jealous husband, the one you *respect* very much. Your ruse will lose all credibility if we spend the nights apart."

"The bed is very narrow." Her voice sounded very small.

"A happy couple always has enough room."

Jamie escorted his little princess back to the Carousel. An uneasy mix of amusement and guilt churned inside him, and something more, something dark and brooding he had no wish to examine. What made him want to needle her so? He was to blame for her situation, and she had shown remarkable courage and resourcefulness in solving the problem of alternative employment. And she seemed to hold true affection for Nora.

"How is the little Skylark?" he asked quietly.

"Getting very weak. I'm…" Miranda drew a shaky breath and lowered her voice, as if reluctant to say the words. "I'm pleased you've come. The doctor says she only has a few days left, and I agree. She didn't seem worried about being able to tell you goodbye. Something to do with her Cheyenne beliefs. I talk to her about God, but I don't discourage her Indian faith. In my view, two sets of religion offer a double dose of comfort."

Jamie felt warmth spread in his chest and feared the sensation was becoming all too frequent in Miranda's presence. He'd been right to get Nora away from Mrs. Van Cleef. The old harridan had scolded the child for talking about animals having a spirit, or anything else that went against the most puritan interpretation of the Christian faith.

When they reached the saloon entrance, Miranda gripped his arm to halt him. "Can we go upstairs the back way?"

Jamie saw her strained expression and felt another rush of guilt over how he had teased her. For a gently bred female, she had handled the saloon crowd well, but now the drunken miners might call out rude comments if they saw her leading her husband up to the bedroom. If he could spare her the embarrassment, he owed it to her.

"Sure," he said. "Let's go round the back."

They left the boardwalk and took the narrow passageway between the buildings. When Miranda stumbled, Jamie offered her his arm. "Hold on to me. I can see in the dark. There's a pothole ahead, and a shovel leaning against the wall, and a broken chicken cage."

He steered her safely through the alley and up the rickety back stairs, through the balcony door, into the upstairs hall. When he tried the door to her room, it swung open.

"I don't lock the door when Nora is alone inside," Miranda whispered to him. "It allows her to come out and call for me from the landing, in case she needs me while I'm downstairs."

Jamie went in. In the bed on the left, a small shape lay tucked beneath a brightly colored quilt. The light through the open doorway fell on the soft features of the sleeping child. Then the quilt rippled, and the big brown eyes flared open. No whoop of joy. No bounce up on the bed. Just quiet words, carried on a mere rustle of breath.

"Uncle Jamie. I knew you'd come."

Terror seized Jamie at how weak his niece appeared. He turned to Miranda, who had tiptoed in behind him. "Should we let Nora sleep?" he asked quietly.

Miranda shook her head. "You talk to her. I'll go and

make a pot of herbal tea. There is always hot water on the stove at the end of the upstairs hall."

She held his gaze for a second, their positions reversed now, the light from the hallway falling on him and leaving her face in shadows, and yet in Miranda's expression Jamie could read the words she could not speak. *Talk to the child while you can, for she might not be with us in the morning.*

Jamie nodded. Tears stung in his eyes, an alien sensation he'd almost forgotten, for it had been almost two decades since he'd allowed himself the luxury of weeping. He turned toward the child on the narrow cot and waited until Miranda's footsteps had faded away.

"Everything okay, Skylark?" he asked. "Is she looking after you well?"

"Miranda is the best Mama you could have brought me. She can do everything she promised. Magic tricks, and she knows how to tell how fast the wind is blowing. It is measured in something called knots, did you know? But it's not the same as a knot on a string, or a knot in my hair."

"I didn't know that, Skylark." While Jamie had been listening to the child, he'd taken a tin box of matches out of his coat pocket, and now he lit the pair of lamps in the wall brackets and took a look around.

The room had been transformed since his last visit. By the door, clothes hung from pegs. On a shelf above each bed, toys and books and ornaments jostled for space. Beneath the window stood a table, and on it sat a selection of crockery from the kitchen and a bundle of folded cloth. Pictures tacked to the walls completed the bright, cozy atmosphere.

"Miranda can draw, just like Mama could."

Jamie settled on the edge of Nora's bed and studied the artwork on the opposite wall. He recognized some of his sister's drawings, animals and Indian symbols. The oil paintings were new. Nora reached out to point at a picture, but her arm fell back to the covers, her strength depleted.

Jamie smoothed her glossy black hair. "Don't wear yourself out, Skylark."

He heard footsteps, turned to see Miranda walk in with a clay teapot balanced in her hands. She didn't say anything, just gave Nora a tender smile and knelt on the floor. Moving with easy grace, she took two mugs from the table and poured tea into them.

Miranda handed Jamie a mug, then gestured for him to scoot along the bed. He moved up and she took his place. Using some kind of tiny beaker carved out of wood, Miranda gave Nora small sips of tea, first tasting each measure to make sure it had cooled enough.

"I put honey in the tea," Miranda said to the child. "It will give you strength."

"I don't need it anymore," Nora replied. "I'm ready to die."

Jamie bolted up to his feet, splashing hot tea onto his fingers. He couldn't do this. Part of him wished he had been delayed along the way. That he'd been injured, or his horse had gone lame. He, who dealt with death every season of the year, could not handle watching a child slowly slide toward her passing.

"Show Uncle Jamie the picture of us on Alfie," Nora said.

Miranda shot Jamie a glance he couldn't interpret. "Here," she said, reached up to take a small painting from the shelf above the bed and handed it to him.

It was an oil painting on a wooden board, and it showed a gray Appaloosa horse and a fair-haired woman in black boots and a short, vaquero-style coat. A little girl wearing a similar outfit sat in front of the woman. The saddle and bridle had silver studs.

"That's us on Alfie when we go out riding," Nora said.

"Does the livery stable rent out the Appaloosa?" Jamie asked. He had sold the horse and had expected it to be resold at once. Appaloosas were in decline since the Nez Perce War ended more than a decade ago and were rarely offered for sale.

"I bought it back," Miranda replied.

"Bought it back?" Jamie stiffened. "But I sold it for two hundred dollars."

Miranda didn't say anything, and Jamie knew he couldn't press for an explanation in front of the child. He made a quick mental calculation. Five dollars a night. The most Miranda could have made while he was away was around a hundred dollars.

His eyes roamed the room, noted the details he'd failed to appreciate before. Expensive toys. Brand-new picture books. Clothes in a child's size—denim trousers and small boots, and a fringed leather coat that would turn a little girl into a miniature bandit princess.

"What have you done?" he growled then fell silent. It would have to wait.

Sensitive as always, Nora reached for his hand. "Don't be angry with Miranda. I love her. I want you to love her, too." Small fingers curled around Jamie's callused ones. "Say you'll love her. Promise you'll love her."

"I'll love her," Jamie muttered through clenched teeth.

"Good." The child sighed and closed her eyes. "Now I am ready to die."

Chapter Eleven

Miranda woke up to a bright summer dawn. She thanked the Lord for another sunny day, in case it might be Nora's last. She wanted to get up, visit the privy, but she didn't know how to get past Jamie, who slept on the floor between the two beds.

Last night, after Nora had drifted off to sleep, a morose mood had seized the bounty hunter. He'd gone out, not to the Carousel, but to the rough, restless Purgatory a few doors down the street. Hours later, he'd returned, reeking of whiskey, and had settled on the floor without a word.

It had been Miranda's plan to tell him about her sisters, but Jamie had set her temper on edge, the way he had suddenly acted full of suspicion when he had understood she'd been spending money. What did he think? That she'd robbed the bank?

Her eyes swept over the man on the floor. He seemed to be sound asleep. The long duster was spread like a blanket over him, boots peeking out beneath the hem. She couldn't see his guns, or the knife he carried in his belt. His warnings rang through her mind. *If you need to wake me up, don't creep up on me and touch me. I'll most likely slit your throat.*

Needs must. The privy called. Miranda folded the quilt

aside. She slept in a baggy gown made from an old flannel shirt with a length of fabric added to the hem. The garment skimmed her toes and served as a day dress as well as a nightgown. Unless she was going out into the town, she kept it on until it was time to change into her stage costume.

Miranda eased one foot down to a vacant spot by the hip of the sleeping bounty hunter. Then the other foot. He didn't stir. She couldn't see his face, for he had propped his hat over his eyes. Gingerly, Miranda picked her way past him. When she was at the door, she heard him speak in a low voice. "Can you bring coffee?"

Miranda nodded her agreement and darted out, unease coursing through her. He must have been awake all along while she crept past him. How could a person wake up like that, making no sound, not moving at all, not even a flinch? And how could he talk as if he could see through the crown of his hat?

Downstairs, Miranda crossed the backyard to take care of her needs, then came back inside and went to fetch coffee from the kitchen. She paused to talk to Moses Freeman, the powerfully built but gentle cook who had sharpened her parasol for her.

In his fifties, Moses took great pride in his breakfast biscuits and the spicy Southern flavors of his cooking. When Miranda first got to know him, she'd asked him why he had left the temperate climate of Louisiana to settle in the Wyoming Territory.

Moses had replied that when he gained his freedom, he had wanted to get as far away as he could without leaving the country. He'd planned to keep going all the way to Alaska, but had stopped in Wyoming when he discovered Canada lay in between.

"How's the little one doing?" Moses asked in his

deep rumble, his fingers busy pinching the biscuit dough into balls.

Miranda gave a slow shake of her head and blinked away the tears. "Maybe today. Maybe another day. Maybe two or three."

Moses nodded, arranged the uncooked biscuits into a pan. "I have the grave all dug out where you shown me, next to where her mother rests in the cemetery."

Miranda touched the back of his huge gnarled hand. "Thank you, Moses."

The former slave, who'd seen more suffering in his childhood than most people saw in a lifetime, felt no shame in showing his grief. Bright trails of tears ran down his weathered face. "The girls is ready for it," he said. "The undertaker's gonna give you no trouble."

"I appreciate everything you've done, Moses, and everything Eve and Jezebel have done."

Moses turned to put the pan of biscuits in the oven. There was weariness in the rigid set of his broad back—the weariness of a man who was getting on in years and had seen every chance of happiness pass him by. He didn't turn toward Miranda again, and she got the impression he needed a moment alone.

"Thank you, Moses," she said softly and picked up the steel jug she'd filled with steaming coffee from the big copper pot on the stove. "Please thank Eve and Jezebel for me when they come down."

The Carousel only had two saloon girls, and they had carved up the market, as indicated by their names. The small, fair Eve dressed in girlish, demure outfits, a picture of virginal innocence. Jezebel had dark hair and striking gypsy features. She rimmed her eyes with kohl and wore low-cut sequined gowns. The arrangement worked well. Each girl had their regular clients, and the men who craved variety could alternate between them.

The undertaker, Mr. Jones, a tall, officious bachelor, had been adamant that Nora couldn't be buried in the church cemetery, since she had never been baptized, her parents hadn't been legally married and Indians had their own burial ground. That Nora's mother had been buried in the churchyard failed to sway him.

Eve and Jezebel had resolved the situation by threatening to withhold their favors permanently if Mr. Jones failed to cooperate. Reluctantly, the undertaker had agreed to turn a blind eye, pretending not to notice if Moses dug a grave and helped Miranda to bury the child in the early-morning hours.

Miranda returned upstairs with the coffeepot, her mind busy figuring out how to explain the situation to Jamie in such a way that he would not be tempted to put a bullet in the unfortunate Mr. Jones.

Jamie had kept still on the floor while Miranda scrambled out past him. His head throbbed and his mouth tasted like a sewer. It was not so much the whiskey, although last night he'd drunk more than he was used to. It was the stale air at the Purgatory, full of tobacco smoke, and the night slept in a warm, stuffy room instead of outdoors.

Once Miranda had padded out in her bare feet, he waited a few seconds before getting up and going to the big cauldron of water on the stove at the far end of the corridor. He rinsed his face and teeth and ran a hand over his jaw. Shaving could wait another day. He didn't care much for his Indian heritage, but the weak growth of beard came in useful.

Back in the room, he opened the window and filled his lungs with the crisp morning air. The northerly aspect would be chilly in the winter but it was a small price to pay for the view of the snowcapped mountains in the distance.

His eyes fell to the bundle of fabric on the table. He shook it open. It was pretty fabric, the kind one might use for curtains or to cover parlor cushions in a wealthy home. Tiny birds in bright colors —hummingbirds, he decided on a closer look—hovered on a cream-colored background.

"You've found my hummingbirds, Uncle Jamie."

Nora had woken, and she was looking up at him, her eyes bright and alert. For an instant, hope flared within Jamie. She seemed so much better now. Then the truth flooded into his mind, cold and unwelcome. It had always been like that—small spurts of vitality when the child had taken care to rest and preserve her strength.

He bent to Nora, gathered her in his lap. "It is very nice fabric. What is it for?"

She gave him a quick peck on the cheek. "It's for me, for when I die."

Jamie's heart wrenched as he watched the child smile. Ten years old but as wise as someone who had lived to a hundred.

The small, frail hands stroked the brightly colored fabric. "The hummingbirds will guide me when I sail up to heaven. Heaven, or *Seana*, like my father did. Mama told me he traveled the long fork of the Milky Way, even though he was killed in battle. He died a good death. Miranda says that *Seana* and heaven are the same place really, so one day she'll be there, too. Will you be there, Uncle Jamie?"

"If I die a good death."

Jamie frowned as he heard his words. Where did that come from? He'd been baptized Christian, he was only a quarter Cheyenne and he took no interest in the Indian legends.

He didn't believe that if you died a good death your spirit traveled up the long fork of the Milky Way to *Seana*, and if you died a violent death your spirit went up the short fork to some other place, or remained stuck on earth. If he did believe that, he'd have one more thing to worry about.

"Mama told me that when I'm ready to die, a hummingbird will come and call for my spirit. That's why Miranda ordered this fabric. We looked together in a big book and chose. It was called a *cataloo*."

A hummingbird, Jamie thought. They were rare this far north but he'd occasionally seen them. Hummingbirds came in May and stayed until September. They were at the end of August. If he kept Nora indoors, away from the flowering plants... Jamie shook his head. What was wrong with him? He didn't believe in all that Indian mumbo jumbo.

A bright, feminine voice came from the doorway. "It was a *catalogue*, Skylark, from a big store called Montgomery Ward."

Jamie turned and saw Miranda walk into the room. How had it happened? All his finely honed instincts had failed to warn him. She'd walked right up to him, and he'd not heard her footsteps, nor had he sensed her presence. If she had been a wanted man and he on the hunt, he'd already be dead, and it would not have been a good death.

Miranda was holding up a steel coffeepot. Her gaze searched his, and Jamie could read uncertainty in her expression. She lifted the pot higher, as if offering to pour. "I hope this is all right. I'll go back downstairs for biscuits in a few minutes."

Jamie met the question in her eyes. "It's fine," he said. "It's good."

He could sense Miranda's anxiety ease. Both of them knew her question had not been about breakfast. She'd been asking him about the hummingbird fabric—if he minded how she had been preparing Nora for the end.

The child did not seem to notice the tension but continued her chatter. "When I die, Miranda is going to line the coffin with the hummingbird fabric, and she is going to put all my favorite toys inside. It might be a few days before I get to Mama in Heaven, and I'll have something to play with while I travel. I'm going to wear my new clothes. Will you stay, Uncle Jamie?"

Nora fell silent and looked up. The naked plea in her eyes was the first time Jamie had seen the child reveal her fear. "Will you stay and help Miranda put me in my grave?" Nora went on. "She is going to do it early in the morning, just when the first rays of sunshine come over the hill. Will you stay, Uncle Jamie? Will you stay?"

Jamie felt as if a heavy weight was crushing his chest, suffocating him. "Yes, Skylark," he replied, his voice rough with emotion. "Of course I'll stay."

Jamie watched Miranda stack away the dirty plates and cups. They'd had biscuits with blueberry jam for breakfast. Nora was already getting tired. He tucked her back into bed with a promise of an outing in the afternoon if the weather held.

"I'll take these downstairs," Miranda said.

He followed her into the hall and closed the door. "We need to talk."

She peered down at her bare toes beneath the hem of the baggy dress she wore and gave a small, uncomfortable shrug. All morning, Jamie had sensed an undercurrent of hostility from her, and he knew it stemmed from his angry, unreasonable reaction last night. How could he explain? For a second, he'd believed she had found a way of contacting his mother's family in Baltimore to ask for their help.

The mere idea had made rage flare up inside him. He never wanted to ask anything from them again. The only thing he felt for his grandfather was a bitter, black hatred.

He didn't know if the old man was still living or had died years ago, and he didn't care.

He might have been able to overcome his resentment if the doctors believed something could be done for Nora, that having limitless funds might make a difference. But over the years, he'd been assured time and again that medical science held no miracle cure. Not unless someone knew how to cut open a human chest, take out a defective heart and put another one in its place.

After his initial flash of anger, Jamie had come to his senses. He knew for certain there was nothing in Nora's belongings from which Miranda could have discovered the Baltimore address. Everything was in his saddlebags—including the thick letter that had come more than a month ago. He'd never opened it, but he'd not had the determination to burn it, the way he and Louise had burned the two other letters that had come before.

However, the question remained unanswered. How could Miranda buy back Alfie and pay for all those things? It occurred to Jamie that the alternative answer—the only one he could think of—might be even worse than his initial thoughts. Out of habit, his fingers felt for the guns at his hip. Startled, he realized he'd left his weapons in the room and was only armed with the spare knife hidden in his boot.

He shifted on his feet. "I need to know. Where did you get the money?"

Blue eyes met his. "It's none of your business."

"I think it is."

When Miranda didn't reply, Jamie hesitated. He knew he could bully the answer out of her, or get to the truth by going downstairs and talking to the people in the saloon. Instead, he spoke in a low voice.

"It is clear to me you love Nora. And I've seen how women can be when they love. They give everything, no matter how high the price. I saw it in my mother, and I saw it in my sister. And now I fear you may have felt compelled to use any means to ease Nora's final days."

Miranda's brow puckered. "What are you talking about?"

"Those men...down in the saloon... You haven't...?"

He could see the shock register on her face. He heard her sigh, saw her shoulders droop as she let go of the resentment that had risen between them. "No! Dear Lord, no," she blurted out. "My sister sent me money. My sister Charlotte."

Attentive and silent, Jamie listened while Miranda explained how their parents had died in a boating accident, and Charlotte, the eldest, had become an heiress. Jamie learned how their unscrupulous cousin had tried to get his hands on the money, and how Miranda had fled into the night, trying to reach Charlotte, who had already gone into hiding in a played-out mining town called Gold Crossing. He'd never heard of the place, but Colorado and Wyoming had dozens of mining towns that vanished almost as quickly as they sprang up.

"So," he said, digesting it all. "Your sister sent you a thousand dollars?"

Miranda nodded, and Jamie didn't press for details. Easy enough to check at the bank. Because they were married, he could find out anything about her business he might wish to know. "And your sister is in Gold Crossing now?" he added. "And everything is fine? Your cousin is no longer a threat? And you'll have someplace to go when you leave here?"

Again, she nodded, but the gesture seemed reluctant.

"Good," he said. "I have things to do. Bank. Livery stable. Marshal's office. I'll be back in the afternoon and we can take Nora out."

"Wait," Miranda said as Jamie turned to go back into

the room to fetch his knife and his pair of guns. "When you said you'll stay, did you mean it?"

She'd been speaking with her face downcast but now she lifted her chin. Jamie could see tears glistening in her eyes as she went on. "I didn't know if you would mind me talking to Nora about dying. She senses the time is near, and I believe it makes things frightening and confusing for a child if adults deny the truth. I wanted to make things less scary for her. Help her accept the inevitable."

"You've done well."

The plates and cups rattled as Miranda adjusted the load across her arm. "I don't think I'll be able to handle things alone…not in the end… I need you here…need someone to lean on… Need your strength to carry me through… Will you stay?"

Jamie blinked. He'd been doing a lot of blinking since he arrived last night. It must be the dust in the air. "Yeah," he said gruffly. "I meant it. I'll stay."

In front of him, Miranda's face crumpled. Her eyes pinched tightly shut. Jamie could see the dampness between her eyelids but the tears didn't fall. Her head was moving in the tiniest of nods, up and down, up and down, and she appeared to be holding her breath.

"Thank you." The words were soundless, a mere movement of her lips.

Jamie wanted to pull her close, bundle her into his arms, but somehow the kiss they'd shared last night stood between them, warning him to stay away. In his mind, he could hear Nora's words. *Say you'll love her. Promise you'll love her.*

He'd told her that he would.

God help him if it turned out to be true.

Chapter Twelve

Miranda had discovered that summer days in Wyoming often dawned bright but clouds could gather by midday and the afternoons might bring squalls. Today the weather remained mild and sunny, and the promised outing could go ahead.

They rode out of town, away from the mine workings. Nora, dressed in her denim trousers and boots and fringed leather coat, sat in front of Jamie on Sirius. Miranda, dressed alike, rode on Alfie, leading the way to their favorite picnic spot beneath a massive oak that offered shelter from the sun and the wind.

She dismounted, and Jamie handed Nora down to her, and then he vaulted off, untied the rolled-up blankets behind his saddle and spread them out on the ground. Miranda's silver-studded saddlebags contained the picnic—cold chicken and ham and creamed potatoes. While Miranda set out the food, Nora kept craning her neck, surveying their surroundings, as if in search of something.

"What are you looking for, Skylark?" Miranda heard Jamie ask.

"I'm looking for the hummingbird that will guide me to Mama."

Grateful she had her back turned Miranda dabbed the

corner of her eye. How great would the pain be later, when she could barely withstand it now? How hollow the emptiness? How deep the longing? She tried to find something to feel positive about.

At least now she knew that she wanted to be a mother one day, wanted children of her own. After her encounter with the Summerton children, she had shied away from the thought, but the brief taste of motherhood with Nora had changed her mind.

Her emotions under control again, Miranda finished spreading out the picnic. Jamie produced an orange out of his pocket, something that must have been transported from California at great expense.

"This is for the hummingbird." He pulled a knife from his belt, sliced the orange in two. Then he took out a piece of metal wire, uncoiled it and stuck one end through the orange half and suspended the wire from a branch on the tree. He did the same with the other half. "The hummingbird has a long, narrow beak it uses to drink the nectar from the fruit," he explained.

Nora smiled. "I'll wait for it to come."

They ate, and soon the afternoon sunshine lulled the child to sleep. Miranda watched Jamie from beneath her lashes. He was sitting on the ground, leaning back on his elbows, one leg folded at the knee. The breeze stirred his hair beneath the brim of his hat.

His silhouette blended against the landscape as though he were a part of it—part of the green grass and the mountains on the horizon and the rustle of the wind in the tree above, and the scents of parched earth and the gurgling of the small stream nearby, even the clunking of the machinery from the mine across the valley.

Once again, it struck Miranda how limited her world had been up to now. Apart from an occasional trip into Boston, she only knew Merlin's Leap and the countryside around the estate. Since their parents died and Cousin Gareth took over, her life had been restricted to the confines of the house.

She wanted more. She wanted to see the world, find her place in it.

She spoke quietly, her attention on Jamie. "What did you mean when you said that you've seen how women can give everything when they love, no matter how high the price? What did your mother give? And your sister?"

Jamie let his eyes rest on the horizon, as if he hadn't heard her question.

"Talk to me, James Fast Elk Blackburn," Miranda said with a touch of impatience.

"I don't find it easy to talk. Not about my family anyway."

"That's what people do, when they want to be friends. They lift the veil of privacy from their lives and let others see inside."

He glanced at her. "Is that what you want me to do? Lift my veil?"

Miranda picked up a twig from the ground and tossed it at him in mock anger.

"You've seen my veil lifted aplenty."

The corners of his mouth tugged up.

Heat crept into Miranda's cheeks. Her mind made a little spontaneous leap, and her gaze fell on Jamie's mouth. He'd kissed her. And she'd kissed him back. An odd spinning sensation had invaded her stomach then, and now, as she kept watching him and remembering that kiss, the same sensation radiated all through her, as if the heat from the sun had suddenly intensified a hundredfold.

"Has any woman ever loved you like that?" she asked softly.

His reaction was not what she had expected. Instead of

telling her to mind her own business, the bounty hunter threw his head back and burst into a roar of laughter.

Miranda's eyes narrowed. "What's so funny?"

"No woman has ever loved me. Not in that way or in any other way." He rocked on his elbow for a moment, as if she had just come up with the funniest thing ever uttered west of the Mississippi. Then he pulled his hat deeper over his head and started talking.

"My mother came from Baltimore. A fine family, like yours. She was on her way to Colorado, to marry the garrison commander in one of the forts. He was a little older, but their families were good friends and she was fond of him. My father was a soldier. Not a scout, but a soldier. He was half-Cheyenne, but he lived like a white man. Cut his hair short, went to church on Sundays. He was part of the escort that took the stagecoach to the fort. By the time my mother got off the stage, she knew she wouldn't marry the man she was engaged to. She'd not spoken a single word to my father, but she had been watching him. She broke off her engagement on the first day and then she told my father that she wanted to marry him."

"And what did he say?"

"He was horrified. He had no intention of stealing his commanding officer's fiancée. He told her that, in clear and absolute terms. So my mother went to the nearest town and got a job as a schoolteacher. It took her a year to convince my father they should be together."

"What happened to them?"

"My father died in an Indian massacre, in a place called Sand Creek. Seven hundred white militiamen killed a hundred and fifty Indians, mostly women and children. My father tried to stop the slaughter, and one of the militiamen pierced his chest with a bayonet.

"He'd left his army post by then. Dishonorable discharge. The garrison commander my mother had jilted brought trumped-up charges of misconduct against him. It was payback for stealing his fiancée. My father was working as a scout for another army unit when he was killed. It was an accident of fate he happened to be at Sand Creek when the militiamen struck. My mother hoped to get an army pension, but they withheld payment, saying that by trying to protect the Indian women and children my father had deserted his duty."

"They punished him for trying to protect women and children? And used it as an excuse to leave your mother penniless?" Aghast, Miranda suppressed a shudder. "How could they do something so cruel?"

"The garrison commander used his influence. I think he still wanted my mother, and he was plotting for her to be destitute, in need of a man to provide for her. She wouldn't marry him, though. We went to Baltimore. I was five. Louise was seven. I don't remember much of it. Only that the journey was long. We only stayed a single day. In the evening, my mother came to get us from the small room where we were waiting. She put our coats on us and we left. I remember that her face was very white and her hands were shaking so badly she couldn't button up my coat."

"Did she tell you what took place?"

"Never. She never spoke about it. Never spoke of her family again. She behaved as if Baltimore had vanished from the map. Louise claims she heard the servants talk and our grandparents had offered to take her back if she put us into an orphanage and pretended we didn't exist."

"What became of your mother?"

"We went back to Colorado and she opened a dress shop. Worked day and night, sewing dresses. About ten years later, she died. Just passed away in her sleep. Worn-out, I guess. Because of us—having two kids with Indian blood—the rich ladies in town didn't buy from her.

She didn't make much money. Not like someone with her skill and good taste could have done, if it hadn't been for me and my sister."

Miranda felt a twinge of shame. She and her sisters had thought they had suffered, losing their parents and then being hounded by Cousin Gareth. In truth they had been blessed, for they had grown up in a happy, secure home until they were on the verge of adulthood.

"Is your mother the one who educated you?" she asked quietly.

"Until she died. I was twelve. Then I went on the road, bounty hunting."

Startled, Miranda sat up straighter, dry leaves rustling under her. "You became a bounty hunter when you were twelve years old?"

Jamie nodded. "Bounty hunting had just been made legal, and it seemed a good way to make a living. I only went after men who were worth as much dead as they were alive. I knew I'd struggle to arrest a grown man and haul him in. But an outlaw destined for a rope is unlikely to surrender, and in a gunfight my youth didn't matter."

"Gunfight... You have to shoot it out?"

"A bounty hunter can only kill in self-defense. Otherwise it's murder. I practiced with a gun until I knew I was good enough to stay alive and then I went out on the road. I earned my first bounty a week after my thirteenth birthday. An outlaw had robbed the mercantile and killed the owner's wife. The owner put up the bounty, and all he wanted was to see the man's dead body brought back to him."

It sounded so violent, so hard and cold. And yet Miranda could detect no cruelty in Jamie. He was simply doing a job. And a bounty hunter was on the side of the law, helping sheriffs and marshals to deliver justice.

In his own way, Papa had been a hard man, too. He'd

had to be, to maintain discipline among the ships' crews. And despite that touch of hardness, Papa had been an honorable man, gentle with his wife and daughters and fair with his seamen and business associates.

"What if an outlaw surrenders?" she asked. "What will you do then?"

"If the bounty is big enough, I'll take him in. Sometimes I might let him go. Either the bounty isn't worth the aggravation of hauling him in, or something about the man convinces me he doesn't deserve to die or go to prison. Some men become outlaws not by choice, but by force of circumstance."

Miranda searched Jamie's face. He was in profile to her, and what she could see of his features gave nothing away, and yet his last comment had revealed compassion and sympathy for men less fortunate than him.

"Do you like it? The life of a bounty hunter?"

"It's the only life I know."

Jamie turned toward her, tilting back his head to peer at her from beneath the brim of his hat. The wind stirred the leaves in the tree above them. The sun broke through and made dappled shadows on the harsh angles and planes of his face. Again, Miranda could see the light in his clear gray eyes, as if a fire burned somewhere deep within.

An odd sinking sensation seized her, and she spoke quickly, in an effort to shake off the strange mood. "I would never have thought that we have something in common, but we do. I was just thinking a moment ago that I only know one life. The easy, comfortable life at my family home in Merlin's Leap."

"You know more, Princess. You know this life now." Jamie snagged a long blade of grass from the ground beside him and used it to point at Devil's Hall. "You've fitted right in. Made friends. Taken care of Nora. I'm proud of you. And grateful."

No words of praise had ever given Miranda the same sense of achievement, the same warm glow of pleasure. That heady, dizzy feeling engulfed her again. Confused, even a little frightened by it, she focused on the conversation.

"What about your sister? What did she sacrifice for love?"

"Louise married an Indian. Half-blood Northern Cheyenne, one who lived like an Indian, on the reservation. Initially, the Cheyenne kept most of their ancestral lands in a treaty with the US government. Later, when gold was found, ninety percent of the reservation was taken away again. That happened before I was born.

"The man my sister married wanted to make a life in the traditional ways, hunting buffalo, but the animals were too scarce by then, and there was always the threat that white militants might attack them if they saw Indians in possession of rifles.

"When Louise fell pregnant and they knew they'd soon have another mouth to feed, he thought, why fight the changing times when you can move on with the progress? So they took to prospecting for gold. They found a claim and staked it, but when they went to record their claim, they were told Indians didn't qualify. Louise had thought she could file in her name. She didn't look Indian, not as much as I do, but the recording officer knew she was part Cheyenne and rejected her claim.

"They went back to where they'd found gold, planning to dig up as much as they could before someone else found the location. The recorder must have tipped someone off, for a week later two men came. They shot the husband and chased Louise away.

"She fled on horseback, seven months pregnant. Nora was born premature, which might be what left her with a weak heart. My sister got the job cleaning at the Carousel, and she continued to work there until she died two months ago. Stray bullet in a bank robbery, I told you about it. Before it happened, she'd asked me to look after Nora, and I promised her that I would."

Even though Jamie rarely betrayed his emotions, Miranda could tell he had loved his mother and sister, just as much as he loved Nora. Apart from the three women who had been his family, it appeared he was alone in the world. Once Nora died, he'd have no one.

Except her, it occurred to Miranda. Legally, she was his wife. An odd excitement stirred within her at the thought. What would it be, to be married to a man like him? There was danger about him, and a hard, uncompromising edge. And yet she'd discovered there was honor in him, and compassion, and a deep sense of family loyalty.

Suddenly a comment whispered in her mind, something her mother had once told her and her sisters while talking about finding a husband. *A man who spreads his love too thinly will rarely love deeply.*

James Fast Elk Blackburn certainly did not spread his love too thinly. Did that mean he possessed the capacity to love unusually deeply? The thought made Miranda's heartbeat quicken, made a strange pressure build up in her chest, as if she could not catch her breath.

"You said your sister asked you to look after Nora," she commented when Jamie seemed to have run out of words. "You make it sound as if she expected to die."

Jamie locked his gaze on the horizon again. "She said a skylark had told her she'd die before Nora. Skylark was her special bird. Her powerful connection with nature. The Cheyenne religion is partly animistic. After Louise went to live on the reservation, she learned about the old beliefs, and she embraced them."

"And do you believe in them?" Miranda studied his

expression as she asked the question. "Do you believe a hummingbird will come for Nora?"

She could see a muscle tug in the side of Jamie's jaw. She knew he wanted to tell her it was nonsense, but something was stopping him. Miranda glanced up at the oranges swinging on the metal wires, and then at the child asleep at the base of the tree. A chill rippled along her skin.

"Let's go," she said. "The air is getting cold. I want to go back."

Jamie looked at her from the corner of his eye, then gave a nod and rolled up to his feet. She knew what he was thinking. What they both were thinking. Perhaps neither of them believed, but they were clutching at anything, even the tiniest source of hope. They didn't want to see a hummingbird. Not yet. Not today.

For the rest of the afternoon, the sky remained clear, building up heat in their small upstairs room at the Carousel. While Nora slept, Jamie helped Miranda hang up more pictures on the wall.

"Another nail," he prompted.

Miranda held out her palm.

Every time Jamie took a nail, his fingertips grazed her skin. There was a new kind of awareness between them now. It was not just the kiss they had shared, or the distraction of constantly brushing up against each other in the confines of the small room.

The attraction was beyond the physical. It was the kind of yearning that could flare up between a man and a woman if both of them had a raw spot of grief inside them, if they both longed for someone to help them heal and forget.

Jamie knew the feeling would grow. It would be at its worst right after they lost Nora and buried her lifeless body in the ground. That's when he'd have to be at his most alert to resist temptation, to stop himself from doing something that could not be undone.

"That's it." He stood back. The wall was covered now, two more of Miranda's oil paintings next to Louise's drawings and pictures cut out of magazines.

Miranda looked up from where she was arranging her brushes and paints. Her hair was spilling free from its upsweep. Perspiration beaded on her brow. She lifted one arm to wipe her face with the sleeve of the shapeless gown she'd changed into after they returned from their picnic. She looked lovely enough to break a heart of stone, let alone one of a solitary man who was about to lose the only living person he loved.

Jamie shifted on his feet. "I'll go and check on the horses."

He went out to the livery stable and managed to keep away for almost an hour, until sundown, when the restlessness inside him drew him back into the room. Nora remained asleep, a small, huddled shape beneath the quilt.

"I'm not going to work tonight," Miranda said. "I'll bring up a tray with chicken casserole. Nora will be too weak to eat, but she might take a little of the broth."

Jamie waited while Miranda went down to the kitchen and came back with a big tureen that released spicy scents into the air. They propped Nora against the pillows and took turns feeding her. Soon Nora fell asleep again and they had their own supper. It seemed wrong for Jamie to enjoy the food, but it was the best meal he'd had in a long time, tender and succulent and full of flavor.

"Moses is a good cook," he remarked.

"He is a good man," Miranda replied. "I think he was in love with your sister."

Jamie nodded. Instinct had told him the same, even if Louise had never said anything. "I think she loved him, too, but Nora was her world. If Louise had lived, maybe one day something might have come of it…"

Startled, Jamie listened to the easy cadence of his voice. He didn't like to talk. In particular, he didn't like to talk about feelings—not his own or anyone else's—and here he was now, speculating about his sister's affections.

They kept up the quiet talk until Nora awoke again, just as darkness fell, and a dusting of stars appeared in the black expanse of the sky outside the window. Jamie lit the lamps in the wall brackets. Miranda took out the book of poems and read Tennyson verses about a brook.

> "I chatter, chatter, as I flow
> To join the brimming river,
> For men may come and men may go,
> But I go on forever."

Jamie watched her as she read, her head bent, lamplight playing in her golden hair. A deep, painful ache rose in his chest. He knew he was falling in love with her. He'd never thought about a woman that way before. He'd turn thirty soon, and vaguely he'd assumed that one day, if he wished for some home comforts, he might marry an Indian girl, or at least one who was part Indian. A woman who didn't have much to lose by marrying him.

But now, the domestic scene filled him with a fierce longing. He'd give anything for the right to have a family of his own, the kind of family Miranda would one day have. A good husband, with a position in the community. Neighbors. Extended family, trusted relations who traveled across the continent when called upon, instead of turning their back with a cold, callous rejection the way his grandfather had done.

He'd have to suffer this strange anxiety for a few more days. Then they'd bury Nora, and he'd put Miranda on the train to Gold Crossing, wherever that might be, and he'd never see her again. Although he couldn't hope to forget her, in time the memory would fade, and he might achieve some kind of a pale imitation of happiness. Or perhaps his luck would run out, and an outlaw's bullet would wipe away all his worries.

Chapter Thirteen

In the morning Nora was too weak to dress or eat, but she insisted on inspecting the oranges hanging from the picnic oak, to see if hummingbirds had been feeding on them. Miranda and Jamie bundled her into a quilt and rode out.

For once, the gusty wind that seemed a permanent fixture of the Wyoming weather had stilled. The mine works were clanking across the valley. The first hint of autumn chill lingered in the air but the sunshine chased it away.

Jamie dismounted first, picketed the horses and held his arms out for Nora. Miranda passed the child to him and jumped down to the ground, grateful for her tall boots and warm coat. Perhaps they should have waited for the afternoon heat, but Jamie had worried the day would grow overcast.

They laid Nora down at the base of the tree, where she could lean against the trunk and have a clear view of the oranges hanging from a branch above. Jamie went to inspect the fruit that had dried a little.

"Something's been pecking at it."

"It's been. My hummingbird has been." Nora's words were faint.

Miranda tucked the quilt more firmly around the child. "Rest now."

Nora closed her eyes. Miranda and Jamie settled to sit on either side of her, shielding the child from the wind with their bodies. Miranda started singing. Her father had liked sea shanties and her mother had liked the opera, Verdi and Mozart and Rossini, and the newcomer Puccini. In her saloon act, Miranda had combined both. She sang Puccini now, her voice lullaby soft.

"Look! Look! He's come."

Nora's excited cry made Miranda pause. She looked down at the child. Nora's eyes were open, her head tipped back. A happy smile lit up her face. Miranda followed the direction of her gaze.

A tiny bird hovered by one of the orange halves, as if suspended in the air. The wings beat so fast, the eye couldn't follow the movement. The long beak dipped inside the fruit as the bird drank the nectar. Spellbound, Miranda stared at the bird that glittered like a flying jewel in the sun. Then it flew backward, beat its wings on the spot for a second before darting off into the distance with a purring sound, a bit like a grasshopper makes.

"She is gone."

Miranda heard Jamie's softly spoken words and turned to look at him. He was bent over Nora, gently closing the child's eyes.

"No!" The cry of denial tore from Miranda, even though she had known it would be today—had known since the moment Nora woke up and had been too weak to even take a sip of the honey-sweetened tea.

"It was her time," Jamie said.

Miranda had never known grief could be so powerful. It swelled inside her, forming a relentless pressure that made tears stream from her eyes. It filled her lungs with a harsh cry that wanted to burst out, that wanted to ripple through the air, all the way up into the sky, and demand that God explain why. Why Nora? Why this child?

Her grief had been nothing like this sharp when her parents died, for then the loss had followed the pattern of nature—that the old should die before the young. Miranda clamped down on the rush of emotion, holding it tight inside.

Beside her, Jamie had not moved. Miranda took her cue from him and sat still, forcing her body to relax. She resumed her singing, in halting, broken snatches, fighting the sobs, fighting the grief. They remained beneath the tree until midday, when clouds blotted out the sun and the wind grew blustery. The hummingbird never returned.

At the Carousel, Nordgren informed the customers the saloon would close after lunch and would remain closed until midday the following day. No one complained. In the kitchen, Moses began to sing in his booming voice, the kind of deep, haunting, spiritual hymn he and his fellow slaves had sung to remind each other that God had not forsaken them.

Eve and Jezebel cleared the bathing room and Jamie and Miranda laid Nora in the coffin with the toys and picture books the child had chosen for her journey. Then they sat down to hold their wake over her. They didn't speak but Miranda drew comfort from Jamie's quiet presence.

Late in the afternoon, a knock sounded on the door. It was one of the ladies from town, a small woman, perhaps thirty, with a purple birthmark the size of a silver dollar on her cheek, a blemish that in medieval times might have gotten her burned at the stake as a witch.

"I'm Miss Vickery. My brother told me the little girl has passed away. The rose bush in my garden is still in bloom. I thought perhaps you might like some roses for the coffin. I could bring them in later tonight, so they'll be fresh in the morning."

"That is very kind of you." Miranda stood aside. "Would you like to see her?"

Miss Vickery advanced into the room, her steps slow and reverent, and paid her respects. After she'd gone, another lady came, and then a husband and wife. All evening, a stream of well-wishers trickled in, the death of a child breaking the barriers of prejudice where all else might have failed.

When the first rays of the sun peeked over the hillside, they carried the coffin to the small cemetery beside the church. Miranda wore her riding outfit. Eve and Jezebel wore brightly colored silk gowns, fringed shawls covering the low necklines. The fabrics glimmered in the sun like the feathers on a hummingbird.

As they walked along the street, people stood on their front porches, men with their hats in their hands, women with their fingers laced in prayer. Respecting their privacy, no one joined the procession.

At the cemetery, Miranda lifted from the coffin the rose wreath Miss Vickery had prepared and held it while Moses and Jamie lowered Nora to her final resting place. They took turns tossing sprays of earth over the coffin, and then Moses picked up his shovel and filled the grave while the rest of them watched. When the earth was closed up, Miranda laid the wreath of roses over the small mound and read out an excerpt of the Tennyson poem that had brought her to Nora.

"Yet all things must die.
The stream will cease to flow;
The wind will cease to blow;
The clouds will cease to fleet;
The heart will cease to beat;
For all things must die.
All things must die."

After she had finished, Moses sang one of his spiritual songs, a haunting lament about the end of earthly toils and eternal joy in the Kingdom of God. Once the final notes had faded away, they turned around in silence and walked back to the Carousel. Miranda leaned on Jamie's arm, relying on his strength, the way she had warned him she would need to do.

At the Carousel, Jamie led Miranda upstairs. She felt cold, so terribly cold. Her body was shivering, her teeth chattering. When they got to their room, she halted in the middle, between the two narrow beds, her mind completely blank.

"Take off your coat," Jamie prompted.

She frowned, unable to comprehend the simple words, unable to move.

"Your deerskin coat. Take it off and get into bed. You look exhausted."

When she didn't react, Jamie unbuttoned her coat and slid it down her shoulders, talking softly as he eased her arms out of the sleeves. "You've been up since yesterday morning. I'm used to going without sleep, but you're not. You are just about ready to collapse on your feet."

"I'm cold."

"I'll warm you up."

Jamie tossed her leather coat on Nora's bed. He curled his hands over her arms and rubbed her skin through her cotton shirt, trying to get her warm. "Your hands are like blocks of ice." He took one of her hands in both of his, blew warm air into her palm and massaged her fingers, then did the same with her other hand, but it didn't help.

"I'm cold," Miranda whispered, her body rigid. "Why is it so cold?"

"It will be all right. I'll go and get you some hot tea."

"Nora likes it with honey to sweeten the taste."

"Nora's gone, sweetheart. She's gone." Jamie put his

hands on her shoulders, peered into her eyes, frowning. "Do you understand? Nora is gone."

She stared at Jamie, saw the black hair and bronzed skin and straight nose and sharp angle of his cheekbones. She'd never really paid attention to it before, but she could see a hint of family resemblance between him and Nora now.

"I know," she said. "I know."

And then the tears came. Great, racking sobs rose in her chest, as if each sound was tearing a piece out of her. Her body trembled. Her hands rose to fist in the front of Jamie's shirt. He bundled her against his chest and held her close. His warmth flowed into her, finally thawing that frozen feeling inside.

On and on she went, her breath flowing in jerky gasps, her sobs growing into angry wails as she struggled to accept her loss, struggled not to resent God for taking Nora away.

Jamie held her tight. At first, he tried to console her with murmured words, but when she ignored him and just kept on crying, he merely held her, his arms wrapped around her, his body warm and strong against hers. Little by little, exhaustion overcame grief, and Miranda's crying subsided to muted sobs.

Jamie withdrew his arms from around her and settled her on the bed. "Let's get you under the covers." He lifted the patchwork quilt and bundled her beneath.

Miranda obeyed, as docile as a child. Her mind was empty. It felt as if all her thoughts had focused on a list of tasks to accomplish for Nora. Now that she had come to the end of the list, her mind had shut down, unable to figure out what should come next.

Beneath the covers, the cold invaded her again. Her teeth clicked together. Her body trembled. "Hold me," she said. "Hold me, so I'll be warm."

Jamie hesitated, rocking on the balls of his feet. Then he climbed in beside her. He eased past her, settling his back against the wall, and fitted her into the curve of his body, her back against his chest, his arm across her waist, anchoring her in place.

"Sleep," he said. "I'll watch over you."

All day, all night, they remained like that, cocooned beneath the covers. Miranda drifted in and out of a restless doze, never quite awake, never enjoying the full respite of sleep. A few times, Jamie got up to take care of some errand—speaking to Nordgren, fetching a glass of water for her, getting a damp cloth to bathe her swollen eyes. Once, he led her down the rear steps to the privy and waited outside, ready to guide her back upstairs.

During the day, Miranda could hear the clanking of the mine, like the heartbeat of the town. When dusk fell, the Carousel came alive again, perhaps more subdued than normal, but the piano played and the gambling resumed and the girls took their clients up to their rooms, their laughter and voices ringing through the thin walls.

Life went on. Her life would go on, too, Miranda knew. Tomorrow, she would have to face her future, leave Devil's Hall, go back to being Miranda Fairfax, instead of Miss Randi who sang in a saloon, took care of a little girl and was married to a bounty hunter with gray eyes that no longer seemed as cold as ice.

Chapter Fourteen

For Jamie, the day of mourning and the night that followed were bittersweet. He held Miranda in his arms, her body tucked against his. He no longer knew which loss would be greater, having said goodbye to Nora, or giving up Miranda.

And yet he knew he'd have to do it, as soon as possible. Trying to hold on would be foolish. Foolish and wrong, and bound to lead to more suffering in the long run.

When the morning dawned, he shook Miranda awake. Jamie felt no fatigue, for the half-awake, half-asleep slumber of the last twenty-four hours was no different from his usual rest.

But he understood Miranda would be drained and disoriented from lack of sleep. Her eyes were puffed from crying, her face pale, her hair in a tangle. Despite looking worn and disheveled, she was more beautiful to him now than she had ever been before, for she had shared her grief with him, had turned to him for consolation.

"Let's get up," Jamie said. "We have things to do."

Things to do. It seemed as if those were magic words, for a sense of purpose sparked in Miranda's red-rimmed eyes. She stirred, scooted up to a sitting position on the bed and swung her feet to the floor.

"I want to see the headstone," she told him.

"Fine." Jamie got up, too, rolled his shoulders to get rid of the stiffness. He took his guns from where he'd placed them, one beside the pillow, the other hidden beneath his hat on the table, and strapped them on. He added the knife to his belt and propped his hat on his head.

"I'll bring you water to wash and then I'll wait for you downstairs."

He was standing by the counter, on his second cup of coffee, when Miranda came down. She seemed more alert now, although still pale and drawn. She halted beside him, made no move to sit down, but did not resist when he led her to a table and made her eat two biscuits heaped with butter and jam.

Autumn seemed to have arrived in a rush. Wind blew across the eastern plains, whistling along the boardwalk, tossing up dust and dry leaves. They made their way to the cemetery. The stonemason from the mine had been to chisel another engraving to the simple headstone.

Louise Blackburn 1857–1889
Nora Blackburn 1879–1889

No "devoted mother and wife" or "beloved child," for a bond as strong as theirs needed no mention. It occurred to Jamie that without the exact dates, a stranger looking at the inscription might assume the mother and child had perished together, perhaps in an accident. It did not matter.

He watched Miranda stand by the grave, her head held high, golden hair whipping in the wind. A little color was coming back into her cheeks. He'd never seen her wear her hair completely unbound before, and it made him realize how distracted she must be, not quite in touch with reality. He called her name to get her attention.

When she looked up, he spoke in a firm, efficient tone. "We'll take today to pack up, say goodbye to the people at the Carousel. If you have any business to take care of, or if you want to send any letters or telegrams, you'll need to do it today. Tomorrow morning we'll ride out. I'll take you to the nearest railroad station and put you on a train to your sister."

Something sparked in Miranda's eyes. Good, Jamie thought. She was returning to full awareness and rational thought. "Where is Gold Crossing exactly?" he asked. "Is it in the Wyoming Territory or in Colorado? Is it east or west of here?"

"Neither," she replied. "It's south. Arizona Territory."

Jamie stared at her. Recollections of conversations rattled through his mind. She'd never said where, it dawned on him. He'd just assumed, because she'd talked about a mining town, and they were in an area with a heritage of gold rushes. "But you were on Union Pacific Railroad," he protested feebly. "On a train headed for San Francisco."

"So?" She gave a small, very feminine shrug that seemed to suggest logic was the preserve of men and fools. "I got on the wrong train in Chicago."

"It's a heck of a long way to go on the wrong train."

"By the time I realized, I thought it might make more sense to go on to San Francisco and then double back on a southbound train. I'd see more of the country that way."

See more of the country. So spoke a woman who a few days ago had told him she only knew one life—the safe confines of her parental home near Boston, along the civilized Eastern Seaboard.

Jamie stepped away from the grave. Crouching down, he picked up a stick from the ground and used it to draw a diagram in the dirt. "Here's Devil's Hall, Wyoming Territory. Here's Gold Crossing, Arizona Territory."

He didn't know if the place was north, near Flagstaff, or south, near Tucson, but it made little difference. He poked the second dot in the ground a good distance below the first one. He added another dot, way over to the right. "Here's Chicago. And here's San Francisco." He punched one more dot over to the left. "You can go this way. Or you can go this way." He drew two big arrowheads, the first pointing to the right, the second to the left.

Miranda squatted beside him. She put out her hand. Jamie passed the twig to her. She drew a vertical line from the dot representing Devil's Hall down to the dot representing Gold Crossing. "I want to go this way. The shortest way. South."

An uncomfortable feeling settled in the pit of Jamie's belly. "There are no trains going south. Trains go east-west, apart from spur lines, and those are dead ends to connect with the main lines."

"The shortest way between two points is a straight line."

"That might be true when you sail a ship on the ocean."

"I want to go south." Miranda scraped the stick over the vertical line again and said the words Jamie had feared she would say. "You have to take me."

"I can't take you. It's almost a thousand miles. It'll take more than a month."

"It will take a long time on the train, too, whichever route I take. I'll be sitting idle for days on end. Alone. With nothing to occupy my mind except grief. I can't take it. And what else will you do for a month?" She turned to look at him, her eyes suddenly sharp.

It didn't seem fair to Jamie for her to switch tactics like that, as if logical argument was suddenly a woman's birthright. "I have business to take care of," he protested.

"You can hunt for outlaws along the way. And you

have no reason to remain in Wyoming now. You might as well head south for the winter, enjoy a milder climate."

Jamie hesitated. He didn't want this complication. Up to now he'd spent no more than a week with her in total. The first three days had been with suspicion and hostility standing between them, and then another four days with their focus on Nora.

How would it be if they traveled together for a month, sharing every moment of the day? If each morning the first sight he saw was Miranda? If each night he sat awake, watching her while she slept, her golden hair like a ray of light in the darkness?

How much harder would it be to stay away from her? How much further into his heart could she burrow? How much deeper would the pain cut when they finally parted?

He couldn't take it. Couldn't take the temptation of constant proximity. Couldn't take the risk of doing something that might tie them together for good. Couldn't take the strain on his emotions.

It occurred to Jamie that his thoughts were like holding up a mirror to what Miranda had said a moment ago—that she couldn't take the solitude and boredom of sitting on the train, immersed in her grief. Deep down, he already knew he'd lose the argument, but he made a valiant effort.

"You'll hate overland travel. You'll freeze on the high ground through Colorado. You'll get saddle sores on your delicate skin. There'll be outlaws. You'll have to learn to defend yourself. Kill, if need be. It'll be more than a month of bad food and sleeping rough and getting wet when it rains. You'll have to go thirsty and hungry and without sleep."

"I don't care. I told you, I've never traveled much. I've only known one life. This is my chance for adventure. I can't make the trip alone, but with you escorting me I can." The twig scraped against the ground in a straight line. "I want to go south."

Jamie didn't reply. Miranda lowered her voice and spoke again. Jamie knew what was coming, even before she said it. Because her words reflected his thoughts. "You owe it to me. You owe it to me not to leave me alone in my grief."

Earlier, when he'd won her in the bride lottery, Jamie had justified his actions by telling himself she was better off with him than she might have been with any other man. She might have been used roughly. She might have been forced to work from dawn to dusk, looking after an extended household of stepchildren or elderly in-laws.

But last night, as he watched her consumed with grief, it had occurred to Jamie that he might have asked more of Miranda than any of those other men could have asked. He owed her. Plain and simple. *He owed her.* And a man of honor paid his debts.

"South it is then, Princess."

He would simply have to find a way to resist the temptation, overcome the risk of doing something foolish and live with the strain to his emotions. Jamie pushed up to his feet, helped Miranda rise. "Let's go to the mercantile. From the way I've seen you shop, it's going to take all day to get you kitted out."

Jamie had never thought it possible to spend so long choosing a bedroll. Miranda stroked the fabrics to test the smoothness. She lifted the bedrolls to her nose and inhaled the scent. She spread them on the plank floor of the mercantile and tried them out. Jamie stood guard, making sure no one entered the aisle where she lay like a drunk passed out.

Next, she tried on several warm coats and rejected them all, in favor of a thick wool poncho that would fit under a rain slicker. Tin plates, utensils, a skillet and pan, every item required a thorough inspection before she made her selection.

It would not do, Jamie decided. He'd die of boredom and it would take a week before they could start the journey. "How much money do you have?" he asked.

"I have four hundred dollars left, but I want to give fifty to Moses and twenty-five to Eve and Jezebel each. That leaves me three hundred."

"Fine. I'll pay for these." He steered her out to the porch and pointed her toward the dress shop across the road. "Go and get some underwear. Whatever it is ladies wear beneath everything else in the winter to keep warm. Long legs. Long sleeves. *Shoo.*"

He finished off with a friendly pat on her bottom and followed her with his eyes until she'd vanished into the Ladies' Fashion Emporium. Then he went back into the mercantile, bought matches and cartridges and a few tools, two oilcloth sheets and a canvas tent, hurrying to get his purchases completed before Miranda could come back and insist that they try out every single item on the shelves.

He need not have worried. By the time Miranda came out again with two parcels under her arm, he'd been to the livery stable to buy a pack mule, and was sitting on the steps of the mercantile, having a cup of coffee, waiting for her to emerge.

"Food," she informed him. "We need to stock up with food."

"Moses will shop for us. He'll know what to get." Jamie got to his feet, looked up into the sky to check the position of the sun. It was past lunchtime. "I suggest you have a bath. It will be a while before you have a chance for another one. Then we can organize our outfit. I'll introduce you to the pack mule."

Her eyes went round. "You bought a mule? Why didn't you wait for me?"

Jamie took the last sip of his coffee. "Sorry. I didn't think."

It was a diplomatic lie. If he'd waited for her, the task would have taken all afternoon, and they would have ended up with two mules, because he'd bought one of a pair, and Miranda would have refused to split up the animals used to having each other for company.

It was nice to have two mules, Miranda thought the next morning as they headed south across the valley. She'd named the beasts Castor and Pollux. Both were chestnut brown, almost as big as Alfie, with inquisitive eyes, long ears and mournful calls—particularly if about to be separated from a lifelong friend.

Being on the road, leaving the sad memories behind felt good. She'd taken an emotional farewell from Eve and Jezebel and Nordgren and Moses. The prospect of one day saying goodbye to Jamie filled her with unease. He had comforted her in her grief, and in some way he had become the anchor that held her together, helped her meet whatever came next.

Soon the landscape flattened and they picked their way through the long prairie grass, careful to keep the horses from stumbling over the shallow streams that crisscrossed the earth. In the afternoon, heavy clouds rolled in, bringing blustery rain. By the time Miranda had pulled on her wool poncho and fastened the oilcloth slicker over it, every layer was damp. As they rode on, the chill seeped into her bones. The smell of wet wool and wet horse and wet leather clung to her, as if it would never wash off again.

When twilight fell, Jamie halted in a rocky clearing bordered by stunted trees with yellowing leaves. "I can see now why it will take so long to get to Arizona," Miranda said after she had dismounted, her legs so stiff they nearly collapsed beneath her weight.

"This is not the worst of it. The river crossings will be the main obstacle. If there is no ferry, it can take days to find a safe spot to get across."

Too exhausted to worry about what lay ahead, Miranda took off her leather gloves and rubbed her hands together, blowing warm air over her fingers that seemed permanently curled from holding the reins.

"What do you want me to do?" she asked between puffs.

Jamie was pulling an oilcloth sheet from Castor's panniers. "Hold this end."

She grabbed the edge of the oilcloth sheet and held it up while Jamie tied two corners into the trees. Then he secured the opposite edge against the ground with metal pegs, making a lean-to shelter.

"Get out of the rain," he ordered.

Miranda darted beneath the lean-to. Even at the high end, the shelter did not allow her to stand up.

Jamie handed her another oilcloth sheet. "Spread that on the ground."

Carefully avoiding tracking dirt on top, Miranda unfolded the oilcloth.

"Here." Jamie held out a rag. "Wipe your boots before you crawl on top."

She did as he told her and huddled beneath the canopy. The rain drummed against the oilcloth. The wind stirred the branches, making them look like ghosts swaying in the twilight. A few paces away, she could see Jamie moving with quick, purposeful motions as he put up a small canvas tent, hacking down saplings to make poles and fastening ropes to the ground.

She ought to be helping, Miranda thought as she

watched him through the deluge. As he bent and straightened, his rain slicker flared wide, letting water saturate his clothing. The ends of his hair pulled into wet clumps. Rivulets ran down the brim of his hat.

He seemed oblivious to the hardships—cold, fatigue, hunger. Perhaps a man developed a hard edge when he took on a profession that required him to face death and be prepared to deliver it. And yet she'd seen tenderness in him. It was that dichotomy of cool exterior and the depth of feeling inside him that fascinated her so. And the air of danger that clung to him. It excited her. What was it like, to be a bounty hunter? Perhaps with him she might get a peek into that life of peril and adventure.

The tent, once it stood up, white canvas flapping in the rain, seemed very small, barely four feet wide. Miranda blurted out the thought as it popped into her head. "Why didn't you get a bigger tent? It's too small for two."

Shame burned on her cheeks the instant she heard her words. Spoiled Eastern girl. That's what she'd sounded like. It would serve her right if Jamie tossed some cutting remark back at her, putting her in her place as the useless creature she was.

"It's meant for one," he said. "I'm not sleeping in it."

She knew he intended to annul their marriage and wished to protect her reputation—even though there was little left to be tarnished. She'd been singing in a saloon, and people had seen them share a room at the Carousel.

"I don't mind," she told him. "No one will know."

"It's not your honor I'm thinking of, Princess. It's your safety, and mine. It's too easy to creep up on a man sleeping in a tent. Can't see out through the walls. The flapping of the canvas muffles the sound of anyone approaching. By the time I wake up to an intruder's presence, whether it's the two-legged or the four-legged kind, it might to be too late."

"I see," Miranda said.

Slowly, the misery of the cold, wet landscape closed around her. As the darkness fell, there wasn't even the majestic line of the mountains to see in the distance. All she could see was the inky blackness settling over them. Rain poured from the sky. Wind howled in the trees. She felt tired and hungry, with a trace of fear creeping in.

It crossed her mind how much she had relied on sleeping beside Jamie, warm and safe, tucked into the curve of his body as they lay together in a tent, the rest of the world far away, the future insignificant compared to the demands of the present. The kiss they had shared played on her mind, making her wonder how it would feel if Jamie did it again—hauled her into his embrace and pressed his lips against hers.

But there would be none of that. She would sleep alone in the tent, while Jamie slept beneath the lean-to, keeping them safe. Without her, he would not have even bothered putting up a tent. She was a burden. The sensation grew as Miranda watched him set out bread and jerky for supper and boil coffee on a fire he'd built beneath a tree, using the leaf canopy and his rain slicker to protect the struggling flames from the rain.

"Do you want hot water to wash?" he called out.

She longed for the luxury of a hot wash. But instead, she said, "I don't need to wash. The rain has taken care of that."

Only spoiled little Eastern princesses washed with hot water on the trail. She did not want to be one of those. Miranda made herself a promise. She would learn to do her share of the chores. Or she would board a train when they reached the next railroad town, even if it meant she might never see Jamie again.

Chapter Fifteen

Jamie couldn't have wished for better conditions to convince Miranda to travel by train. Day and night, the wind howled across the prairie. Rain battered the earth until the horses struggled to keep their balance on the water-logged trail.

Their clothes were damp. The food unappetizing. The nights wet and cold. *Miserable*. That was the best word to describe it all. Except Miranda. For her, Jamie had another word.

Stubborn. Stubborn as hell.

"Get under the overhang," he told her when they pulled up for the night beside a wall of red rocks, just before the cliffs narrowed into a canyon.

"No. I'll help you with the lean-to shelter."

Jamie muttered a curse. Miranda kept insisting that she *carry her weight, do her share, earn her keep*, whichever in her repertoire of arguments she might toss at him while ignoring his commands to get out of the rain.

"Start supper," he ordered. He had contrived a division of labor that allowed her some measure of protection from the weather. When they halted for the night, he lifted the panniers from the mules to the most sheltered spot. Then he did the same with the saddles and saddlebags. It was Miranda's task to take care of their provisions and maintain the tack for the horses.

"Look for soot stains on the cliffs above the overhang," he advised her. "That will be the best place to light a fire, tried and tested by other travelers."

Miranda jumped to her feet. "I'll go and collect firewood."

"Stay where you are!" Jamie roared, then gritted his teeth. The damn woman had reduced him to yelling. For a second, he let his gaze rest on her. Thank heavens he'd bought her the expensive leather hat that repelled water. Her face and hair were dry. Nothing else was. Her skin was marble white, with an almost bluish tinge, and she was shivering.

But she never complained. Never. It seemed forever ago that they had first set out on the journey to Devil's Hall after he won her in the bride lottery. He recalled how he had expected his little Eastern princess to whine about every hardship. He could not have been more wrong.

"Check the coffee and sugar to make sure they're dry."

"I've already done that. I'll go and get firewood."

"No!" Jamie bellowed. He finished tying one side of the oilcloth to the wooden stump he'd beaten into the ground. The lean-to was barely three feet high, but it would keep them out of the rain. Tonight, he could not put up the tent, for there were no saplings he could cut down to make poles.

"Check the saddles and bridles," he ordered. "Wipe them dry."

Each night, he contrived to keep her busy in a sheltered spot while he put up the lean-to and got a fire started. He dreaded the thought of a campsite without firewood. If he didn't manage to keep Miranda warm at night, she might catch pneumonia.

Jamie felt his body go rigid. No. He refused to dwell

on the possibility that something might happen to her. Refused to admit that he'd come to care about another person. Caring for someone brought the prospect of loss, and he'd had enough of losing loved ones.

While they ate, Miranda plagued him with questions.

"How does a bounty hunter find the outlaws?"

"With patience."

"Patience with what?"

"Listen in saloons. Ask around. Pay for information."

"And how does a bounty hunter track down his quarry?"

Quarry? It was a new word to him, but it seemed to fit. "Follow the information."

"Follow the *information*?" she echoed. "You don't look for hoofprints on the ground and broken twigs and other signs to see which way the outlaws have escaped?"

"It's not like that. If the outlaws know you're coming, you don't stand a chance."

"So you need to figure out where the outlaws are hiding, and then you'll have to sneak up on them and catch them by surprise?"

"Yes." Jamie scooped up the last of the beans from his plate. "That's it."

At his reticence, Miranda huffed in frustration. Jamie turned away and held his plate out to the rain to clean it. As he listened to the drumming of the drops against the tin platter, he suppressed the sense of inadequacy. He knew Miranda wanted to talk. She found comfort in idle chatter, but he didn't have it in him.

That long talk beneath the picnic oak, when he'd told her about his mother and his sister, seemed to have depleted the store of words inside him. And somehow, as if by common consent, neither of them had mentioned Nora since the day of the funeral. It might have been to allow the grief to heal, or perhaps out of respect for the

Indian belief that one should encourage the dead to pass into the next world.

Miranda spoke again. "Where can you get wanted posters?"

"Sheriff's office. Town marshal. Sometimes a post office or a store."

Miranda gave a slow nod. There was an eager look in her eyes that worried Jamie. He was starting to get some idea of the path her thoughts were taking. He had already figured out that her thirst for adventure was greater than her common sense.

"Forget it, Princess," he muttered. "Women can't be bounty hunters."

"Why not?" she shot back. "You said patience is the most important requirement, and the ability to coax information out of people. In those, women are better than men."

Jamie did not reply. He knew arguing would only serve to spur her on.

Jamie lay beneath the oilcloth, his clothes almost dry from the flames, his hunger chased away by the dull staple of beans and jerky. In the darkness, he could feel Miranda's restless fidgeting beside him.

"Can't you sleep, Princess?"

"I'm cold." She wriggled closer, bumping against him. "Hold me, like you did before."

Jamie tensed. Then he rolled over to his side and pulled Miranda into his arms. It was a dangerous thing to do, but he couldn't deny her the comfort of his warmth. He could feel her trembling. Instead of burying her face in the crook of his neck, she tipped her head back. Despite the lack of light Jamie could make out her features and the faint glimmer of her open eyes.

"You won't get to sleep unless you close your eyes, Princess."

"How do you know they're open?"

"I told you, I can see in the dark. You're looking at me."

She spoke very softly, a mere rustle of sound in the night. "I've been thinking of how you kissed me on the floor of the Carousel… It was not how I expected a kiss to be…and I've been wondering if it would be the same if you kissed me again…"

She could not have come up with anything that would have startled Jamie more. For an instant, his mind went blank. Then it sprang into a chaotic flurry of doubt and hope and need. He could feel his heart pounding in his chest. His brain screamed a warning, just as it had that other time. And just as at that other time, he ignored the warning. Sometimes a temptation was too strong for a man to resist.

Threading his fingers into Miranda's unraveling up-sweep, Jamie cupped the back of her head and leaned forward. Even after three days on the trail, the scent of floral soap clung to her, tantalizing his senses.

"Like this?" he asked and pressed a gentle kiss on her brow.

"No."

"Like this?" He brushed a kiss on the crest of her cheek.

"No."

"Like this?" He settled his mouth on hers. He intended to keep the kiss light, but Miranda's lips were warm and soft and willing beneath his. Despite the thick layer of clothing between them, he could feel her feminine contours pressing against him.

A rush of emotion went through Jamie. He'd never before understood how tightly his life had been bound to that of Louise and Nora. Providing for his sister and his niece had given him a purpose, had added a sense of honor to his grim and dangerous profession.

Now they were gone. He had no one. No feminine softness to balance the hard days out on the road, no welcoming smiles to return to. Just the great big emptiness inside him and the slow, tedious wait for it all to one day come to an end.

But Miranda was alive and vibrant against him. The beautiful, compassionate Miranda, whose presence lit up his gloomy world like sunlight banishes the darkness. Jamie breathed in her scent, felt her warmth and softness in her arms and gave in to his hunger.

Rising up on one elbow, he eased his body half on top of hers and deepened the kiss. This time, Miranda was with him at once. Her lips parted, offering him access. When his mouth slanted greedily over hers, she made a tiny moan deep in her throat, an erotic sound that enflamed his need.

On and on the kiss went. The rain beat in a sharp tattoo against the oilcloth. The wind blew across the prairie with a dull, mournful howl, sending a chilly draft beneath the lean-to canopy, but their bodies thrummed with heat.

There was passion in his little princess, Jamie discovered, and it seemed all too easy to make that passion spark out of control. The night was cold, wet and miserable, yet he doubted Miranda would protest if he tried to ease her out of her clothing.

Clinging to the last vestiges of his sanity, Jamie broke the kiss and lifted his head. "Princess, we have to put a stop to this. Do you understand how perilously close you are to getting hitched to me for the rest of your days?"

He could see the faint glimmer of her eyes in the darkness and knew she was looking at him. "It might not be such a bad idea," she replied in a voice as light as a butterfly's wing.

Jamie settled on his side again and bundled Miranda tight against his chest, her head tucked in the crook of his neck. A hollow sense of despair filled him. Why did she have to say it? Why did she have to tempt him to dream the impossible?

"Wait until we get into the next town and need to find a place to stay." His tone was grim. "Then you tell me if you still think it might not be such a bad idea to stay hitched to me for the rest of your days."

The sharp, lashing rain had finally ceased. Riding at the end of their small procession, Miranda saw the line of the railroad that bisected the prairie a moment before she spotted the cluster of buildings in the distance. The place didn't seem much of a town. Water tower, perched on four legs, like an enormous spider. A station house with a wooden platform. A few other buildings lined up in a single row.

She longed to get dry and warm. Eat a decent meal. Sleep in a bed. The thought gave her pause. The kiss last night had been more than just a kiss. What would happen if they shared a room with a bed? Was she ready for such intimacy? She didn't know. Perhaps no woman knew for certain until the moment was upon them.

All she knew was that every day she found her eyes drawn to Jamie as he rode on Sirius ahead of her, his posture graceful in the saddle, his touch on the horse gentle but sure. At the rest stops, she would covertly watch him and feel an odd kind of restlessness.

But was that enough? Had she been foolish to put forward the idea they could make their marriage real? Was what she felt for him the start of something true and lasting? Or was it merely a means to ease the grief of Nora's passing, a yearning for the comfort and warmth he could offer?

Casting aside the questions for which she had no an-
swers, Miranda followed Jamie and the pack mules along
the mud-churned street between the railroad station and
the rest of the buildings. The tallest one had a sign that
said Palace Hotel. Miranda didn't dispute the boast. Right
now, anything with a roof and a bed would qualify.

Jamie reined in Sirius and turned around in the saddle
to look at her. His hat shadowed his features and the upturned collar of his duster hid part of his face, but in his
eyes Miranda could see a hard glint, as if he anticipated
some kind of trouble.

"Go and get a room," he told her. "I'll take care of
the horses. There's a sign for a livery stable at the end
of the street."

"Can we leave the packs? Or should we take them up
to the room?"

"I'll see if they have a guard at the livery stable over-
night."

Miranda dismounted, hurried to Pollux and took out
her canvas bag where she had her spare clothing and a
few personal items. As she crossed the street to the hotel
entrance, the short, stocky man who'd been standing on
the boardwalk went inside and took up position behind
the curved reception counter in the corner of the lobby.

"I'd like a room," she told him. "The warmest you
have."

"You're here for the train?" Dark-haired, with small
brown eyes set deep in their sockets, the man appeared
curt, almost hostile.

"Just passing through on our way south."

"That your husband? The Indian with them two pack
mules?"

Miranda smiled, her head cocked to one side with a
touch of feminine appeal. "Yes. That's my husband. And
he is only a quarter Cheyenne."

The man muttered something Miranda didn't catch, and then he flicked open his ledger. "I'm afraid we're fully booked tonight."

"But…" She surveyed the lifeless lobby with limp velvet curtains and dusty chandeliers and fraying padded chairs. "You can't be. It seems very quiet."

"There's a party arriving on the evening train. And some of the rooms are closed for renovation."

I expect they need it, Miranda thought tartly. It seemed as though the place had been thrown together in haste when the railroad came through two decades ago, and only as an afterthought had people realized the furnishings had to stand up to wear and tear.

"Is there…" Miranda took a deep breath, her dreams of a warm room and soft bed in danger of turning into a mirage. "Is there some other establishment that might have vacant rooms?"

"You could try the saloon. Two doors down." The man pointed along the row of buildings, to the opposite direction of the livery stable.

Miranda gave him a tired nod. "I'll try there. If my husband comes in, can you tell him where I've gone?"

"I'll wager he'll figure it out on his own," the man muttered.

Puzzled by the comment, Miranda left the Palace Hotel and made her way along the boardwalk, her boots clattering with forlorn steps. The saloon seemed equally quiet as she pushed in through the batwing doors, her canvas bag draped over one shoulder.

The Gold Nugget was a rough, functional place, with scarred wooden tables and chairs. Gas lamps burned in brackets along the wall. There were no guests, only a man who seemed like a cardsharp. He was sitting alone at a table, flicking playing cards between his fingers, fanning the deck open and closing it, practicing his tricks.

Behind the counter, a voluptuous blonde in her forties was polishing glasses with a towel, holding each glass to the light to inspect it before stacking it on the shelf.

Miranda walked over to the counter. "Do you have a room for the night?"

The woman gave her a cursory inspection, then picked up the next glass to polish. "This place isn't suitable for the likes of you. Try the Palace Hotel. Two doors up the street."

"I've just been there. They told me they are fully booked."

"Fully booked." The blonde hooted with laughter. "That'll be the day."

Miranda frowned. "They said there's a party arriving on the evening train."

One corner of the woman's rouged mouth curled into a smirk. "He can be a bit funny, Karl Lomax, who owns the Palace. Thinks a woman traveling on her own is the devil's bait, sent to lure good men straight to hell. You sure you want to stay here, love? This is a saloon. When the train pulls in, this place will fill up with a rowdy crowd."

"I don't mind," Miranda said with a smile. "I'm no stranger to saloons. I used to sing in one. The Carousel, in Devil's Hall. It's a mining town, four days' ride to the north."

The blonde lowered the glass and towel, surprise and delight brightening her tired features. "I know Devil's Hall. That big Swede, Nordgren, still own the place?"

"He does. And Moses does the cooking. The girls are Eve and Jezebel."

"I'll be damned." The woman swept another glance over Miranda. "You can stay here for free, love, if you sing for the customers tonight. What do you call yourself?"

"My stage name was Miss Randi."

The woman gave another hoot of laughter. "Randi? I can see why the men might have liked to call you that."

A blush crept to Miranda's cheeks. The clientele at the Carousel had given her good-natured ribbing over the name, and she understood the double meaning. "It comes from my given name, Miranda," she explained. "I'm Miranda Fairfax. I mean, Miranda Blackburn. I am married now, and I'm not traveling on my own."

It crossed Miranda's mind that she was giving out a lot of information. Bounty hunters probably just tossed a few coins on the table and grunted a demand for a key, but it was lovely to talk to a person who actually seemed to enjoy conversation.

"I'm Aggie," the woman said. "Aggie Nugget, can you believe it? Got me a good few customers when I was younger, with my yellow hair and all. Gold Nugget, they used to call me. The saloon's named after me."

"You are not old, Aggie," Miranda said. "You are a lady in your prime."

"Oh, aren't you a smooth one…" Aggie pulled a face, but there was pleasure in her mocking tone. "The stage is over there, behind the red curtain. Go and take a peek, love. There's a piano, too, but there's no one here who knows how to play."

Miranda turned. The lone cardsharp was sitting with his back toward her, still practicing his tricks. He was dressed very well, in fawn trousers and a peacock blue frock coat, pristine white shirt cuffs peeking from the sleeves. He had light brown hair. A walking stick leaned against the side of the table.

A walking stick with a silver handle in the shape of a wolf's head. Miranda gasped at the familiar sight. The gambler must have heard her, for he turned around.

"Gareth!" she cried out as she stared into the face of Gareth Fairfax, or at least a man who looked just like him—just like him, and yet subtly different. For if it was her cousin, he had changed since she'd last seen him at the railroad station in Chicago, where she'd fled from him almost two months ago.

Chapter Sixteen

⟨∾⟩

Miranda steeled herself for a confrontation as Cousin Gareth bolted to his feet. He'd lost a great deal of weight. No longer puffed, his features looked handsome now. The straight nose and blue eyes and elegant posture reminded Miranda of her father, the older brother to Gareth's father. There was a fresh scar on Gareth's forehead, a livid red welt that ran from the hairline to the temple.

He charged up to her and fisted his hands in the front of her wool poncho, rattling her so hard her teeth knocked together. "Who am I?" he yelled. "What is my name?"

When she didn't reply, when she merely stared uncomprehendingly at him, he shook her harder. His eyes were wild, his expression fraught. "Do you know me? Do you know who I am? Gareth? You said Gareth. Who am I? Tell me? Tell me?"

He didn't know who he was. Startled, Miranda gathered her wits. Cousin Gareth must have lost his memory. The scar on his forehead might be from a blow.

"I'm… I'm sorry," she muttered. "I made a mistake… I saw the walking stick… I thought I'd seen something similar before but I can see now it's not the same."

The man uncurled his fists from her clothing and sank

back down on the wooden chair that had scuttled backward when he jumped out of it. "I thought... I hoped..."

Miranda avoided meeting his eyes. "I'm sorry."

He gave a small shrug, as if of acceptance, and spoke quietly. "They found me on the train with this gash in my head." He touched the scar on his forehead. "The doctor says it is just a severe concussion. No real damage to my brain. He thinks eventually I'll remember. There'll be some trigger that lifts the mist in my mind."

He shook his head wistfully. "When you said Gareth... it seemed so familiar... Suddenly I thought I could smell the salty ocean breeze instead of this infernal prairie wind..."

When he fell silent, Miranda felt compelled to say something. "Perhaps your home is by the ocean. You speak like an educated Easterner."

"Yes. Yes. I've been told so." He fastened his gaze upon her. "People have been calling me Wolf, because of the emblem on my walking stick, but I like Gareth. Do you mind if I adopt it? Use it as my name until I find out my real one?"

"By all means," Miranda said. "It suits you."

Cousin Gareth picked up the deck of cards with one hand, spread them into a fan, then shuffled them with a mere flick of his wrist and twist of his fingers.

"I might not know who I am, but at least I know *what* I am. I'm a professional gambler. Cardsharp. Good at it, too. Must have always been, for I don't seem to know how to cheat. I only play an honest game. That's good, because in these parts a man gets shot if he is caught cheating at the card table."

Miranda realized he was talking to her just to keep up the conversation, to connect with another human being. It must create a terrible sense of loneliness when all memories are wiped out, friends and family forgotten, every part of one's personal history lost.

She ought to tell him. She could be the trigger he needed to lift the curtain of mist in his mind and regain his memory. He posed no danger to her now. She could tell him that Charlotte had married and claimed her inheritance.

But…if James Fast Elk Blackburn resented escorting her all the way to Gold Crossing…telling the truth now would give him the opportunity to foist her off on Cousin Gareth, who was her closest male relative. Miranda shivered at the prospect. She didn't want to put Jamie to the test, didn't want to find out if he wished to be rid of her.

Moreover, Cousin Gareth might be furious about losing his grip on the Fairfax fortune. He might take his revenge out on her. Even if he didn't, most men lumbered with responsibility for a female who had run away from home to become a saloon singer would believe the proper course of action was to send her back home again.

And she didn't want to go back to Merlin's Leap. Charlotte was in Gold Crossing and Annabel was on her way there. She wanted to join her sisters, and she wanted the adventure of overland travel with Jamie, even if it meant leaving Cousin Gareth to his fate.

In truth, Cousin Gareth seemed to be doing remarkably well in his new incarnation. He was dressed in fine clothes. Making a good living. From the way Aggie looked at him, he appeared respected. Liked. Perhaps even loved.

Apart from the scar, he looked physically fit and healthy. A great improvement from his hard-drinking, dissolute ways of the past. He had changed from a failed scoundrel into a successful one, even though he was still a scoundrel. The best plan was to leave him be, Miranda decided, with only a small twinge of guilt.

"I'm sorry I can't help you, Mr....Gareth. I wish you luck."

Cousin Gareth laughed. Despite the undertone of sadness, the sound seemed to convey less bitterness than the harsh, braying whine that had served him for laughter at Merlin's Leap.

"Luck is one thing I seem to have," he replied. "At least at the card tables."

Miranda gave him a wan smile and turned to Aggie. "I'm sorry. I don't think it is possible for me to sing here tonight. My husband wouldn't approve." *My cousin might recognize my sea shanties and regain his memory.*

"Husbands." Aggie rolled her eyes. "The bane of my business."

At the sound of the heavy footsteps of a man struggling with a weighty load, Miranda glanced over to the batwing doors. "Here he comes now."

"Ah," Aggie muttered, observing James Fast Elk Blackburn's progress across the floor. "I can see now why there is no room at the inn."

Jamie strode into the saloon and dumped the first set of mule panniers on the floor next to the long counter. The aging but attractive blonde behind the bar welcomed him with in an indulgent, almost maternal smile. "Your wife tells me she used to sing at the Carousel in Devil's Hall."

"She isn't singing here," Jamie replied. "I don't have the energy to play the jealous husband." One corner of his mouth kicked up in a smile as he darted a look at his little Eastern princess. "Although, as I recall, the role had its benefits."

Miranda didn't react to his teasing. She seemed preoccupied, her forehead in a frown, her hands clenching and unclenching in that agitated manner she had when she struggled to control her temper.

Jamie felt a sting of regret at the humiliation she must have suffered at the hotel, being turned away on his account. She would soon learn what it meant for a white woman to take up with an Indian husband, even if it was a husband in name only.

"You got a room yet?" he asked Miranda.

"No, I..." Miranda's eyes darted to the gambler who sat alone at the table. "I haven't had time... I was talking to Aggie."

"Miss Aggie." Jamie nodded at the barmaid to acknowledge the introduction. "How about a room for two weary travelers? One with a stove, if you have one."

"The honeymoon suite has a stove."

Jamie suppressed a wry grin. "That'll do."

Aggie perked up. "Firewood is two bits extra."

"Charge us four so we don't have to skimp. And a bath for the lady? I assume there's a bathing room downstairs?"

"There is, but it has rats. The honeymoon suite has a private bathtub. For two bits extra, I can have someone carry hot water upstairs."

"Make it another four. I want the water piping hot, and plenty of it." Jamie poked the panniers heaped on the floor with the toe of his boot and spoke to Miranda.

"Everything's damp. I'll bring over the rest. Get settled in the room and I'll haul the luggage upstairs. You can spread your clothes out to dry, and you'll need to check the provisions, to make sure nothing spoils."

The gambler at the table had turned to watch them. Jamie took stock of the man. Light brown hair, regular features, the kind some people might describe as aristocratic. The scar on his forehead appeared recent. Something about the man seemed familiar, but Jamie couldn't quite figure out what it was. He would have to check through his store of wanted posters. Maybe he was an outlaw with a bounty on his head.

"I'll get the rest of the gear," Jamie said and headed back outside.

When he returned to the saloon, Miranda was gone. Aggie pointed to the staircase. "Honeymoon suite. Last door at the end of the hall. Has a private balcony."

Jamie shifted the panniers to his right shoulder, leaned down to grab the other set from the floor and swung them over his left shoulder. Staggering beneath the weight, he climbed the stairs, sympathy for the pack mules flickering through his mind.

He would have knocked but his hands were occupied balancing the load on his shoulders. "Coming in," he called out and lifted one booted foot to kick the door open.

Lurching into the room, he lowered the panniers to the floor. It was an odd thing, he admitted, the masculine stubbornness that made a man believe it would be easier to carry one heavy load up the stairs instead of making two journeys with a lighter load.

He looked around. The room was a pleasant surprise. Clean and airy, with thick drapes at the tall window that gave out to the balcony. The bed was an enormous oak affair, with a pair of nightstands to match, and an armoire on the wall opposite. The bathtub must be behind the curtain that separated a small alcove from the rest of the room.

In the corner, Miranda was kneeling in front of a cast-iron potbellied stove, blowing at the kindling to get the flames going. Jamie couldn't help noticing how nicely her rounded buttocks strained against her denim trousers.

He squatted next to her and spoke in a low voice. A man did not like to put his inferiority into words, even if that inferiority was only in the minds of others.

"I'm sorry," he said. "You'll get more of that as we travel on. It's worse in some places than others. Mostly they just refuse to serve Indians. Sometimes they might pull a gun from beneath the counter, to make you leave quicker."

Miranda looked puzzled, so Jamie spelled it out. "I'm sorry they turned you away at the hotel. Sorry if they said anything to insult you. It's not your fault, or even mine. That's just the way it is."

He could see her brow furrow, then smooth out again as she understood his meaning. "They told me they were fully booked, so I left. I guess they might have become unpleasant if I had refused to leave." She picked up another piece of firewood and tapped it against the floor, her eyes downcast. "Why is it like that for Indians?"

"I reckon it's partly because some folks just need to hate. They target the weakest group around them. Or it might be because white soldiers and militiamen slaughtered so many Indian women and children. It is easier to justify those deeds if you convince yourself the people you killed were savages, no better than animals. Otherwise you were guilty of murdering innocent women and children, for no other reason but because you wanted their land. No one wants to feel like that, so it is easier to keep up the hate."

"Do you hate them back?"

"Sometimes. Mostly I just walk away. Like my hair. I don't really like it long, but it is too much trouble to find someone to cut it."

"I don't mind it long." Miranda shifted on her knees, turning toward him. She raised one hand and slid her fingers into his hair, stirring the raven locks.

Jamie kept still, enjoying the caress. Ever since he kissed Miranda in the tent last night and she responded with such abandon, he had been fighting his hunger for her. Tonight, they would sleep in the honeymoon suite, cozy in the warmth. Already, he could smell the pungent pine resin from the stove, could hear the flames crackle and pop as they caught, adding to the intimate atmosphere.

But Miranda seemed ill at ease. Being turned away from the hotel must have upset her more than she was letting on. He'd warned about the hardships in store for a woman who took up with an Indian husband. Perhaps Miranda had come to her senses, saw the folly of her suggestion that they might make their marriage real.

Doubt and want collided within Jamie, stirring him into reckless action. He pushed up to his feet, curled his hands beneath Miranda's arms and pulled her up to face him. Slowly, he eased her backward, until she came flush against the wall. She kept peering past his shoulder, as if looking for an escape.

Jamie dipped his head. When their mouths were only a fraction apart, he halted. Instead of kissing her, he pressed his hips against hers, letting her feel the swell of his erection. Did she understand the significance of such masculine reaction? She must, Jamie decided. Although gently bred, she had spent a month in a saloon.

For a moment, Miranda appeared reluctant. Again, she peeked past his shoulder, edgy and restless, as if worried someone might barge in. Then she made a small sound of arousal and arched her back to fit her hips more snugly against his. She tipped her head back to look up at him. Her lips were parted, her cheeks flushed. It fascinated Jamie how easily passion sparked between them.

"Princess, we have a room with a nice, soft bed and a long night ahead of us. Don't tempt me to do something you might regret."

Miranda reached up and raked her fingers into his hair

again. Jamie gripped her wrist to stall the gentle caress that was adding to the heat between them.

He spoke harshly. "You've had a taste of racial prejudice this afternoon. Wait until we get into a few more towns, need to find a place to stay or buy a meal. Then you tell me if you still think it might be a good idea to stay hitched to me for the rest of your days."

He released her wrist and cupped her chin, stroking his thumb across her lips, the way he had done once before. "Marriage is not just sleeping together in the darkness of the night. I'm sure we'd manage that part very well. It is standing by your man when the world is against you. Being married to me means getting turned away from hotels and being refused service in stores and people pointing a gun at you to chase you off their property."

Miranda made no reply, merely watched him, her blue eyes big and round.

Jamie dropped his arm down his side and took a step away. "You think on it while I go and see if I can find a barber to cut my hair at gunpoint. Then I'll see if there's a lawman in this sorry excuse for a town, or at least someone who knows about the routes south. Have your bath, get ready for bed. I'll be a couple of hours."

He walked out of the room, his body taut with tension, his heart pounding in his chest.

Why did Miranda insist on tempting him? Was she just being reckless in her curiosity about men and women, or did she truly believe in the foolish notion they could have a future? He knew better, but if he came back to find Miranda waiting up for him, he might ignore his misgivings and end up putting the honeymoon suite to the use it was intended for.

Chapter Seventeen

Jamie returned to find the room hot and stuffy and Miranda sound asleep beneath the covers in the big oak bed. Filled with a confusing mix of disappointment and relief, Jamie eased over to the bedside, his footsteps soundless on the plank floor.

Miranda's hair fanned over the pillow in damp strands, like golden snakes, and her skin was glowing from the bath. He could smell the floral soap she used. For a long moment, Jamie watched her, his eyes tracing her flawless features.

This was for the best, he told himself. No need to fight the temptation tonight. He could simply go to sleep. Perhaps by tomorrow morning, Miranda would have come to her senses, would take the train to her sister and put an end to the emotional torment that was tearing him apart.

Crossing the room, Jamie went to the balcony and opened the double doors to let in fresh air. Then he went back to the bedside. Miranda was wearing the shapeless gown made from an old shirt. Rough and baggy, it served as a contrast to her beauty, enhancing it even more than silk and lace might have done.

If he peeled off his clothing and slipped beneath the covers, could he stop himself from touching her? No, he could not, Jamie decided. Just the thought of sleeping beside her made his gut clench and his heartbeat quicken.

Perhaps if he just stripped down to his undergarments? No, the risk would still be too great. Miranda might awaken during the night. Her mind fuzzy with sleep, her passions might rise, and they might end up doing something she would regret in the morning.

Satisfied he was demonstrating some of that chivalry Miranda set so much store by, Jamie stretched out beside her on top of the covers. He closed his eyes, then opened them and rolled over to his side. If sleep failed him, he might as well enjoy looking at Miranda.

Miranda pushed closer to the bulky warm object beside her but some obstacle prevented her from tucking comfortably against it. She gave her hips a wiggle on the mattress and inched forward, fumbling to wrap her arms around the thing. Something restrained her. Another wiggle of her hips. Another fumble with her arms. But she never got closer, because that lovely, warm presence slid away each time she advanced toward it.

"The bed too small for you, Princess?"

Her eyes flared open. She blinked away sleep. Gray eyes met hers across the pillow. Jamie lay beside her, but he was on top of the covers and she was under them, his weight trussing her into a parcel beneath the thick quilt.

Miranda craned her neck to glance past him. They were right on the edge of the bed. She must have been doing that for hours—edging forward on the mattress, in an effort to cuddle up against Jamie, unaware that the bedding created a barrier between them.

"One more shove and I'll hit the floor," he warned her.

"Do you always sleep with your boots and clothes on?"

"You think an outlaw will stop and wait for me to get dressed?"

Instead of replying, Miranda yawned and stretched beneath the covers. The room was toasty warm. The balcony curtains stood open. The clouds had cleared and sunshine sparkled on the grassy meadow outside and gilded the mountaintops on the horizon.

"Heavens," she said. "I only intended to lie down for a minute after my bath but I must have slept right through the night. I didn't hear you come in, or the train go past."

She turned back toward Jamie and studied him, marveling at the transformation. His hair was not as short as most men wore theirs, but it was cut in a conventional masculine style. Still a bit too long, it fell to his collar in neat layers. A few coal-black strands flopped across his forehead. She detected a spicy scent, some kind of barber's soap.

"You don't look Indian anymore," Miranda said, startled at how much his native appearance had been a mental suggestion, triggered by his long hair. "You just look foreign. Papa had business partners. A Greek gentleman, and another one who was Creole. You look a bit like them, although they wore ruffled shirts and fancy neckties."

"Don't expect to see me dressed like that." Jamie pushed up to sit on the edge of the bed and raked his fingers through his hair. The layers settled neatly around his head. His features looked less fierce now, without the straight curtain of hair to contrast with the sharp angle of his cheekbones. He looked very, very handsome, Miranda realized. And women all over the world would think the same.

"Did Aggie see you when you got back?"

Jamie glanced over his shoulder and nodded, amusement glittering in his eyes.

Miranda frowned. "Did she comment on your haircut?"

"No," Jamie replied with a grin. "But she pursed her

lips into a circle and blew out a long, slow whistle as I walked in through the saloon doors."

Miranda picked up a pillow and hit him with it. Jamie snagged it from her hands and hit her back. For a moment, they tussled like two children. Then Jamie tossed the pillow aside. He gripped Miranda's wrists and eased her down on her back, pinning her arms against the mattress. He leaned over her, his eyes searching hers with an unspoken question in them.

Tension knotted in Miranda's belly. Her breathing, swift from the pillow fight, came to a complete halt. He would kiss her again. Anticipation tingled on her lips, thrummed in her body.

But then a door slammed in the corridor outside, breaking the morning quiet. Footsteps thudded past their room. A male voice called downstairs for hot water.

Cousin Gareth!

Miranda flinched. The image of him invaded her mind, ruining the moment.

Jamie spoke in a low voice. "Something wrong, Princess?"

"No…nothing…" Her tone was strained.

For a long moment, there was only silence. Something flickered in Jamie's expression, something dark and closed and hard. In a sudden motion, he released her wrists and swung up from the bed. He eased back a few paces and stood there, watching her through narrowed eyes.

"Decision time, Princess. A month of rough traveling. Cold and rain and bad food and being turned away from hotels because no matter what I've done to my hair, I'm still part Indian, and I'll never deny the fact. The alternative is a railroad ticket. Comfortable travel, with warm rooms and beds like this."

"But alone."

Jamie's mouth tightened. "If it's important to you, Princess, I'll escort you to San Francisco. Or even all the way to Gold Crossing, and hand you over to your sister and her husband."

Miranda hesitated. Jamie seemed cool and withdrawn now. And yet there was a current of attraction between them they had yet to fully explore. A month on the trail would give her the chance to get to know him, to see if there truly might be a chance to make their marriage real. And boarding a train would mean losing that chance.

"South," she told him. "On horseback."

"South it is, Princess," Jamie replied, his gaze intent on hers. "But be clear on one thing—I expect you to obey orders. I'm experienced in rough living. You're not. I know outlaws and desperate men. You don't. I can kill without remorse. You can't. After we ride out of this two-bit town, my word is the law. Do you understand?"

Miranda wanted to roll her eyes. What was it with men? Why did Jamie feel compelled to make a big speech about something he'd been doing all along anyway?

"Aye, aye, captain," she told him. "Your crew promises not to mutiny. Or at least the human element of it does," she added. "I can't vouch for the horses or the mules."

"Fine." He picked up his hat from the nightstand and put it on. "I'll go and order breakfast while you get ready."

Miranda munched on a piece of bread slathered with honey and tried to concentrate on the tattered map Jamie had put down on the table between them. The saloon was crowded, mostly with men in rough clothing. It must have been noisy after the train arrived, but she'd slept through it all.

"This is the choice of routes," Jamie was saying. He traced his finger along the map. "The problem will be getting across the Grand River—Colorado River, some call it. It runs through a maze of canyons for hundreds of miles along the border between Utah and Arizona."

He tapped his finger on the map. "Here. Canyons, like huge scars in the earth. Or we could go this way." His traced another line. "Both routes have waterless stretches. We should be all right, though, with the two pack mules. I'll try to buy a small water barrel before we leave."

"Uh-huh." Miranda was only half listening, trying to strain her ears to hear what Cousin Gareth was saying. He was sitting at the next table with a uniformed man who looked like a railroad conductor. She wondered if they kept records of people who'd been caught traveling without a ticket.

"I'm not sure which route is better," Jamie went on. "I've asked around about ferries, but no one seems to know for sure. Because we don't have a wagon, we could swim across if the current is not too strong."

"Uh-huh."

He looked up. "You can swim, can't you? You grew up by the sea?"

Cousin Gareth shot a look in their direction. *Blast and damnation.* He'd been listening, just as she had been listening to him. She needed to get away from him, as fast as possible. Miranda got to her feet, drained the last of her coffee standing up. "I can swim. Let's go and pack."

Jamie folded the map and put it away in his pocket. "We'll take the western route, through Utah into Arizona." He rose from his seat, propped his hat on his head. "You get started. I'll go and see if I can buy a water barrel."

Miranda nodded and hurried toward the stairs. She had barely started up when the clatter of footsteps chased after her. "Miss Fairfax." She turned to see Cousin Gareth standing at the base of the stairs, head tipped back, his expression pleading.

Miranda darted a glance in the direction of the ba-twing doors. Jamie had already gone out, the doors swinging in his wake. "Mrs. Blackburn," she amended. "I'm married now."

"Of course," Cousin Gareth replied. "I heard you talking to Aggie yesterday. You introduced yourself as Miss Fairfax and it stuck in my mind."

Her hand tightened over the balustrade. "What is it, Mr....?"

"Wolfson," he supplied. "Gareth Wolfson. I've settled on Wolfson, because of the wolf's head on my walking stick. And that is what I wanted to ask you about." He climbed the few steps that separated them and halted beside her.

Again, the transformation in him struck Miranda. The slackness was gone, not just in his facial features but the flabbiness in his body. The peacock blue frock coat draped elegantly over his wide shoulders. His complexion was tanned, his eyes clear and alert. Still young, in his early thirties, he was an attractive man.

A flurry of memories unfurled in Miranda's mind, going back to when she and her sisters were small and Gareth a teenager. He had been a welcome visitor at Merlin's Leap then, one who taught them card games and magic tricks. What had gone wrong with him? What bitterness had poisoned his mind?

"How can I help you, Mr. Wolfson?" she asked.

"It is about my walking stick. You said you thought you had seen one like it before. Did you know it has a hidden compartment? Look." He gripped the silver wolf's head, pressed a hidden catch beneath and twisted up the handle to reveal a hollow space inside. "Had you seen something like this before?"

Miranda shook her head. "No. I had no idea."

The hope in Gareth's eyes died. "I spoke to the railroad official. The walking stick was clasped in my hand when they found me. It was the only thing of value the robbers left me. I'm certain it has always belonged to me. I found the hidden compartment. There was money there, banknotes rolled into a tight bundle, but no documents. Nothing to shed light on my identity. I thought perhaps, if you'd seen a similar walking stick before, you might know where it had been obtained and I could investigate. There can't be too many of these made."

"I'm sorry, Mr. Wolfson. I know of no other such walking stick."

"Well." Gareth gave a wistful smile. "It was worth asking. I bid you good day. And good luck for your journey. And congratulations on your marriage. I understand it was recent. He seems a fine man, your husband."

With those parting words, Cousin Gareth turned around and went back to his table, where the railroad man was tucking into his breakfast. Miranda scampered up the stairs. She had to get away from him, before Gareth regained his memory, or before she let compassion and honesty brush aside the instinct for self-preservation and told him who he was.

Chapter Eighteen

You are a fool, Jamie told himself as he pointed Sirius back north, the pack mules and Miranda following him. He should feel nothing but frustration that Miranda had refused to board the train, and yet the sensation that filled him seemed dangerously close to relief.

Why had he gone to the trouble of getting his hair cut? Was it because he liked it short, or had he really done it to show Miranda he could fit into her world? That he could be a husband worth keeping, as she had so innocently suggested? Judging by her behavior in the morning, he had succeeded in making her understand how impossible the idea was.

From now on, whatever feminine nonsense she threw at him, he'd do better at resisting temptation. He was an escort to get her safely from point to point, nothing more.

Jamie halted his horse, waited for Miranda to catch up. "Are you happy with the route I've chosen?" he asked. "West and then south through Utah into Arizona."

Miranda glanced back toward the railroad where the cardsharp from the saloon was standing outside the livery stable, inspecting the horses for sale.

"It's fine," she replied. "Can we keep going?"

"There are forded crossings and a ferry across the

Colorado River. We can decide how to cross when we get there."

"Fine." Miranda flapped one hand to usher him along. "Let's go."

Jamie frowned as he nudged Sirius into motion. Something was wrong, something more than what had taken place between them. Miranda had been edgy since they came into town. At first he'd assumed it was the railroad, the tension of making the choice that committed her to the long overland trail, but now she seemed more nervous than ever. It bode ill for the journey.

Miranda seemed to have snapped out of her anxiety, but some kind of plan was germinating in her mind, Jamie could tell. She was too eager to learn, too ready to obey his commands. Instinct warned him that when a stubborn woman suddenly turned meek, it was merely a smoke screen for some outrageous demand she intended to spring on him the instant she considered him adequately primed.

Traveling was pleasant now. Sunny autumn days with blue skies and a cool breeze. In the sky, migrating flocks of geese headed south. The trail meandered across the Sweetwater River, crossing it nine times in all, but the fords were easy, the current light.

They stopped for the night by Independence Rock, a huge gray boulder, like a giant turtle. Two decades ago, it had been a landmark on the Oregon Trail. Scratched names and initials covered the surface. It was said fifty thousand migrants had left their mark.

After they finished clambering over the rock, studying the history recorded there, Jamie left Miranda to light a fire and walked off to shoot a rabbit for supper. When he squatted to gut and clean the carcass, eager footsteps pounded across the grassy meadow toward him.

"Show me how to skin the rabbit."

Jamie slanted a sideways look at Miranda, who'd crouched beside him. Easier to let her stay than to order her to leave. He pulled out his knife, sliced the rabbit from throat to tail and shook out the entrails. If he was not mistaken, he heard gagging sounds.

"Your face has gone green, Princess."

"I…am…all…right." The words came between clamped teeth.

"Leave this to me. Oil my saddle instead. The leather is drying up."

"I want to learn how to prepare a rabbit for supper."

"You can't learn with your eyes closed."

Jamie waited for Miranda to open her eyes again. He poked at the entrails with the tip of his knife. "This is the kidney. Best part of the rabbit. This is the liver. That's good, too. The rest of the bits inside you throw away."

Beside him, Miranda rocked forward in small, sharp jerks, accompanied by strangled sounds. "Go away," Jamie ordered. "Some things you are not meant to handle."

"I…can…learn."

"Maybe, but it will have to be another time. I'm hungry, and I don't like the idea of having to shoot another rabbit if you throw up all over this one." He jerked his chin toward the camp. "Go put the coffee on."

Miranda scrambled to her feet, hurried off. Jamie followed her with his eyes. She made ten yards before she came to a halt and doubled over behind a bush. He shook his head. *Stubborn* was not a strong enough word but he couldn't think of a better one.

He reckoned he'd figured out what outrageous demand she planned to spring on him. She had aspirations to be a bounty hunter. Of course, it was impossible. Just as impossible as the idea of making their marriage real.

And yet there was no mistaking the attraction between them. It was there, in the quickly snatched looks. In the long, emotion-filled silences. In the accidental brush of hands that left a tingling in its wake. In the way she asked him to help her into the saddle and in the way he held on to her longer than was necessary as he fulfilled her request.

He had no regrets about escorting her on the journey. He'd enjoy her company while he could and after their parting he'd cherish the memories. It was good for a man to have a woman to dream about when he rode the lonely trails.

Jamie finished preparing the rabbit, pierced it with a skewer from a piece of hickory and returned to the camp where he set the carcass to roast over the flames. When the meat sizzled, he cut a piece and offered it to Miranda. She shook her head. Her throat moved in a frantic swallow, accompanied with one of those gagging sounds. Jamie suppressed a rueful smile. Rabbit might have to remain off the menu for some time to come.

He pushed up to his feet. "I'll get you dry biscuits. They'll settle your stomach."

He went to rummage in the saddlebags, found the tin of biscuits. Back at the fire, he made coffee, added a few spoonfuls of sugar.

"Here." He handed her the mug, then paused to massage the small puckered mark on his palm. It had been itching today, for the first time in years.

Miranda had recovered enough to speak. "What gave you that scar?"

Jamie sat down, looked up into the sky where a million stars glittered. If he hadn't been feeling so guilty about letting her watch while he gutted the rabbit, he might have kept his silence. But talking seemed an easy way to make amends.

"I got it when I was a kid. We went to school in town for a year. Me and Louise. They didn't take Indians, but we didn't really look Cheyenne, so our mother thought we might get away with it. Of course, we didn't. Some kids guessed, and I got into a fight. The other boy picked up a piece of timber from a woodpile and hit me with it. He didn't realize there was a nail sticking out of it, and when he swung it, he nailed my hand to the schoolhouse wall."

"That's awful. Did it hurt terribly?"

"I don't remember it hurting, but I remember being furious because I was stuck. It took me a while to wrench the piece of timber loose. By the time I got my hand free, the other boy had run off and I had no prospect of catching him."

"Does the scar bother you?"

Jamie held his hand in front of him, curled and uncurled his fingers. "Not normally. I was lucky. The nail went between the bones and tendons. The wound healed in no time. I never think about it, except..."

He fell silent. To his surprise, Miranda didn't prompt him. It seemed as though she realized it was something he struggled with in his own mind, and she wanted to give him the freedom to talk about it or to keep his thoughts private.

"After Louise went to live on the reservation, she became a great believer in the Indian superstitions. According to her, the scar holds my fate. One day, it will change the course of my life." Jamie sent Miranda a tense smile across the flickering firelight. "It's nonsense, of course."

"Do you miss your sister?" Miranda asked softly. "Do you mind not being able to visit her grave, or Nora's grave?"

The tension in Jamie grew. He didn't talk about his emotions, let alone admit to weakness. And yet somehow, the words tumbled out. "Of course I miss them. For years, providing for them was my purpose in life. But I have no need to visit their graves. Their spirits are not there. They are all around us. Every time I see a skylark, I'll think of Louise. Every time I see a hummingbird, I'll think of Nora."

As Jamie fell silent, it occurred to him that what he had just explained about the spirits of his sister and his niece contradicted his claim that he regarded Indian superstitions as nothing but nonsense.

Miranda didn't probe further, and Jamie pushed the prediction about his scar out of his mind. But that night he had the dream again. It came perhaps three or four times a year, usually right after he'd been in a gunfight.

In the dream, he was holding a gun aimed at an outlaw. When he tried to pull the trigger, his fingers refused to work. One by one, he heard the small bones in his hand snap. His hand broke apart, like something made of clay, and the fragments rained down to his feet.

In the dream, he only had the one gun, and when his hand was no longer there, the gun fell to the ground, leaving him to face the outlaw unarmed. He always woke up before the outlaw shot him. He wondered what might happen if he remained asleep. Did dreams have the power to kill? He wasn't familiar enough with Indian legends to know the answer.

It took Miranda a while to realize the white blobs on the horizon were covered wagons. There were two of them, and ahead of them she could see a heavy open wagon, filled with barrels and crates, drawn by a string of mules.

They were half a mile away when gunshots cracked through the air. The team of mules burst into a run. The wagon filled with barrels and crates hurtled to the riverbank, where a ferryboat stood waiting. A pair of men jumped down from the wagon and drove the mules onto the ferry, forcing the animals into a tight group to allow room for the wagon.

The ferry, drawn by a steel cable, set in motion and inched across the wide expanse of the river. On the other side, the mules jumped off. The harnesses pulled tight and the wagon rolled off on its way. The ferry remained moored to the riverbank.

When Miranda and Jamie reached the pair of covered wagons, they found a woman and three men standing in a cluster, yelling at each other. The woman, a heavily built brunette dressed in a mud-brown gown, a gunbelt strapped around her waist, was hurling insults at the men. Her eyes narrowed as they settled on Jamie in his long duster.

"You a gunfighter?" she demanded to know.

"Could be," Jamie replied.

The woman pointed across the river. "Two outlaws stole my whiskey wagon. A hundred dollars if you retrieve it."

Jamie jumped down from Sirius. "How much whiskey?"

"Ten barrels. Twenty crates of French champagne, too."

Miranda sat on Alfie and watched Jamie lift the saddlebags from his horse and set them down on the ground. By the time she had dismounted and gained her footing on stiff legs, Jamie had already unsaddled Sirius, unhooked his gunbelt and was wrapping it into an oilcloth pouch.

"We don't need the money," she told him.

He glanced over at her and spoke quietly. "If my guess is right, much of that whiskey will make its way to the Indian reservations. If it does, it will rob Indians of what little money and dignity they have left. I won't let it happen."

He took off his long duster and the buckskin coat beneath, but kept on his shirt and denim trousers, and the boots that never seemed to leave his feet. He vaulted on Sirius again, bareback. Holding the oilcloth pouch that contained his gunbelt high above his head, he rode down to the riverbank and urged the horse into the stream.

"When you get to the other side, untie the ferryman," the feisty brunette shouted after him.

Miranda hurried to the edge of the water, leading Alfie by the reins. The current whirled and foamed around Sirius and Jamie as they eased into the stream. The water rose up to Jamie's boots. Then up to his thighs. Then higher still. Sirius began to swim, his neck craning out of the water, his powerful body moving in a steady rhythm.

When they reached the opposite bank, the horse scrambled up to dry ground. Jamie jumped down from the saddle, took his gunbelt from the oilskin pouch, tied it around his hips and hopped onto the ferry. Miranda saw him bend to a man trussed up in ropes. A blade flashed in the sun, and an instant later Jamie jumped back to dry land, vaulted on Sirius and took off, crouched low over the horse, his speed making a mockery of Miranda's claim that she could ride faster than him.

Her eyes followed the horse and bareback rider until they shrank to a speck in the distance. It felt as if a cord attached to her heart was stretching tighter and tighter. She could barely breathe. When Jamie finally vanished out of her sights, the world seemed empty and cold and full of shadows.

Chapter Nineteen

⟨~~~~~⟩

The brunette came to stand alongside Miranda and waved at the ferryman across the river. Freed from his ropes, the ferryman got to his feet and rubbed his wrists to get the blood circulating. A few seconds later, he went to work with the steel cable and the ferry set off toward them, fighting the current.

"What's he called, the gunfighter?" the brunette asked.

"Jamie Blackburn," Miranda replied. "He's my husband."

"A married gunfighter?"

Miranda nodded, her gaze strained into the distance where Jamie had vanished.

"Well, Mrs. Blackburn, I'm Stella Stevens." The woman turned and pointed at each of the three men in turn. "And these no-good pieces of human junk are my brothers. Stan, Simon and Seth."

Miranda glanced over. She could see the family resemblance. Dark hair and sallow skin. Small eyes and prominent brows, in faces that were almost as wide as they were long. On Stella, the looks gave an air of shrewd cunning. On the men the impact was the opposite, a primitive, simian appearance that suggested lack of intelligence.

The men were all dressed the same, battered bowler

hats and dark wool trousers and ill-fitting suit coats over faded shirts that might have once been blue. Miranda made no attempt to guess which was Stan or Simon or Seth. They all seemed around the same age, middle thirties. Stella looked over forty, clearly the eldest and used to giving orders.

Stella clapped her hands. "You can come out now, girls."

Before Miranda's astonished eyes, a girl jumped out from one of the wagons. Then another. And another. And another. Four girls. The sight brought back memories of how the little Summerton girls had emerged from their stranded carriage in Boston.

However, Miranda hoped those little girls wouldn't grow up to join the profession of these ones, for it was easy to recognize them as saloon girls. All four were dressed in high-heeled slippers and low-cut satin gowns, identical except for the color.

"This is Scarlet," Stella said. "And this is Olive. Violet. Sandy."

Bright red dress. Muted green dress. Violet dress. Light brown dress.

Stella beamed like a proud mother hen. "I reckon men might forget which girl is which, but they'll remember by the color of their dresses. These are my Color Girls, for my saloon in Gold Hill. The best watering hole in all of Utah, it will be."

"If we get the whiskey back," one of the men muttered.

"And if we don't, I'll take it out of your hide," Stella shot back. "You were supposed to guard the shipment." She spat on the ground. "Cowards, the lot of you. I'm glad Pa isn't alive to see what kind of lily-livered chickens you've turned into."

"Should've taken the train to Salt Lake City," another one of the brothers mumbled.

Stella gave an angry flap of her hand. "You know we can't take the train. I owe money to the Rio Grande railroad company. They might impound the goods."

While they'd been talking, the ferry had made its way across the river. Stella sprang into action. Gathering her mud-brown skirts, she climbed onto the bench of one the wagons—not the one the girls had emerged from, but the other one. She twisted around to shout inside.

"Time to come out, gentlemen."

Two men scrambled down, one tall and thin, the other short and even thinner. Unlike most men in the West, neither wore a hat. It might be out of vanity, Miranda decided, for both had glossy black curls, long enough to pull into ringlets—the most attractive feature in their appearance, for their faces were bony, with beaked noses and receding chins.

The tall man, in his fifties, gave a courtly bow, one hand sweeping the air, the other hand pressed to his chest. "Jobai, Laszlo. Master musician, at your service."

The short man, around twenty, cradled a violin case in his arms like one might hold a cherished child. The older man prodded him in the side. The younger man slanted an alarmed glance at him, then gathered himself and bowed with the same flair. "Jobai, Istvan."

Stella cracked the reins. The mules set into motion. "Do you want to take the first crossing or the second, Mrs. Blackburn?" Stella called out. "We'll have to cross in two lots."

"First crossing," Miranda shouted back. The other side was where Jamie was. It might only be fifty yards closer to him, but it was an important fifty yards.

Trusting Seth and Stan and Simon to look after the pack mules, Miranda guided Alfie into the narrow space left free behind Stella's wagon. The Color Girls had already hopped aboard. The ferryman, a compact individual who moved with short, jerky steps, probably from years of having to take care not to trip over the edge, detached the ramp and they set off.

Halfway across the stream, the current seized the primitive vessel, sending it into a swirl. The steel cable overhead sprang taut. "Grab hold of the cable!" the ferryman yelled. "Help me stabilize the craft."

Miranda reached up. The steel line, tight as a bow, cut into her palms. The ferry spun and jerked, fighting the current. The girl in a scarlet dress toppled over and rolled along the bottom of the vessel, her red silk skirts flaring out like a bullfighter's cloth.

Alfie gave a frightened whinny. The timbers shook as the Appaloosa reared up and slammed down again. His heavy flank hit Miranda in the shoulder, knocking her off balance. Instinctively, her hands tightened around the steel cable. As she clung on, the ferry went into another spin and fell away from beneath her feet, leaving her dangling on the cable.

Terrified, Miranda fought to get back on board. Swinging her body, transferring her grip along the cable, she chased the vessel as it pulled away. Cold sweat rose on her skin, making her hands damp. She could feel a snag in the steel wire cutting into her palm. Blood trickled from the wound, warm and slippery, mixing with the sweat.

Her hold grew precarious…slipping…slipping…

She lost her grip and plummeted down to the water, the momentum of her fall plunging her beneath the surface. Cold darkness closed around her. She held her breath as the torrent seized and spun her, pulling her into the icy depths.

Legs kicking, arms thrashing, Miranda battled the rushing water, upward, upward. Her lungs strained. Blood pounded at her temples. She broke through to the surface, sucked in gulps of air. She was floating, the current carrying her downstream, the ferry already ten yards away... twenty...thirty...

Her deerskin coat weighed her down. Water filled her boots. Miranda tried to reach down to her legs and pull off the boots, but the current seized her and spun her again, sucking her back down into the icy darkness.

Forget the clothes. Miranda filled her lungs to help her float and started swimming, each stroke taking her closer to the shore as she drifted downstream. Ahead of her, the river narrowed, the banks rising into sheer walls of rock. If she didn't reach the shore soon, she might never be able to climb out.

With every ounce of her strength, Miranda swam, arms churning, legs kicking, lungs heaving. The muddy bank drew closer. Five yards. Four. Three. Two. No trees, no boulders, no protruding roots, nothing to grip, nothing she could use to haul herself out of the water. With a desperate lurch, Miranda buried her fingers into the mud and clung there, battling the force of the current.

The strain on her muscles easing, she summoned the last of her strength and managed to flip onto her side and roll out of the water. Panting, she sprawled on the muddy slope, her feet still in the current, the stream gushing over her boots.

For several minutes, Miranda lay there, letting relief slide over her. Then she realized the river had not released its hold on her yet. The mud beneath her was eroding away. She was slipping backward, the water already lapping at her hips. Exhausted, her entire body shaking, Miranda teetered up to her hands and knees and clawed her way up the bank.

"Jamie," she whispered as she knelt on the grass, weighed down by a mix of terror and relief and exhaustion. She found the strength to lift her head and stare ahead, along the trail where the bareback rider had disappeared, chasing the whiskey wagon. She could see no horse, no rider, no sign of him. Just the river snaking its way across the rugged landscape.

Jamie drove the mule wagon back down the trail, Sirius trotting behind. Ahead, one of the covered wagons and Miranda's gray Appaloosa had already crossed the river. The ferry, loaded with the second wagon and the pack mules, was docking at the shore.

"Jamie! Jamie!"

He saw Miranda hurtle along the bank toward him. She was covered in mud, her hair in a tangle. With every step, water sloshed from her boots. Jamie halted the mule team, set the brake and climbed down. Miranda threw herself against him, her arms sliding around his neck in a wet, muddy embrace.

"Oh, Jamie." The words came on a sob.

"What happened?" He hugged her tight. "Did you take a tumble when you got off the ferry?"

"I fell into the river. I had to swim. Look. Look." She drew apart from him and held out her hands. Her palms were scratched, with a bleeding cut on one of them. "I tried to hang from the steel cable but I lost my grip. I thought I was going to drown."

The ferry had finished unloading and the others hurried up, crowding around them. "Did you kill the thieves?" the woman asked.

"No," Jamie replied, his attention on Miranda's palms. "I nicked one of them in the arm and they ran off."

"We heard gunshots," one of the men said.

Jamie shifted his shoulders in dismissal. "They were new to the business of thieving. Panicked and wasted a lot of ammunition." He glanced up. "Can someone get me a drop of whiskey?"

One of the men produced a metal hip flask from his pocket. Jamie took it, pulled his shirt free from his trousers, unscrewed the flask and dampened the hem. Gently, he patted Miranda's palms clean with the whiskey-soaked fabric. "It's only a scratch," he said. "It won't bleed much, but it might hurt to grip things for a day or two."

Behind them, a muffled explosion and the tinkle of shattering glass disturbed the quiet. The woman in a mud-brown skirt swore.

"Sorry," Jamie said. "The champagne got shook up when they raced off with the wagon. The bottles are breaking and popping open."

"Don't move the wagon," the woman yelled at the man who had climbed up to the bench and gathered the lines. "Get a couple of buckets," she ordered the gaggle of girls in brightly colored gowns. "We'll save what we can from the broken bottles. We'll have ourselves a party tonight."

She turned back to Jamie and Miranda. "Can you stay? We have a side of beef to cook. It doesn't exactly go with champagne, but I can promise you music and merriment."

Jamie glanced up into the sky. The sun was sinking, the light fading, the air getting cool. Beside him, he could feel Miranda shivering. He wrapped one arm around her, pulled her close to his side and held the slim flask of whiskey out to her.

"Drink," he told her. "It will stop you from getting a chill." He watched as Miranda tipped her head back and took a deep gulp. Her face puckered with distaste. A ripple traveled down the length of her.

"I think champagne might be just what my wife needs," Jamie said to the strangers. He gestured at the edge of the forest about a hundred yards back from the river. "If you collect some firewood and build a fire, we can forget about the hundred dollars. As long as you help me get my wife warm and dry."

* * *

Jamie stood between the two covered wagons, talking to Seth Stevens. He'd been introduced to Stella and her brothers, and to the two Hungarian musicians who were father and son, and to the Color Girls.

Miranda was in one of the wagons, getting out of her wet, muddy clothes. Jamie had already changed, but the process appeared to take much longer for a female. He'd seen the Color Girls dart in and out of the wagon, bearing crystal flutes of champagne. Giggling and a flurry of feminine voices burst out every now and then.

"The bounty for the Hardin brothers is four thousand dollars," Seth was saying.

"Not interested," Jamie replied. "I'm on vacation."

He tossed back the last of the whiskey in his glass, savoring the trail of heat down his chest, and nodded at Seth. "Excuse me. I need to go and find my wife."

He kept saying that, Jamie realized. *My wife.* And every time he did, a wave of warmth greater than the glow from Miss Stella's top-grade whiskey flowed through him.

He paused by the covered wagon. The girl in a green dress, Olive, was passing two full champagne glasses into the wagon and taking away two empty ones. Jamie had to admire Miss Stella's logic. Without the colored dresses he'd never have remembered the names of four women who all looked much the same to him.

Another stream of feminine laughter rang out. Jamie grinned into the twilight. If he wasn't mistaken, he might have a tipsy wife on his hands tonight. He moved closer, was just about to call out for Miranda when he heard one of the Color Girls talking.

"How did you end up married to a bounty hunter?"

Jamie's feet stopped moving. Eavesdropping was second nature to him. That's how he gathered information about where a wanted man might be hiding. Miranda replied, her voice bright and lively. Good, Jamie thought. The champagne was doing its job of wiping away any lingering residue of fear and shock.

"He promised to bust me out of jail if I married him," Miranda was saying.

"You were in jail!" the Color Girl gushed. "What for?"

"Train robbery."

"Train robbery! You robbed a train?"

"I robbed several trains," Miranda boasted. "But they also tried to pin a robbery on me that I hadn't committed."

Jamie shook his head, a rueful smile tugging at his lips. Now his little Eastern princess was fashioning herself into the Queen of the Outlaws.

"Heavens." The Color Girl lowered her voice. "What is he like…the bounty hunter? He is part Indian… Are they like other men…you know…in the boudoir…?"

Jamie winced. There were limits to eavesdropping. He didn't want to hear what answer Miranda's imagination might furnish to a question about his bedroom prowess.

"Miranda," he called out. "Are you ready? I have ointment for your hands."

Silence. Then a burst of giggles. The wagon canvas rustled, as if someone was struggling to find their way out through the flap, and then Miranda tumbled down in a careless leap. Jamie caught her and restored her balance before she toppled over. She was wearing her light blue dress, like another Color Girl, but with a shawl tied around her shoulders to add a touch of modesty.

"Jamie!" A huge smile spread on her face. "We were just talking about you."

He ignored the comment. "I have ointment for your hands. It will stop infection."

Miranda inspected her palms, lifted them closer to her

face and lowered them again, as if they were some strange objects instead of a part of her body. "They don't hurt."

Jamie took the small stone jar from his pocket, unclipped the lid and dipped his finger into the cooling salve. "This will make sure it stays that way. Give me your hand."

He massaged in the herbal paste, rubbing his thumb over the scrapes. "Train robber, huh?" His wife's hands were tiny in his, her skin soft. Jamie kept rubbing longer than needed, just for the pleasure of touching her. "You robbed several trains?"

Miranda lifted her chin in that haughty angle he'd noticed the first time he set eyes on her. "I was traveling without a ticket. That's robbing the railroad company. And I did it on several trains. All the way from New York City."

"I see."

Swaying on her feet, Miranda sniffed at the air. "I'm hungry."

The two wagons were set at an angle to each other, and on the open side of the triangle a big bonfire burned, with hunks of beef roasting over it, releasing succulent scents.

"Me too," Jamie said. "Let's go and eat."

"And drink," Miranda replied. "I'd like more champagne."

Behind her back, Jamie grinned in anticipation. He knew the prim Miranda, and the angry Miranda, and the grieving Miranda, and the stubborn Miranda. With an interest tinged with affection, he waited to get to know the drunken Miranda.

Chapter Twenty

~~~~~~~~~~

The violin struck a lively tune. In the covered wagon, a piano joined in. A midnight concert under the stars. Miranda tipped her head back and laughed, letting the sound ripple toward the sky. She took another sip of champagne, giggled as the bubbles tickled her nose. Her belly was full of good food and her head buzzed with the nectar of kings. It was time to be merry, time to rejoice in being alive.

"Go easy on the champagne, Princess," Jamie warned her.

"It's all right. Our parents let us have champagne at Merlin's Leap." One small glass, she might have added. Not gallons of it flowing freely. But she'd be a good little wife and obey. She drained the glass and set it down on the trestle table behind her.

When the Hungarian father and son took a break to have their supper, Miranda plucked a glass of tawny liquid from the table and took a sip. Jamie had told her to go easy on the champagne but he'd said nothing about whiskey.

The liquor burned like a stream of fire down her chest. Emboldened, her mind in a pleasant swirl, Miranda burst into a boisterous sea shanty, something to break the boring silence that had settled when the notes of the piano and violin faded away.

"Whiskey here, whiskey there
Whiskey almost everywhere

I drink it hot, I drink it cold
I drink it new, I drink it old."

Jamie grabbed her arm and interrupted her just as her feet were about to master the pattern of the merry jig she'd been improvising. "Go easy on the whiskey, too, Princess."

"Spoilsport," Miranda muttered, but she sat down on a rickety wooden chair and waited for the music to resume.

It didn't take long for the party to liven up again. The violin and piano sent out a catchy tune. In the space between the wagons, three of the Color Girls settled into formation with Stella's brothers and began to dance, the flames of the bonfire reflecting on their shiny satin gowns.

The scarlet girl remained standing aside, waiting for her turn. Wasn't she the one who'd been asking about Jamie? And she was staring at him now. With big, eager eyes. *Oh, yes, siree, I do notice,* Miranda thought. If Scarlet planned to satisfy her curiosity about men with Indian blood in them, she could think again. Hopping from the chair, Miranda waved her hands at the girl, as if shooing away a sheep or a goat. *Hands off my man.*

"What's wrong, Princess?"

"Huh?" She spun toward Jamie, stumbled.

He reached out to steady her. "You're flapping like a chicken attempting to fly."

His hand closed around her arm in that strong, firm

touch she'd felt many times before, and a need seized Miranda, as sudden and powerful as a lightning strike. She wanted to feel Jamie's arms around her, wanted to feel the warmth of his body against hers.

She turned to him. "Dance with me."

He tilted his head in a gesture of regret. "I don't know how."

Miranda shifted her attention to the couples making elaborate patterns of advance and retreat between the wagons, skirts twirling, feet skipping, boots thudding. "Wait here," she said to Jamie. Weaving a little, she made her way to the young man with a violin, whispered a request into his ear. He smiled and nodded, not interrupting his playing.

Miranda returned to stand beside Jamie. A moment later, the tune changed into a soft lullaby. She turned to face Jamie. The light was behind him, his features shadowed, his expression guarded. All of a sudden, her heart was beating too fast and her hands seemed to be shaking. Her mood no longer felt in a pleasant swirl but on the brink of danger.

"This is easy," she said despite her misgivings. "You just shuffle your feet."

For an instant, Jamie met her gaze, his gray eyes dark and serious. Then he opened his arms and Miranda stepped into him. They had embraced before. The night after Nora died, she'd lain in bed curled up against him, and he'd held her when she was cold under the lean-to canopy, but that had been for consolation and comfort and warmth.

This was different, and they both understood it.

This was a woman issuing an invitation to a man.

The music soared around them, and Jamie pulled her close, anchoring her body against his. Miranda's hands swept up to his neck. She shifted her fingers through the thick strands of glossy hair. His skin was warm beneath her touch, his hair cool and crisp.

She could feel each movement as they danced. The slow rocking of his shoulders. The subtle rise and fall of his chest with every breath he took. The pressure of his hips against hers. The toe of his boot eased between her slippers. She could feel her skirts tangling around his leg.

The notes from the piano and violin swarmed around the clearing like dragonflies, rising and falling, rising and falling, caressing her skin. Blood thrummed through her veins, delivering a rush of heat that defeated the cool of the night. A hunger ignited deep within her, a hunger that demanded more than just two bodies gently swaying to the music.

"Kiss me," she said. "Why do I always have to ask?"

Jamie missed a step, stumbled. Miranda giggled. Stars seemed to be winking at her in the sky. A pleasant lassitude swirled through her mind. Elation filled her—elation and an irrepressible joy, a lightness of spirit, a sense that life was a magical gift from gods.

"You've drunk too much champagne, Princess."

Keeping one arm around her, Jamie lifted his other hand to her face. He traced the curve of her cheek with the back of his fingers. He caressed her chin, trailed his fingertips along her eyebrows, lingering over each feature, as if paying homage to her beauty.

"Kiss me," Miranda said once more.

With excruciating slowness, Jamie lowered his head. His hair, raven black in the night, fell forward, framing his face. Just before their lips met, he paused. Miranda felt the need prickle on her lips, felt the longing swell and soar inside her. She put her hands on his shoulders and rose on tiptoe, closing the distance, her lips settling against his.

Jamie made a rough sound that rumbled low in his

throat. His arms banded around her, anchoring her close to him. Miranda could feel the hardness of his body against hers. The music seemed to fade, the night shadows deepen. It felt as if time had suspended itself, as if everything in the clearing had vanished except their bodies molded together, their mouths feasting on each other.

The kiss seemed to go on forever. The hunger inside her grew and grew and grew, even while it was satisfying itself. Breathless, dazed, Miranda clung to Jamie, her fingers fisted in his shirt, her legs too unsteady to support her weight.

Finally, Jamie eased their bodies apart. His hands slid up from her waist to caress her throat. Miranda could feel the frantic hammering of her pulse beneath his questing fingers. Darkness and firelight cast deep shadows across Jamie's features, and again Miranda got the oddest impression that a secret heat burned in the cool gray of his eyes.

"Will you sleep in the tent with me tonight?" she asked. The question came without thought, born of boldness that rose not just from champagne, but from the euphoria of survival. Life suddenly seemed too short, too precarious not to live it to the fullest, not to seize every source of comfort and pleasure, not to chase after every dream, however fragile or distant that dream might be.

Jamie contemplated her in silence. "Why?"

Startled by the blunt question, Miranda fumbled. "I…"

"I mean, why now? Why tonight?" he clarified. "A few days ago we shared the luxury of the honeymoon suite but I got the impression you couldn't get away quick enough. Why now? In a tent?"

Slowly, Miranda marshaled her thoughts through the buzz of champagne in her brain. Her eyes grew wide as she recalled the crisis at the railroad town. She made a sweeping gesture, swaying a little on her feet from the force of the motion.

"Had to get away from Gareth, of course."

"Gareth?"

"Cousin Gareth." Forgetting the romance of the moment, Miranda giggled at the memory of the encounter. She'd been so clever. She'd fooled him good.

"The cardsharp," she explained. "He was my cousin. The one I was running away from when I left Boston." She gave a flap of dismissal with her hand and spoke in a tone of contempt. "Of course, he is no danger to me now. Charlotte is married. Bye-bye, Cousin Gareth," she chanted. "You lost. We won."

Jamie clasped her by the shoulders and peered into her face. "What are you talking about? The cardsharp in the saloon barely spoke to you. I saw him nod to you and say hello, and little more."

"Well, of course. Cousin Gareth doesn't know he is Cousin Gareth." Miranda's shoulders jumped with a hiccup. She swallowed, sent Jamie a triumphant smile. "He's lost his memory. He doesn't even know his own name."

Miranda didn't resist when Jamie sat her down on an empty champagne crate and fired questions at her, his face furrowed with concern. The interrogation seemed too tedious an occupation for such a fine night. Music and dancing and kissing were much more fun than being questioned about Cousin Gareth.

"So he didn't recognize you?" Jamie pressed.

"No-o." Another hiccup broke free.

"But he overheard you saying that you sang at the Carousel in Devil's Hall?"

Miranda nodded and trapped the next hiccup before it could get out.

"And he heard you say that your name is Miranda Fairfax."

"Was. Now I'm Miranda Blackburn. A bounty hunter."

"Train robber, last I heard," Jamie muttered.

Miranda giggled, then clamped her mouth shut, swaying on the makeshift seat.

Jamie curled his hands around her arms. Leaning over her, he searched her eyes, his expression serious. "That cardsharp was looking to buy a horse when we left. I reckon he'll ride out to Devil's Hall and ask questions about you. Think, Princess. Did you send telegrams or letters to your sister? Did you leave any trace that would lead him to Gold Crossing, Arizona Territory?"

Miranda hiccupped. "Letters. Telegram. Money order. Records at the bank."

A grim look settled over Jamie's features. "I reckon you'll catch up with your cousin in Gold Crossing. Maybe you ought to send a telegram to warn your sister. If your cousin takes the train, he might get there before us."

"He can't harm her now. Charlotte is married and has Papa's money."

"Perhaps your cousin no longer has power over you or your sisters," Jamie argued. "But if he gains his memory, he might be furious that you didn't tell him. It must be hard for a man to lose his identity like that," he added quietly. "Bad enough when you lose one person you care about. Losing everyone and everything at the same time must drive a man to despair."

He slanted a curious glance at Miranda. "Why didn't you tell him? Let the man out of his misery? He is family after all, and you said he is no longer a danger to you."

A shiver rippled over Miranda. She'd been feeling guilty about it, but she had suppressed the feeling. Now the champagne was letting the regret loose, just as it was letting loose the longing for Jamie she normally kept locked away behind the gate of propriety.

Perched on the wooden crate, kicking her heels against

the side with a drumming sound, Miranda lowered her gaze and spoke in a mutter. "I thought you'd get rid of me. Dump me on Cousin Gareth and save yourself a thousand-mile journey across the continent."

"Oh, Princess."

Miranda peered up. Jamie was shaking his head but the darkness hid his expression. She could hear his heavy sigh, could see his shoulders shift. "I'll go and talk to Seth," he said in a low voice. "If he and his brothers agree to keep watch, I can sleep with you in the tent tonight."

Four feet of space shared between them. Fully clad, boots on his feet, Jamie cradled Miranda in his arms, his lips nuzzling hers. Even if he'd wanted to, it wasn't possible to put any distance between them. He'd resolved to stop after one kiss, but that kiss was stretching minute by minute. His mouth never seemed to get enough of hers.

"Princess," he breathed against her lips. "We have to stop."

"I don't want to stop."

Jamie pulled back, studied her face. The light from the bonfire filtered through the tent canvas, casting a warm yellow glow that allowed him to see the languid expression on Miranda's face.

The music was still playing, but only the violin now, a lilting tune that soared and dipped like a bird in the sky. The temperature had fallen, but the tent was trapping the heat from their bodies, enveloping them with the haze of their own desire.

"You've had too much to drink, Princess."

"I know…" she whispered. "But I want…"

Jamie eased up on one elbow and leaned over Miranda, propping his other hand on her opposite side. One of his legs bent at the knee and straddled hers, pinning her down. He could feel the toe of his boot dipping between her legs.

"What do you want, Princess?" he asked roughly and wedged his boot deeper, emphasizing the intimate intrusion. "Is this what you want?"

Alarm flashed in Miranda's eyes, just the way Jamie had intended. He feared he might not have enough strength to resist her, and he wanted to make sure she would stop him if he tried to go too far.

"Apologize," Miranda demanded. Her tone was petulant, full of hurt, not angry or indignant, as Jamie had expected.

"What for?" he replied. "I haven't done anything... yet."

"I want you to apologize for what you said about me riding astride. It was crude and mean and nasty."

"Oh, Princess... Miranda." Jamie lowered his head and let his forehead come to rest against hers. The tone of her voice spoke of a long-nursed grievance. How much had that one callous comment been niggling in her mind?

"I'm sorry," he muttered. "I was angry with you, and..."

He wanted to roll onto his back, wanted to avert his face, but he owed it to Miranda to let her see his expression while he talked. If revealing his feelings was the price he had to pay to make his apology complete, so be it.

"That's the way it has always been for me...with women. Perhaps not crude...but functional...efficient. I've never been with a woman in a way that involved anything more than just satisfying the demands of my body."

"And me?" she said. "What is involved when you are with me?"

Jamie met her gaze and held it, allowing Miranda to see into his thoughts. "With you, everything is involved,

Princess. My body, my mind, my heart. Everything that I am. Everything that I hope to be."

Miranda lifted a hand and touched his cheeks, his chin, his lips, in much the same way he had traced her features earlier while they danced under the stars in the clearing. Her fingers were gentle, her touch as soft as a spring breeze.

"You are forgiven," she whispered.

"Thank you." Jamie dropped one final kiss on her mouth, light and tender now. "Go to sleep, Miranda. This is not the time or place."

Even if she hadn't been drunk on champagne, her recollection of his callous comment had spoiled the moment, reminding Jamie of how far apart their worlds were. Part-Indian bounty hunter and an educated Eastern princess. He was becoming dangerously close to thinking it would be possible to bridge that gap.

Chapter Twenty-One

❧❧❧

Jamie got up in the moonlight to take his turn for a two-hour watch. When the first glimmer of dawn painted the sky pink, he lifted the tent flap and peeked inside. He found Miranda awake, pale and bleary-eyed. She sent him a grimace of nausea and discomfort.

"I'm thirsty," she croaked. "My head hurts."

With a grunt of sympathy, Jamie straightened on his feet and fetched her a cup of coffee. By the time Miranda had drunk the thick black brew and freshened up in a secluded spot by the riverside, she appeared more alert.

As they moved around the campsite, preparing for their departure, it seemed clear to Jamie that Miranda was avoiding meeting his eyes. He got the impression that she wished to forget the intimacy of the night, and he chose not to remind her.

With routine born of three weeks of traveling, they folded down the tent and packed their belongings and loaded the mules and saddled their horses. After saying goodbye to Stella and Seth—the others were still asleep—they resumed their journey south.

During each rest stop, Miranda seemed a little livelier. The awkwardness of the morning faded, like the autumn sunshine dispersed the chill of the night. Jamie was relieved. It had crossed his mind that if Miranda was look-ing for a reason to be angry with him, she could choose between construing his reticence as a rejection and claim-ing that he had been taking liberties.

In the evening, as they struck camp, it became evi-dent to Jamie that although Miranda might not wish to acknowledge what had happened between them, a subtle change had taken place in their relationship. Up to now, Miranda had worked hard, but her efforts had been tense, as if she were being tested. Now she seemed to relax. In-stead of dividing up the tasks, they worked side by side. There was nothing said or done to declare that they had become more than traveling companions, and yet things felt different between them.

Miranda declined the shelter of the tent, telling him she preferred sleeping under the stars while the weather remained mild. After supper, when they sat by the fire, Miranda bombarded him with questions, as if she had acquired a right to probe into his mind.

To his surprise, Jamie found he was not only allowing Miranda to pull aside the veil that shielded his privacy, he was letting her knock down the walls that protected it.

"How did you learn to track outlaws?" she asked.

Jamie adjusted the soot-black coffeepot on the flames. "An old man taught me. He was a full-blood Cheyenne. He turned up at my mother's house one day when I was around eight. My mother let him take me out for the af-ternoon, and he kept coming back. He never spoke about himself. Only about nature. How everything had a spirit. Not just animals, but every rock and tree and flower, and every grain of sand."

Leaning forward, Jamie lifted the scalding coffeepot from the circle of stones and poured the thick brew into the mugs Miranda held out. "He had long straggly hair and skin more wrinkled than the leather on my glove.

He must have been some relation from my father's Indian side. My mother had never seen him before, but her instincts told her she could trust him. Then, when I was around ten, he stopped coming round. He must have died, although we didn't know for sure. There was no one we could ask."

"What happened to your sister when you went on the road, bounty hunting?"

"Louise tried to continue my mother's business of sewing dresses, but she didn't have the skill for fine work. Women wouldn't pay her as much. She couldn't pay the rent on the house, not even with what I could bring in. When she was eighteen, she got interested in her Indian heritage. She went to live on the reservation and met her husband there."

Jamie tossed the dregs of his coffee into the flames and listened to the hiss they made. He glanced at Miranda. She was sitting on the ground, her legs tucked under her. Firelight played on her features, reminding him of the passion she'd shown him last night. Regardless of the consequences, she'd offered herself to him. With others present, she had shared a tent with him, making it difficult to claim they were married in name only.

Once before, she had suggested they might make their marriage real. At that time, it had seemed to Jamie she regretted her words almost as soon as they were out, but now he'd discovered it was the encounter with her cousin that had caused her anxiety to flare.

In his mind, Jamie went through every incarnation he'd witnessed of Miranda. She'd adapted herself to every situation, met every challenge with valor and determination. Bride to a stranger. Mother to an Indian child. Saloon singer. Bereaved parent. Pioneer on the trail. His wife in the eyes of the world, a social outcast according to many.

She was a woman of courage. One prepared to take risks. Perhaps even on him—a quarter-Cheyenne bounty hunter who owned nothing but a horse, a saddle and a pair of well-used guns.

Jamie spoke slowly, hesitating over each word. "I stayed in Wyoming because I wanted to be close to Louise and Nora. There are a lot more outlaws in Arizona and New Mexico. Big bounties. I've been thinking…after we get to Gold Crossing, I'll stay down south… Now that I don't have doctor's bills and other expenses to worry about, I can start putting money aside. I'd like to get some land eventually…raise horses…"

"I thought you liked bounty hunting."

He was silent for a moment, then allowed another crack in his armor. "It's a dangerous job and it keeps a man on the road. If he wants to take on the responsibility for a family, he needs to find a safer occupation that allows him to settle down."

"I see." Miranda looked pensive.

"It might take some time to build up a stake. Maybe a couple of years."

"So you'll remain a bounty hunter for now, and when you've saved up enough money, you'll retire, buy a piece of land and raise horses?"

"That's about it."

"I think it's a good plan," Miranda said quietly.

Jamie gathered his courage. Miranda had asked him to kiss her. She had asked him to sleep in the tent with her. She had taken the first step to bring them together. She had laid herself open for rejection. He owed it to her to do the same.

"What I'm saying, Princess, is that I'd like us to stay married… I'm asking you to stay married to me. You don't have to decide now," he hastened to add. "It will be another two weeks before we get to Gold Crossing.

And if you're not sure, you can stay with your sister and think about it while I get the money together for a piece of land."

Miranda gave him a secretive, feminine smile that made Jamie think of a cat with a bowl of cream. "I'll think about it," she said with laughter in her tone.

Jamie breathed a sigh of relief. If proposing marriage to a woman was so daunting when they were already legally wed, he pitied any man who had to do it without the comfort of a marriage certificate in his pocket.

For another few moments, they talked about his plan to raise horses. When it came time to settle down for the night, Miranda arranged their bedrolls side by side in the lee of the rocks that bordered the riverbank.

Jamie watched her in the firelight. He wished he were a man with fancy words, capable of giving a woman a pretty speech, but perhaps it didn't matter. He had managed to say everything that needed to be said.

Day after day, Miranda rode at the end of their small convoy, happy despite the monotony and hard work of traveling. At night, they slept side by side. Sometimes Jamie kissed her and held her in his arms, but as he had to stand guard, intimate moments were infrequent and brief. Miranda did not mind. She wanted her wedding night to be in a comfortable bed behind closed doors.

Ahead on the riverside trail, Jamie called for a halt. Miranda reined Alfie to a stop. Dark clouds were rolling across the sky, threatening a storm. Although it was only afternoon, daylight was already fading.

Miranda watched Jamie dismount and take Sirius by the bridle and lead him along the riverbank, studying the horse's gait. Pausing, Jamie leaned down, curled his hand over one hind leg and pushed against the flank until Sirius allowed him to lift up the hoof.

"The shoe is loose," Jamie called out. "It won't last much longer."

He climbed back into the saddle and rode over to Miranda, turning the pack mules around to face north again. "We passed a town a couple of miles back. Didn't look like much of a place but I expect they'll have a blacksmith."

The town was called Three Guns and it did have a blacksmith—a huge, swarthy man with a broken nose and a completely bald head. According to the sign above the entrance to his forge, he also pulled teeth, offered an antidote to snakebites and cured all manner of aches and pains. Miranda suspected that anyone who purchased his treatments would claim an instant improvement because they would be too afraid to say anything else.

Jamie twisted around in the saddle and pointed along the dusty street. "There's a telegraph office. Why don't you send your sister a telegram? You ought to warn her that your cousin might be turning up."

Accepting the advice, Miranda rode to the general store that housed the post office and the telegraph. She hopped down outside the weathered timber building and tied Alfie to the hitching rail. Her footsteps clattered on the boardwalk but came to an abrupt halt outside the open door as she spotted the row of wanted posters tacked to the wall.

She paused to study the fuzzy images printed on yellow paper. Some were barely more than sketches, but one poster had two photographs. *Alvin and Alonzo Hardin.* She recalled hearing those two names before. Seth Stevens had been talking about them. The men had robbed a gold shipment from the mines in Gold Hill, killing two express messengers.

And the bounty was four thousand dollars.

Her eyes fixed on the amount on the poster. Settling down to raise horses was a fine idea, but it worried her Jamie couldn't do it right away. She recalled the fear she'd felt when he rode after the whiskey wagon, vanishing out of her sights. Could she tolerate two years of such fear while he went out on the road, bounty hunting?

No, she could not. And perhaps she was staring at a solution.

Miranda leaned closer, read the small print on the poster: "Wanted alive by the Gold Hill Mining Company." Tempted to rip the poster from the wall, she looked around. Two men loitered outside the saloon, and a third one sat smoking on the hotel steps. It might be unwise to reveal her interest. She pulled her hand back, adjusted her deerskin coat and marched into the post office.

The clerk, a pretty young woman with chestnut hair coiled on top of her head, sat reading a penny dreadful behind the counter. Crammed into a corset that almost cut her curvy figure in half, she wore a dress too revealing for daywear.

"Do you have copies of the wanted posters?" Miranda asked.

The woman ducked beneath the counter, straightened and slammed a poster on top. She'd only produced one—the one with the Hardin brothers. Her gesture was defiant, as if daring anyone to catch the criminals.

"Do you have any other posters?" Miranda asked.

"Only that one." The clerk twisted a chestnut curl around her forefinger, eyeing Miranda with disdain, smirking at the unladylike outfit of denim and deerskin.

Miranda picked up the poster. "Can I keep this?"

"What's it to you?"

We are bounty hunters, Miranda was about to blurt out but curbed her tongue just in time. Her stream of prattle to Aggie Nugget while Cousin Gareth was listening had taught her about the dangers of loose talk.

"Merely curious," she said. "They seem to be worth more than anyone else."

"That's because Alvin Hardin is more of a man than all the others put together. No one will catch him alive, and they won't shoot him either, because he ain't worth a single dollar dead."

"Why is he wanted alive even though he murdered two men?"

"He stole a gold shipment. If someone kills him, the mining company will never get their gold back. Nobody knows where he has hidden it. He hasn't even told—" The girl cut off her tirade and bit her lip, then went on petulantly, "What is it you came in for?"

"I'd like to send a telegram."

With an arrogant flick of her wrist, the girl tore a sheet from a telegram pad and slid the piece of paper across the counter. "Print the message here. Twenty cents a word."

"That's too much!"

"That's our price. The law allows up to thirty cents per word. Take it or leave it." She gave Miranda a condescending look. "Can you write, or do you need me to do it for you?"

Miranda clamped down on a burst of temper. "I'll guess I might manage to scratch down a few words."

The girl flustered. Her fingers went back to twirling her hair.

From the back of the shop came an angry bellow. "Rose!"

The girl rolled her eyes. "That's my pa. More ornery than a donkey with a burr in his tail. I'll be back in a minute. Pa will have to send your telegram anyway. I've only just started learning the code."

Miranda attempted a friendly tone. "That must be difficult."

"It sure is, but I've got to learn. I promised—"

Again, an abrupt silence. Miranda got the impression that Rose harbored important secrets she longed to share with a female confidante but did not dare to disclose.

If she wanted to help Jamie to go after the Hardin brothers, Miranda realized, she would have to learn to gather information, lure people into confiding in her. The thought made her uncomfortable. Betrayal was betrayal, even between strangers.

But four thousand dollars would be enough to buy a piece of land, she reminded herself. It would mean Jamie would never have to place himself in danger again. And because the Hardin brothers must be captured alive, there would be no killing.

Brushing the moral dilemmas aside, Miranda focused on composing her telegram. At the high cost, she did not wish to waste words.

Journey going well. Cousin Gareth maybe coming. Lost his memory. Not know his name. Goes under Gareth Wolfson. Accidentally revealed your location. Sorry. Be careful. Love. Miranda.

"Amnesia" instead of "lost his memory" might have saved two words but it didn't make the point as well. Miranda would have liked to have mentioned that Cousin Gareth seemed a nicer person now, more like he had been when they were small, but she couldn't justify the added expense.

She waited for Rose to return. It took the girl three attempts to count twenty-seven words, and even longer to work out the cost, including the address. Miranda waited patiently by the counter, then watched the girl disappear into the back and listened until the telegraph key started clicking.

* * *

Back at the blacksmith's forge, Sirius was prancing about, unhappy with all the poking and prodding about his hooves. After leading the horse by the bridle in a circle to calm him down, Jamie stepped into the saddle and rode over to join Miranda.

"There's going to be a storm," he told her, peering up into the sky, now blanketed with angry clouds. "We'd better stay in a hotel tonight."

They made their way down the street. As they dismounted and tied their animals to the hitching rail outside the hotel, the man who had been sitting on the steps rose. He stubbed out his cheroot and settled to wait in the open doorway. Tall and lanky, he had a sharply pointed chin and nervous, darting eyes. Miranda could smell the sweet, cloying scent of the greasy pomade he had used to slick back his hair.

Reluctantly, the man moved aside to let them enter. He crossed the lobby to the small desk along the wall. Once behind the desk, he slammed his hand down on the domed bell in front of him. The shrill ring echoed around the lobby.

It seemed an odd reaction to Miranda. Surely, the bell was for clients to summon the innkeeper, not the other way round? She noticed Jamie fall a few steps behind her. He was moving slowly, skirting the lobby, keeping his back to the wall.

"We'd like a room," Miranda told the innkeeper.

The man's mouth twisted. He spat out his words, as if they tasted foul in his mouth. "I don't rent rooms to Indians. You'd best leave."

"What about a room for the lady?" Jamie asked calmly.

The man jerked his pointed chin at Miranda. "She belong to you?"

"I'm his wife," Miranda replied, anger rising inside her.

The man reached beneath the desk, took out a big revolver and held it in his hand, gesturing at her—not exactly pointing the barrel at her, but his manner carried a warning that any second he might. "That makes you an Indian squaw."

Miranda tensed. From the corner of her eye she observed Jamie. He was not wearing his long duster, only his tan buckskin coat. His gunbelt was in plain sight, and she could see his hands hovering by his hips.

A female voice came from behind them. "Don't even think about it."

Miranda spun around. A woman, dressed in a long skirt and a white shirtwaist, her auburn hair scraped into a bun, had entered through a side door. Tall and thin to the point of looking emaciated, she was aiming a rifle at Jamie.

"We don't want no trouble," the woman said. "Your kind can sleep in the hayloft at the livery stable. If you pay for your horses, they don't charge you extra."

Jamie raised his hands in a gesture of surrender. "No trouble. We'll go."

The woman didn't lower her rifle. "Indians killed my two babies. It might be twenty years ago, but the pain is still as fierce as if it had been yesterday. I've sworn never to have an Indian in my house. Nothing personal, mind you. Just bad memories."

Miranda nodded. She inched toward the entrance. Instinct made her shuffle her feet backward, keeping her attention on the woman. She felt Jamie's hand curl over her arm and he pushed her behind him, shielding her with his body as they retreated.

When they got to the doorway, Miranda spoke up. "We lost my husband's niece a few weeks ago. She'd been ill a long time, so we knew to expect it, but it didn't ease our grief. I can't imagine how terrible it must have been for you. You have my sympathies. Please don't worry about us. We'll be fine in the hayloft."

The woman lowered her rifle. Deep lines marred her gaunt face, as if nature had painted a mask of suffering on her features. "Thank you," she said in a strained tone. "I'd like to make an exception for you but I can't. I'm afraid to let go of my hate. It's the only thing I can do for my children now—keep hating what killed them."

Jamie followed Miranda outside. Before turning around, he kicked away the stone used to prop the door open. The heavy timber panel swung shut with a muted slam. Miranda could feel Jamie's body shaking with pent-up rage as he ushered her a few yards along the boardwalk and pressed her against the side of the building. Eyes sharp, he turned to watch the window, to see if a rifle barrel poked out of it.

"I don't mind the hayloft," Miranda told him. "We can keep an eye on the horses and mules."

Jamie's only response was a grunt. A few seconds later, when they could detect no further reaction from inside the hotel, the tension in his body eased. He tugged Miranda down the steps to the hitch rail where their mounts and pack mules stood waiting.

"Let's get settled at the livery stable," he said curtly as he untied the animals.

In morose silence, Jamie led their small procession along the rutted street. Miranda could read his thoughts as clearly as if he were shouting them into the twilight. He didn't care for himself. He was used to such treatment. But it was making fury burn inside him that their marriage had branded her an outcast along with him.

Chapter Twenty-Two

A flash of lightning woke Miranda. For an instant, it bathed the hayloft with an eerie blue glow. Above her, the timber rafters stood out like ribs on a skeleton. Then darkness fell again. Seconds later, thunder rolled in the sky. Heavy rain drummed against the roof.

Earlier, when they settled down, light had spilled in through the gap between the walls and the roof, but as the night fell, solid blackness had swallowed up everything. Miranda could see nothing—not even Jamie, who had stretched out at the top of the ladder, where he could protect her if anyone climbed up.

To compensate against the lack of light, Miranda's other senses had sharpened. Every time she turned, she could hear the rustle of straw beneath the oilcloth she lay upon. Crisp, dry scents of hay mixed with the pungent animal odors from the stable below.

Another flare of lightning. Another boom of thunder. Again. And again. The storm was moving closer, the interval between the flashes of blue glow and the cracks of thunder shrinking, until they came almost simultaneously, the storm directly overhead.

Down in the stable, the horses grew restless, whinnying in their stalls and stomping their hooves. The two pack mules were in a corral outside and their frightened braying filled the brief silences between the thunderclaps.

"Are you awake?" Jamie asked.

Miranda had not heard him move, but the next flash of lighting showed him crouched beside her. Reassured by his presence, she smiled into the darkness. "I'd have to be deaf and blind to sleep through the fireworks."

She felt a touch on her arm. "I'm going outside," Jamie said. "Castor and Pollux are about to panic. They might bolt against the corral fence and get hurt. I'll move them into the stable."

"I'll come with you."

"No." Jamie's tone was firm. "You stay here."

Another flash of lightning illuminated the hayloft, allowing Miranda to see him for a fraction of a second, no more than the blink of an eye, but it was enough to reveal the worried frown on his face. Before she could protest against his orders, Jamie was gone.

Miranda couldn't tell how quickly the time passed. The storm continued to rage overhead. Down at the stable, the horses became fretful, kicking against the stalls, neighing in fear. Perhaps the livery stable owner couldn't come out and reassure the animals.

Gingerly, fumbling in the darkness, Miranda pushed up to her feet. She used the lightning flashes to guide her to the ladder, moving a few steps at a time. At the edge of the trapdoor, she crouched, gripped the top rung of the ladder and climbed down by feel.

When she reached the stable, Sirius was calm but Alfie was kicking and thrashing in his stall, his head swinging left and right. Every time the lightning flashed, Miranda could see his eyes rolling with terror. She slipped into the stall, wrapped her arms around Alfie's neck to restrain him and crooned at the frightened horse. "Easy, boy. Easy now."

Slowly, the familiar voice soothed the gray Appaloosa. He stilled, his breath blowing, his nostrils quivering against Miranda's palm. By now the lightning flashes were growing less frequent, the thunder more distant. Miranda glanced around. Pollux was in a stall, but she could not see Castor or Jamie.

She gave Alfie a few more comforting pats, eased out of the stall and made her way to the entrance. Pushing the rickety door ajar, Miranda slipped outside. The rain had thinned to a drizzle. The next lightning flash illuminated an empty corral. The gate stood wide-open.

Miranda edged along the wall, keeping beneath the eaves that protected her from the rain. She passed the water trough. A trickle from the roof splashed into it, the sound like the merry gurgle of a brook. Ahead, a shadow loomed in the darkness. Despite the lack of light, Miranda sensed the cautious movement of a man advancing in her direction.

Whispered words drifted toward her, too muffled for her to hear.

"Jamie?" she whispered back, then raised her voice. "Are you there?"

The shadow lurched. Burly arms closed around her, pulling tight against a masculine chest. A man spoke in a gruff, throaty whisper. "I thought you'd never come."

Panic shot through Miranda. The body that enfolded hers felt all wrong. The chest was too bulky, the arms too high up around her, the thighs that brushed hers too sturdy. She tipped her head back to look at his face but could see nothing in the darkness.

"Rose," the man whispered. "I've missed you so much."

Lightning forked in the sky. The stark blue-white glow fell upon them, the way a spotlight might illuminate a pair of actors on a stage. Miranda gasped, her gaze riveted on the heavy features and thick beard of a dark stranger who was staring back at her.

Jamie dragged Castor along the waterlogged street, the hooves of the mule splashing in the mud. While he'd been leading Pollux into the stable, Castor had kicked the corral gate open. The frightened beast had bolted, running blindly into the night.

Luckily, instead of charging into the desert, perhaps never to be seen again, the mule had headed for the only source of light in the darkness. He'd crashed into the wall of the saloon and remained there, quivering in the rain, letting out a plaintive whinny.

A sharp sound pierced the rain-soaked darkness. Jamie froze. What was that? Like a feminine scream? He yanked Castor to a halt, cocked his head to listen. The sound didn't come again. Had he imagined it? He'd told Miranda to stay up in the hayloft, but since when did she obey his orders? Instinct, honed from years of living with danger, told Jamie the sound had been a woman's scream, and it had been Miranda.

With frantic steps, he set in motion again, using the mule for cover. When he reached the side of the building, he released his grip on Castor's halter, dipped a hand inside his rain slicker and pulled out the gun he'd tucked into his waistband to keep it protected from the rain.

Darkness surrounded him. There were no sounds, except the steady patter of the rain against the sodden ground and the trickle of water from the roof into the water trough and the restless shuffling of the animals in the stable.

"Miranda!" Jamie called out.

No reply. Jamie cocked the hammer and pointed his gun, waiting for the next flash of lightning. His heart beat in the heavy rhythm that always accompanied a gunfight.

His mind grew sharp. Sounds magnified. Raindrops hit the ground like cannonballs. Gravel rustled like a landslide.

Gravel rustled. Someone was moving in the darkness! An icy chill enveloped Jamie. When he was on a hunt, ready to kill or to be killed, it always seemed to him that all warmth of life left him, as if his body was anticipating the arrival of death.

Lightning flashed. A white glow flared over the landscape. For a second, it painted a tableau. Miranda, in the clutches of a big, bearded man. Jamie aimed his gun, but before he had a chance to call out a demand for the man to release her, the stranger shoved Miranda aside, pivoted on his feet and fled in the opposite direction.

Once again, darkness fell. Jamie thumbed the hammer down, took the precaution to rotate the cylinder to set the hammer on an empty chamber before he pushed the revolver back into his waistband. It was not a location on his anatomy where he wanted an accidental gunshot wound.

"Jamie? Jamie?" Miranda cried out, and then she crashed into him.

For an instant, Jamie hesitated, tempted to give chase. Then he closed his arms around Miranda and cradled her to his chest. She mattered more. Anyway, he couldn't shoot a man without knowing if the man deserved to die, and it would have been too much of a gamble to chase after a stranger in the darkness, with only the lightning flashes for illumination.

"It's me," he reassured Miranda. "It's all right. It's all right."

"I came down to see Alfie and then I looked for you. You weren't there. I saw a shadow and I went to him and he hauled me into his embrace. He wasn't trying to hurt me. He thought I was someone else." Miranda's breathless stream of words held more confusion than fear. "He must have had a tryst with a sweetheart and he thought I was her."

Relief coursed through Jamie. Miranda was warm in his arms, warm and vibrant and full of life. Her lungs were heaving, as if she'd been running, and he could feel her body shaking, but instead of the crippling aftermath of true terror, it was the release of tension from a sudden fright.

"Are you sure you're all right?"

"Yes. I'm fine. I'm fine."

Lightning flared again. In its brief glare Jamie studied Miranda's upturned face, artificially pale in the white glow of the light. Her eyes looked huge and dark, her mouth a slash without color, but her lips were curling into a shaky smile.

"Go back upstairs," he told her. "I'll track down Castor. He tried to get into the saloon. Must have wanted a shot of whiskey to calm his nerves."

Miranda's laughter rippled in the darkness, just as Jamie had intended. He eased their bodies apart and searched along the wall beneath the eaves, until he came upon the storm lantern he remembered seeing on a hook.

He lifted down the lantern and sloshed it side to side, testing for fuel. A whiff of kerosene drifted at him. He fumbled for Miranda's hand, guided her fingers to curl around the handle of the lantern. "Hold this."

His hands free now, Jamie wiped his fingers dry against his shirtfront. He took out a metal matchbox from the pocket of his buckskin coat, extracted a match, struck a light with his thumbnail and lifted the glass to light the lantern.

"Promise to be careful with the lamp," he warned Miranda. "If you burn the place down, you'll kill not only yourself but the horses. And I'll have nowhere to sleep."

She gave another chuckle. "I'm humbled by your concern for my welfare."

It crossed Jamie's mind to complain that she hadn't obeyed his orders to stay inside, but he decided to save the sermon for another day. "Go back upstairs," he prompted her. "I'll join you in a minute."

Miranda lifted the lantern higher, shining the light on his face. "Promise? You won't chase after the man who grabbed me."

"Chase after a man who has done nothing but seek a tryst with his sweetheart?" Jamie shook his head. "I'll leave him alone. He's had enough disappointment for one night. He doesn't want to tangle with me."

Standing guard by the door, he waited until he saw Miranda's boots vanish out of sight at the top of the ladder. Soon, a yellow glow spilled out through the gap between the stable walls and the roof, giving him just enough light to locate Castor huddling in forlorn silence by the water trough.

While Jamie prodded the recalcitrant beast indoors he shifted through the events in his mind. It had puzzled him how the mule had managed to open the corral gate, but now he knew the stranger must have done it, in order to lure Jamie out of the way while he waited for his sweetheart to arrive. But why would a man arrange to meet his woman behind a stable at midnight, and expect her to keep the tryst despite the onset of a thunderstorm?

Chapter Twenty-Three

Miranda dreamed of the face of the bearded stranger. In her dream, the heavy, dark beard fell away. The strong features morphed into the flat surface of a photograph. Below the image, numbers appeared.

Four. Zero. Zero. Zero. And a dollar sign in front of them.

She awoke with a start. Her eyes flared open. The storm had passed, and the warm rays of morning sunshine poked into the hayloft, painting a golden glow over the bales of hay and the mountains of straw. Jamie was sitting beside her, cross-legged, Indian style, watching over her.

Every nerve humming with excitement, Miranda lurched up to a sitting position and grabbed her canvas bag from the end of the oilcloth bed. She rummaged inside, pulled out the wanted poster. After a quick inspection to make sure her hunch had been right, she pushed the picture at Jamie. "It's him. The man who grabbed me."

Jamie studied the image. "Alvin and Alonzo Hardin."

"He was the one on the left. Looks like the older of the two brothers. Four thousand dollars they are worth." Miranda lowered her voice. "And I know how to track them down."

Talking fast, in a confidential murmur, she told Jamie

about Rose, the clerk at the post office. *Alvin Hardin is more of a man than all the others put together,* the girl had boasted, with a feminine pride that implied ownership.

The man who'd grabbed her had whispered, *Rose. I've missed you so much.* Those two had planned to meet last night. And if they had missed each other last night, they would be impatient for another tryst. "All we need is to keep an eye on Rose," Miranda finished triumphantly. "She'll lead us to him."

"No," Jamie said. "It's too risky. Two men against one."

"I can help," Miranda argued. "We can plan how to capture them."

"I don't want you involved in a bounty hunt. There could be shooting."

Cheeks flushed, pulse racing, Miranda leaned closer to Jamie. "Can't you see? This is our big chance. Four thousand dollars. If we succeed you can buy a piece of land and settle down."

She watched Jamie's expression darken. He handed the poster back to her. "No."

Miranda shifted her shoulders, a stubborn gesture of feminine frustration. "I want to help you. Be a team. Like my parents were, sailing their boat together."

"And they died, didn't they?" Jamie said quietly. An angry frown emphasized the sharp angles of his features. "It's not like going on a picnic. You've already proved you won't obey my orders. I'll not risk your life, or mine. End of discussion."

"But—"

Jamie spoke through gritted teeth. "End. Of. Discussion."

Miranda bit her lip, peered at him from beneath her lashes. "I can't bear the thought of waiting at home for years and years while you go on the road, risking your life. I want us to be a team, and there'll be no better chance than this for a big bounty."

Jamie picked up a piece of straw, rolled it between his fingers. Miranda could see the mental struggle on his face. What if something went wrong? She suppressed the flash of fear. Her trust in Jamie's ability to keep them safe overruled her sense of caution.

"Can you shoot a handgun?" Jamie asked finally.

"I am an excellent marksman."

"You'll need to prove that to me first. Then we'll see if Rose leads us to the outlaws. If she does, we'll evaluate the situation. I'll decide if it's safe to make an attempt to capture them. My word is the law. If I believe it's not safe, we'll ride away and leave Rose to her man. You'll have to obey me—not just say you will. You'll have to give me your cast-iron guarantee that you'll do exactly as I tell you."

Miranda laid a hand over her heart. "I promise."

Jamie snapped the cylinder out of his revolver and shook the cartridges onto his palm. Leaving the pack mules to enjoy a day of rest, they had ridden a short distance out of town, to a sunny desert clearing surrounded by prickly pears in fruit.

He held up the weapon and talked like a schoolteacher in front of a class. "This is your gun. A Remington New Model Army Revolver converted to take metal cartridges. It is too heavy for you but it will serve to test your skill." He held out his other hand. "These are your cartridges."

He waited in silence while Miranda gingerly wrapped her fingers around the smooth wooden grip of the revolver. Twenty years old, the weapon had seen much use but remained in excellent shape.

He had bought the pair of guns secondhand, and had

never found anything better to replace them, particularly after he'd had them converted from ball and cap to the metal cartridges that were quicker to load and did not release acrid smoke when fired.

"How does it feel?" he asked.

"Sleek and lethal." Miranda peered into his cupped palm and glanced up at him, frowning. She made no move to pick up the long, shiny cartridges.

Jamie heaved out a sigh. "Don't tell me you shoot like you ride—you know how to aim and pull the trigger but have no idea how to load or maintain a gun."

"I've only shot with an old-fashioned pistol, or a musket. The kind that only takes one lead ball at a time. The grooms loaded for me."

"If you don't know how to load fast, you'll only have six bullets. If you don't kill the outlaws with six shots, you'll die. If you don't clean your gun and it jams, you'll die. If you hesitate before you pull the trigger, you'll die. If your aim is off, you'll die." He lifted his eyebrows. "You still want to be a bounty hunter?"

"Show me how to put the bullets in."

"Cartridges. A bullet flies out and the empty shell is left in the gun."

He helped her fill the cylinder and slot it back inside the weapon. "This gun is single-action. That means you'll have to cock the hammer first, and then you pull the trigger." He took the revolver from her, aimed from the hip and shot off a ripe prickly pear. The blue jays feasting on the fruit flapped their wings and screeched but didn't fly away.

Holding the gun safely, Jamie put it in Miranda's hand. "You try."

Miranda raised the gun, squinted along the barrel. She used her left hand to cock the hammer and squeezed the trigger. A ripe prickly pear exploded. Jamie stared. It had to be a fluke. A lucky accident.

"Try again."

Tense now, on full alert, he watched as Miranda repeated the motion. Another splatter of seeds and pulp. The blue jays screeched. The sweet smell of ripe fruit drifted toward them on the breeze. Miranda fired off two more shots, barely pausing to aim.

"I'll be damned," Jamie muttered.

He reloaded, made her repeat the entire sequence.

Six shots. Six exploding prickly pears.

"Try shooting from the hip," he instructed as he switched in the spare cylinder he'd loaded with cartridges while Miranda had been busy shooting. "Pick a bigger target. Aim at the paddle-shaped leaf instead of the fruit."

Curious, he watched as Miranda adjusted her stance, feet slightly apart, knees bent. A gunfighter's pose. Holding the revolver pointed down, she concentrated, then lifted the gun in a smooth move…and gave a cry of frustration as the weapon failed to fire.

"You forgot to cock the hammer," Jamie told her. "You're not strong enough to do it with your thumb. We'll have to get you a double-action revolver. With one of those, it will automatically cock the hammer when you pull the trigger."

Miranda tried again, this time cocking the hammer before she aimed and pulled the trigger. A hole appeared in the middle of the fleshy paddle of the cactus. Jamie swore under his breath. His wife was a natural with a gun.

He'd agreed to give her a trial because it had been easier than arguing against the bounty hunt, and he had expected her lack of proficiency would allow him to reject the idea. Now he found himself committed to the plan. Not even to keep Miranda safe could he face the dishonor of going back on his word.

Instead of regretting his careless promise, Jamie allowed his mind to dwell on the possibility of actually going after the outlaws. "Let's go back into town and see what kind of weapon we can buy for you."

Despite being called Three Guns the town had no gunsmith. In the hardware store, they inspected the display case with revolvers for sale on commission from the manufacturers.

Miranda pointed through the glass. "That one."

"Dat is nice gun for a lady," said the shopkeeper, a short man with florid skin who spoke with a heavy German accent. He ducked down to withdraw the revolver from the glass case and handed it to her. "Double-action, point forty one caliber. Two-and-haff-inches barrel."

Surprised, Jamie lifted his brows at Miranda. "You don't want to try them all?"

She admired the nickel-plated, pearl-handled Colt. "I want this one."

Of course you do, Jamie thought. *It's the most expensive one.*

"Why?" he asked.

"It's pretty."

Jamie winced. For a moment, her startling skill had made him forget she was not an experienced gunfighter. He must be out of his mind, even thinking of going after a pair of dangerous outlaws with a female partner who carried a *pretty* gun.

Being forced to sleep in the hayloft turned out to be good luck, for Jamie and Miranda discovered two of the horses at the livery stable belonged to Rose Donaldson and her father. Donaldson was a widower, confined to a wheelchair. In Miranda's view, that helped to explain Rose's haughty arrogance. Not only was she the prettiest girl in town, and likely the wealthiest, but she could run around without parental supervision.

According to Jamie, Rose's beau would have drummed caution into her. She wouldn't ride out to him if she thought a stranger was observing her. They came up with a story that Miranda had caught a chill and needed to stay in bed, which allowed them to keep vigil in the hayloft, standing on bales of hay, staring out through the gap at the top of the wall.

On the second morning, right after they had seen a stream of people in their Sunday best file out of the small white church on the edge of town, they heard noises downstairs. The jingle of a bridle. A feminine voice speaking in an impatient tone. Then the clatter of hooves as a horse was led outside. A moment later, they heard the steady thud of a rider breaking into a canter. Peering out through the gap, they could see a woman in flowing yellow skirts leave the town behind and disappear off into the distance.

Miranda scrambled down from the bale of hay. "Let's go."

"Not yet," Jamie warned her. "She'll halt a piece down the trail to make sure no one is following. We'll need to give her a proper head start. Half an hour at least."

Twenty minutes later, they went downstairs and loaded their mules, pretending to be ready to resume their journey. Jamie sought out the owner of the livery stable, and settled their bill.

The man pulled a pencil from behind his ear and scrawled a receipt on a scrap of paper. "Your wife better now?" he asked, with a covert glance at Miranda, who was fussing over Castor and Pollux. He'd been sneaking looks at her ever since they arrived, with the shy admiration of a man who longed for a wife of his own but expected he'd never get one.

Jamie put away his receipt. "She's fine. We'll push on south."

They traveled at a leisurely pace until they were out of sight. In places, Rose's trail was clear, with fresh hoof-prints in the earth, still soft after the storm. Once or twice, Jamie had to dismount to inspect the ground. "Her horse has a nail sticking out on the left hind shoe," he commented as he vaulted back on Sirius. "Easy to tell apart from any other tracks."

To disguise her destination, Rose had taken a route that twisted and turned. They trailed her across the plateau, up into the foothills where aspens blazed in autumn colors. In the cover of the forest, they paused to find a safe place to tie the mules and went on without them. As they gained height, the aspens gave way to hardy evergreens. The air grew cool, the ground moist and springy.

Weaving along the narrow path, they came upon a clearing, set in a depression in the hillside. A log cabin huddled at the base, and tied to a post outside stood Rose's dun gelding. On the left, where a small stream rippled down the slope, two more horses grazed in a small corral.

Jamie twisted in the saddle to look at Miranda. "Go back."

Miranda urged Alfie into reverse. A thick coat of moss and pine needles covered the ground, muffling the sound of the horses' hooves. What little noise they made could be attributed to deer or elk roaming in the forest. After they had backed away, they dismounted and left the path, picking their way between the trees until they were hidden from the sight of anyone passing.

"We'll leave the horses here," Jamie said.

Miranda nodded. Her mouth felt dry. Her heart was beating fast, her entire body tingling in the grip of tension. This was it. A bounty hunt. Nerves churned inside her, like a bout of nausea. For a moment, she wanted to tell Jamie to forget the idea, to forget the bounty. Then he was beside her. He clasped her by the arms and held her still while he studied her face.

"All right?" His voice was gruff, his brows gathered in a frown.

Miranda swallowed, took a deep breath. "Yes."

"The aim is to take them alive," Jamie said. "But if your life is threatened, you must shoot. Remember this. A bounty hunter can kill in self-defense, and it may come to that." His eyes held hers, sharp with concern. "The first time killing a man is the hardest, but if it's a choice between your life and his, you must be prepared to do it."

Her throat too tight to speak, Miranda gave a silent nod.

Jamie released his hold on her and crouched down to the ground. Picking up twigs and a few pinecones and a stone, he arranged them to make a model of the clearing and the house, gesturing over the objects as he spoke.

"I'll have to circle around and crawl down the hillside behind the house. The approach is too open on this side. They have selected their hideout well. On this side, there is a rock halfway between the house and the edge of the clearing. A man would struggle to hide behind it but you are small enough to manage it."

He raked his gaze over her. "Your deerskin coat is good. It blends in. You'll have to decide about your hat. I keep mine on, in case the sun is in my eyes when I shoot. You'll be hiding behind a stone, and the hat will add to your height. I suggest you take it off. Cover your hair with a cloth. Something that will blend against the rock."

Miranda pushed up to her feet and went to Alfie, who was standing placidly next to Sirius, both of them nosing into the dead leaves on the ground. She took off her wide-brimmed hat and hung it on the saddle horn, found a green-and-brown-checkered neckerchief in Jamie's saddlebags and tied it around her upsweep.

"Is this all right?" she asked when she returned to him.

Jamie nodded. He picked up a pinecone and placed it next to the stone on his map. "You'll have to crawl on your belly to get here. Then you'll have to stay still and wait for Rose to leave. I'll be here." He placed another pinecone by the cabin. "There's a pile of firewood against the wall. I'll have to hide behind it. There is no other place."

"But there's no cover." Miranda spoke in an agitated whisper. "You'll be seen."

"The part of me that is Indian knows how to blend in."

Jamie dropped two more pinecones in front the square of twigs that represented the house. "When the men come out, if there are more than two, we'll let them ride out. You do nothing. You just keep your head down, remain hidden. If there are only the Hardin brothers, I'll jump one of them when he goes for the horses. I'll grab him from behind and put my gun to his head. I'll yell at his brother, order him to drop his gun. If he doesn't—if he tries to shoot me—you'll have to shoot him. Shoot to kill."

"They are wanted alive."

"Taking one of them alive will be enough. I can't see one of them allowing the other to bury the gold without telling him the exact location. They'll both know. If we have to kill one of them in self-defense, it will not impact the reward."

Another shiver of fear rippled over Miranda. Once more, she felt the urge to call the whole thing off, but she conquered the burst of nerves. "There won't be more than two." She leveled her anxious gaze at Jamie. "There are only two horses in the corral. It will be just the Hardin brothers."

She watched Jamie give a reluctant nod. The cold, sick feeling in the pit of her stomach stirred again. Once

Rose said goodbye to her sweetheart and headed home, she—Miranda Fairfax of Merlin's Leap, the gently bred daughter of cultured parents—would have to aim her gun at a man's heart and be prepared to pull the trigger, if it meant saving Jamie's life or her own.

Chapter Twenty-Four

Miranda squatted behind the stone, her sights trained on the cabin door. A small groove at the top of the rock gave her a gap to peer through, allowing her to keep mostly out of sight. She'd scattered dead leaves and pine needles on her head, adding to her disguise.

An hour went by. Her legs grew numb. There had been no sign of Jamie. Perhaps he truly could blend into the landscape, the way he had claimed. The sun began its descent in the sky. A cool breeze swept over the hillside.

Earlier, when she'd crawled into position, like a snake twisting along the ground, Miranda's denim trousers had gotten damp, and now the chill made her shiver. Lifting her hand to her mouth, she blew warm air on her fingers to stop them from stiffening around the grip of the gun.

Go home, Rose, she ordered in her mind.

As if by magic, the front door eased open and Rose appeared in the frame. She spun around, yellow skirts awhirl, and flung her arms around the neck of the big, bearded man who stood behind her. They shared a long, lingering kiss. Finally, the man curled his hands around Rose's waist and set her apart from him.

The tedium of waiting had allowed Miranda's fear to dissipate, but now, as she watched the lovers say goodbye, she felt a stab of regret. Whatever Alvin Hardin had done, Rose loved him. She would suffer when her beau was hanged. An outlaw chose his path, but it seemed wrong that a woman would pay for his crimes with her tears.

Heels clattering on the flagstones by the entrance, Rose turned around and hurried to the dun gelding waiting a few yards away. She untied the horse, mounted and set off at a canter across the clearing. Miranda ducked deeper behind the stone as the girl rode past.

Another ten minutes passed. The door inched open once more. The big, bearded man came out first, followed by a smaller one. Slighter and shorter, the second man had the same broad face and dark hair. Both walked with a swagger—the arrogant gait of a man who knows he can dominate others and doesn't care if his power stems from violence.

Miranda lifted her head, raised her gun and lined the barrel to point at the smaller man. Both brothers were moving swiftly, on guard, their eyes sweeping the clearing. When they spoke, they kept their voices low, and she couldn't hear what they were saying.

The smaller man nodded and headed toward the corral. The bigger man darted back inside and came out carrying a saddle, which he dumped on the flagstones. He brought out another saddle, then went inside once more and returned hauling two sets of saddlebags, one draped over each arm.

Like a ghost, Jamie separated from the woodpile. The smaller man had just passed him, leading the pair of buckskin geldings from the corral toward the entrance where the saddles waited. Jamie darted past the swishing tails of the horses and glided smoothly between their flanks.

"Drop your guns or your brother dies," he yelled.

Miranda eased higher behind the rock. She could see

the smaller man raise his hands above his head in surrender. The bigger man stood still by the open doorway, saddlebags dangling on his arms. Miranda aimed her gun at his chest.

The man moved, a sudden, urgent jerk of his body, and the saddlebags tumbled to the ground. Spooked by the fracas, the two buckskins shifted back, exposing Jamie to full view.

The world slowed. With utter clarity, Miranda could see the big man's hands fall to his hips and dart up again, holding his guns. She checked her aim, squinting down the barrel of her pretty pearl-handled Colt.

Now, her mind screamed. *Shoot.*

But her finger froze on the trigger. All she could see was the joyful swirl of Rose's yellow skirts as the girl spun around to embrace the man she loved. Nausea surged in Miranda's belly, clogging her throat. Her mind grew dizzy. Sounds roared in her ears, escalating into the boom of gunfire.

One shot. Two. Three.

And none of them from her gun.

Her hand shook so hard the barrel of her gun rattled against the top of the stone. She saw the big man fall. Saw the horses bolt across the clearing. Jamie remained on his feet, standing behind the small man who had spun around and lowered his upraised arms.

Then the small man toppled over and Miranda could see the hole that marked the front of Jamie's tan buckskin coat. Around the black hole, a crimson rim was spreading in a circle, like petals around the center of a bloom.

Silence fell over the clearing.

Utter, deathly silence.

The two horses had halted by the big man's fallen body, patiently waiting for someone to saddle them. *Jamie,* Miranda tried to shout, but her voice was trapped inside her head. She could not breathe. Could not breathe. Cold sweat covered her skin. Icy, icy cold.

Miranda pushed up to her feet, swayed on rubbery legs as she tried to run toward Jamie. Another surge of nausea swelled up inside her. She fell to her knees, doubled over and retched her breakfast onto the carpet of moss and pine needles. Empty and desolate and torn with remorse, she collapsed to the ground.

What had she done? In her hurry to secure their future, in her foolish pride over her own daring, she had endangered her own life and the life of the man she loved. Her courage had failed. Jamie had a bullet in his chest. And she was to blame.

Like always, when Jamie knew the wrong move might cost him his life, his mind was clear and sharp. Alert, focused, absolutely still, he had waited behind the woodpile, blending like a shadow against the wall of the building.

The right moment never seemed to come.

Finally, for a fraction of a second, everything aligned. Soundlessly, as invisible as the wind, Jamie detached himself from the timber wall, slid between the pair of buckskin geldings and grabbed the smaller man from behind, coiling his left arm around the man's neck and squeezing tight. With his right hand, he rammed the barrel of his gun against the man's temple.

"Put your hands up," Jamie growled in the man's ear.

For a moment the world stood poised between life and death. It seemed to take forever, but Jamie knew only a second had passed before the man slowly raised his arms. The instant the movement became obvious, Jamie bellowed out his threat.

"Drop your guns or your brother dies." It was as much a signal for Miranda to get ready to pull the trigger as it was a demand for Alvin Hardin to unbuckle his gunbelt and let it fall to the ground.

The bigger outlaw stood frozen on the doorstep. Jamie held his breath. He could see the hesitation on the man's face, could see the tension in his tall frame. With expertise born from a dozen similar standoffs, Jamie knew the man would refuse to surrender.

Even before the burly arms moved, even before the saddlebags tumbled to the ground, even before the outlaw's hands fell to his hips, Jamie knew to expect a gunfight. The horses had shifted back, no longer covering him. His eyes darted toward the stone. The sun glinted on the nickel-plated barrel of Miranda's gun.

Now, Jamie screamed in his mind.

No shot came from behind the stone.

The big man's guns rose, the pair of them. The smaller man had reassessed the situation and flung himself backward, fighting Jamie's hold. Jamie had no choice. He uncoiled his left arm from the outlaw's neck, pulled out his left gun, aimed at the big man standing on the doorstep and fired.

A single shot, but it was enough. Alvin Hardin jerked, twitched, toppled backward through the open doorway. Jamie felt a burn in his chest. The air around him shimmered, like dark shadows dancing. His breathing grew labored. Hot and cold. Hot and cold. A burning pain in his side, an icy coat of fear on his skin.

By instinct, without a conscious command from his brain, his left arm snaked back to close around the smaller outlaw's throat. Jamie squeezed, tightening his grip, but the motion made pain twist in his chest. His arm lacked strength and Alonzo Hardin could feel it. The outlaw broke free from Jamie's hold and reached for his gun. The barrel flashed in the sunlight as it cleared the leather holster.

There was no choice.

Jamie took aim with his right hand and pulled the trigger, saying goodbye to four thousand dollars. It was a cheap price to pay for holding on to his life. A spasm shook Alonzo Hardin as the final spark of life rippled through him, and then he crumpled to the ground.

Even before the outlaw had fully fallen, Jamie leaped over his slumped body and ran toward the stone where Miranda had ducked out of sight. There had been no other gunshot, but images of potential disasters flickered through Jamie's mind.

A snake, disturbed beneath the stone. The soil was too damp for scorpions, but what about a poisonous spider? *God, let it only be a dead faint,* Jamie prayed in his mind. Miranda had succumbed to a swooning fit and had been unable to fire her weapon.

As he rounded the stone, he found Miranda hunched over on her knees, heaving her guts out on the mossy ground. Jamie knelt beside her. The scarf covering her head was slipping and a tangle of golden hair had spilled forward, obscuring her face.

"All right, Princess?" Jamie said softly and swept her hair aside.

Miranda gave no response. It appeared as though she didn't even hear him. Her face was ashen, the blue eyes staring blindly ahead. The pupils had contracted into small black dots, as if suddenly exposed to bright light. Her breathing was light and swift, her body rocking gently. With each breath she took she emitted a tiny wailing sound.

"It's okay, Princess," Jamie said and bundled her into his arms. At first, her body was rigid but gradually the tension melted away. Her head settled on his shoulder. Her rocking ceased and she stopped making that terrible wounded-animal sound that had been tearing him apart.

How could he have been so stupid? How could he have let her take part in a gunfight? He recalled his first time killing a man, the surge of fear and guilt and self-loathing that came after. How could he have asked the same of her? How could he have expected Miranda to aim her gun at another human being and be prepared to pull the trigger to end a life?

"I'm sorry, Princess. I'm sorry." It was him who was rocking now, kneeling together with her, one arm wrapped around her shoulders, the other hand stroking the tangle of golden hair in a rhythmic, soothing motion.

Finally, Miranda spoke, in a small, fragile voice. "I couldn't do it."

"Of course you couldn't do it, sweetheart. You're no killer."

"It's not… It's not that… I think I could have…killed the smaller man…but with the bigger outlaw… I aimed at him, but I kept seeing him with Rose…her arms around his neck, kissing him…in my mind… I saw her collapsed beside his dead body, weeping for him… I could almost feel her grief… I couldn't do it…not because of him… but for her…"

Miranda lifted her head. To Jamie's relief, her eyes had lost that glazed look. Her breathing seemed easier but he could feel her body trembling. Ignoring the throb in his side, he tightened his arms around her to pull her closer, into his warmth, but she resisted the gesture and leaned away. She settled her hands on his shoulders, pushed him back and met his gaze.

"I nearly got you killed." Her tone was flat, emotionless.

"I'm fine, Princess. Just a scratch."

In truth, it was a bit more. Jamie could feel the pain throbbing where the bullet had grazed his side. A flesh wound, perhaps a cracked rib, but his lungs were intact, and there was no severe bleeding. Provided he got any bone fragments out and managed to keep the wound clean, it would leave no permanent damage.

"Let me see." Miranda fingered the bullet hole in his tan buckskin coat. Puzzled, she inspected the tear. "I don't understand. The hole is right over your heart."

Jamie smiled, trying to lighten the mood. "You think I have one?"

She sent him a frown of irritation. Jamie breathed another sigh of relief. Good. His quick-tempered, stubborn little Eastern princess was coming back to him.

"Look," he said. Wincing at the pain, he eased his arm from around her. "My coat is a loose fit. When I shot the man who stood on the cabin doorstep, I was holding my left arm out, like this." He lifted his arm to demonstrate. The small hole in his coat shifted over to the left, no longer marking his heart but the side of his rib cage.

"Just a scratch," he added, fighting the dizziness.

"I almost got you killed."

"When you're talking about dying, Princess, *almost* doesn't count. I'm right here, very much alive. And now," he said, pushing up to his feet, "we need to get going."

"Shouldn't we...?" She glanced toward the two slumped bodies.

"Take them in? No point. They're not worth a plugged nickel dead."

"I meant, should we not bury them, and take care of their horses?"

"The horses have grazing and water. They'll be fine until someone comes. And we'll leave the burial for Rose. She can decide if she wants to bury them out here, or in the cemetery in town. Then she'll know for certain that her man is dead. If she comes here to find him gone and a burial mound in the ground, she'll never know for sure unless she digs up the grave to inspect the bodies. She might spend years waiting and hoping."

"I could write a letter, tell her what happened."

"I don't think you should do that, Princess," Jamie said with a touch of irony. "The mining company won't be too impressed with the fact that I shot the only two people who know where their gold is hidden."

He held a hand out to Miranda. "Let's go."

She laced her fingers into his, but when he turned to lead her away, she tugged him back. Jamie paused, waited. She was frowning, as if puzzled over something. Her words were spoken awkwardly, with the gravity of some new idea she couldn't shake out of her mind.

"While I was waiting behind the stone—"

"That's what bounty hunting is mostly," Jamie cut in. He wanted to prevent any ideas of another stakeout, in case Miranda was entertaining some foolhardy notion of showing him another wanted poster and going after more outlaws.

His tone sharp, he continued, "Bounty hunting is lots of time wasted drinking in saloons, trying to pick up bits of information and then patient trailing that culminates in a long, boring wait, and a few seconds of staring death in the face. It's not exciting. It is ugly and bloody and wearing on the nerves."

"I know." Miranda stole another glance at the fallen Hardin brothers. "What I was going to say is, how did you know that the three of them wouldn't leave at the same time? That the men would not ride out with Rose?"

Jamie hesitated. He owed Miranda an answer to her question, but it troubled him to tell her something that so plainly summed up his shortcomings as a protector.

"An outlaw, like these men, never relaxes. He is constantly aware of danger, prepared to defend his life. You saw how they opened a cabin door. Slowly, peering out to make sure everything was quiet outside before they emerged."

He paused, then finished. "Alvin Hardin would not have left the safety of the cabin until Rose had ridden away. If he loved her, he would not have taken the risk of her getting caught in the cross fire if a bounty hunter or a lawman ambushed him."

Jamie led Miranda up the slope, out of the clearing, through the pine forest to where the horses stood waiting. A crushing sense of failure settled over him. He had just explained to his wife that he had shown less concern for her welfare and safety than the outlaw had shown for the welfare and safety of his sweetheart.

Chapter Twenty-Five

Jamie sat on Sirius, one arm around Miranda, anchoring her to his chest. He had decided to ride double, for she seemed quiet and withdrawn, almost disoriented. Twilight was falling when they emerged from the cover of the forest to the grassy foothills. On the right, the river murmured with a steady ripple. Bats darted in the air, like black flashes that vanished before the eye had time to focus on them.

Jamie kept going at a slow walk until it became too dark to ride safely. He reined in on a flat stretch of riverbank bordered with big boulders. "We'll camp here for the night."

In silence, Miranda slid to the ground. Instead of tackling the chores with the brisk efficiency she'd worked so hard to develop, she stood aimlessly on the spot. Even in the darkness, Jamie could see the rigid set of her shoulders and her fraught expression.

What was she thinking? What images were flashing before her eyes? Would her mind ever be free of the bloody scenes of the afternoon?

"Could you unsaddle the horses?" he asked, hoping the familiar routine might snap her out of her withdrawn state.

Miranda gave no response, not even a nod. Jamie waited, was about to repeat his request when she moved. In odd, jerky steps, almost like a puppet controlled by some unseen force, she went to the horses, unsaddled them and led them down to the water to drink.

Jamie kept an eye on her while he fried beans and jerky for supper. He might have shot a turkey while they were in the forest, but he had not wanted to fire his gun, for the sound might have brought the terror of the killings back to Miranda.

Finished with the horses, Miranda resumed her aimless pose.

"Food's ready," Jamie called out to her. "Come and sit down."

She shuffled over and sank down beside the fire, not pausing to inspect the ground or select the most comfortable spot. When he handed her a plate and fork, she took them without comment. Still and silent, she stared into the flames, the beans and jerky going cold on the tin plate balanced in her lap.

His own appetite was no better. Jamie scraped the food back into the pan, took Miranda's plate and did the same, then clipped a lid on the pan. The food would serve for lunch tomorrow.

"Why don't you set out the bedrolls?" he asked.

Miranda got up. Jamie went to rinse the dishes in the stream and took the opportunity to deal with his wound. He ought to have attended to the injury earlier, but he had wanted to keep the extent of damage to his body hidden from Miranda.

He took off his coat and stripped away his shirt. The fabric was stiff with blood but the bleeding had ceased. Lifting his arm, Jamie inspected his side. There was no entry or exit wound, merely a groove that ran along his side, like a furrow in a freshly plowed field.

Jamie hopped onto a flat stone by the edge of the water, leaned over the swirling current and bathed the wound, slowly washing away the dried blood. Pain hovered on the edge of his mind. Stoically, he kept it there, refusing to acknowledge the sensation.

A thought crossed his mind. *There's more of the Indian in me than I realized.* He possessed the ability to endure greater pain and more hardship than most men did.

When the gash in his side was clean, Jamie went to his saddlebags, applied a coat of herbal salve to prevent infection and put on a dressing and a clean shirt. Miranda lay huddled on a bedroll next to a big boulder. At least her mind had not completely shut down. It may have been subconscious, but she had settled in the safest place, protected by the rocks. And she had spread his bedroll beside hers. Relief flooded through Jamie. She was not rejecting him, horrified by the visions of him as a ruthless killer.

He walked over and lay down beside her. He wanted to ask her to swap places with him, so he could lie on his good side while he cradled her close to him, but she seemed asleep. He curled up beside her, the pain in his side aggravated by the pressure against the hard ground. *Penance,* he thought. But it wouldn't be enough. Nothing would ever be enough to gain absolution from having exposed Miranda to danger.

Carefully, he slipped his arm around her. Perhaps sleeping on his injured side was better after all. It hurt more, but his good arm could hold her tighter against him. Jamie pulled her into the shelter of his body. She was stiff, unresponsive. He could feel her shivering.

"Are you cold?" he whispered.

"Yes."

So she was awake. Jamie tucked the blankets more snugly around her. For the rest of the night, he lay awake, accepting the bitter truth. He had acted rashly, without proper judgment, something a bounty hunter could never afford to do if he wished to remain alive.

He had followed the lure of the image he could see in his mind—a piece of land, with horses prancing in corrals. A house on the land—a proper house with papered walls and lace curtains in the windows—and Miranda in the house.

The dream had grown in his mind, like the desert came alive after a burst of rain. He had seen her belly rounded with his baby, a passel of children racing around the yard, their laughter and joyous voices ringing through the air.

A happy family. And he had wanted to be four thousand dollars nearer to that dream. He had succumbed to the idea that the gulf between him and Miranda was no more than a narrow ditch he could jump over with ease, when in truth it was a rift as wide as the great canyon of the Colorado River they had yet to cross.

He was a bounty hunter, a man who lived by his gun, a man whose survival depended on luck and a split-second advantage against an outlaw prepared to kill him. It was the only life he knew—just as he had once told Miranda.

Miranda had wanted to team up with him in his dangerous profession, to help him reach out for that dream. And what had he done? Instead of giving her the taste of adventure she had been seeking, instead of giving her the secure future he had promised, he had plunged her into his dark world of violence and death.

There was only one penance great enough.

He had to give up the dream. He had to give up Miranda.

For he could think of no other way to keep her safe.

Miranda lay in Jamie's arms. She wanted his warmth, wanted to be comforted by his strong body pressed against hers, but the peace and contentment didn't come. Cold shivers rippled over her as she struggled with the knowledge that had revealed itself during that terrible instant framed by the roar of gunfire.

She'd been foolish, foolish in her quest for adventure. She'd been lured by the excitement, by the thrill of danger. Bounty hunting had seemed like a game, where those on the side of the law always won. Instead, it was real and bloody and ugly and lethal—a gamble with one's life.

She loved Jamie. And she had failed him. She had appealed to his love for her, to the longing for a home and family he hadn't been able to hide. She had encouraged him to dream. And then she had almost gotten him killed.

Why hadn't she pulled the trigger? The answer was simple. And it was complicated. When she'd aimed her gun at the outlaw, she'd pictured Rose embracing him, but another mental image had superimposed itself over it—herself and Jamie, dancing and kissing in the firelight.

What would it feel like, if he died? The mere thought had filled her with a sense of loss so tearing it had felt as if her heart had ceased beating. She couldn't do that to another woman. Couldn't be responsible for plunging Rose into that dark world of grief. And, through her hesitation, she had almost brought that grief upon herself.

What future could she and Jamie have?

How could their worlds unite?

It would be impossible…impossible…

She had insisted they could be a team, but it was not in her to face death or be prepared to deliver it, however honorable it might be to bring an outlaw to justice. It would never work for her to join Jamie as he hunted for outlaws, courting danger while he saved money to buy land of his own. And yet she could not tolerate the idea of waiting in Gold Crossing while Jamie went away, "taking care of business" as he called his deathly trade.

It might take years for him to save enough money for his dream. During all that time, fear would rule her life. Every letter, every telegram, every sight of a stranger who might ride in with news would fill her with terror, until fear overshadowed everything else. Until she almost welcomed the news of Jamie's death, for that meant she could stop being dominated by fear and get on with the grieving.

Of course, Charlotte had money...

Miranda frowned into the darkness. Papa might have been wrong to follow the English custom of leaving everything to the firstborn, but he had been adamant that the fortune tied up in the shipping line must not be broken up. It would be unfair to ask Charlotte to ignore their father's wishes. And Miranda very much doubted Jamie's pride would allow him to accept money from his wife's relatives.

There was only one answer.

She must give him up.

She must sever all ties with Jamie.

Once he was gone, she would find some worthwhile activity to occupy her days. In time, the memories would fade. She would build a satisfying life as a spinster aunt. Or, perhaps one day she might forget Jamie enough to settle down with someone else. Even as the thought formed in her mind, Miranda knew it would never happen. She would grow old alone.

Jamie had feared that once Miranda recovered from the horror of the shootings she might insist on another bounty hunt. He could not have been more mistaken. Instead of making demands, she withdrew into herself.

Each day, she performed her chores in melancholy silence. In the evenings, as they sat by the firelight, she no longer bombarded him with questions. The distance between their bedrolls grew each night, until they were sleeping so far apart Jamie could no longer hear the words to the forlorn melodies Miranda sang softly in the darkness.

"We'll cross the Colorado River today," he said as they broke camp.

Miranda nodded and slipped the silver-studded bridle on Alfie.

"We'll take Lees Ferry," he added. "It's operated by Mormons."

"Men with many wives."

Good luck to them, Jamie thought. He hadn't been able to keep one wife safe, let alone several of them. "I hear the Mormons cultivate the valley on both sides of the river," he went on. "The horses will have alfalfa, and there'll be fruit and vegetables to buy."

"That's nice," Miranda replied.

Jamie frowned as he tried to think of something more to say. Things seemed to have reversed between them. Miranda had become the quiet one, and he was desperate to talk, to shake her out of the shell she had formed around herself.

In the past week, they had shared the trail with other travelers, mostly Mormon settlers, spreading from Utah into Arizona, but not even the company of friendly strangers had restored Miranda's former liveliness.

Jamie wished he had a nimble mind, the kind that could spin funny stories and tell jokes. In some way, the journey now reminded him of the ride to Devil's Hall after he won her in the bride lottery. The same strained atmosphere, the same doubt over what would happen when they reached their destination.

At Lees Ferry, they rode down the steep slope of rust-red earth, into the narrow valley where the river gushed between its banks with a mighty roar. Ahead of them, a party with a dozen head of cattle was chasing the frightened animals onto the craft.

The ferryman was called Johnson. Jamie told him they would wait for the next crossing. He paid the fare, one dollar fifty for a horse and rider, and two bits each for the pack mules.

"Don't go anywhere," he warned Miranda, leaving her to feed the horses with the bundles of freshly cut alfalfa he'd bought from a farmer's stall.

He came back with a melon that had cost too much. Something eased inside Jamie when he saw a smile brighten Miranda's face. He sliced the ripe, sweet-smelling fruit for her and watched her eat it, only tasting some when he was sure she'd had enough.

"Ready?" he asked when the ferry inched back across the river.

"Ready," Miranda replied.

The ferry was a big scow, twice as long as it was wide, with knee-high sides. There was no steel cable to guide it across. Jamie recalled hearing stories of how the current had once seized the craft and hurtled it downstream, drowning everyone on board.

They led the horses on board first, and then the pack mules, their hooves echoing on the timber planks. One of the Mormon wagons filled the remaining space.

"Come and stand beside me," Jamie called out to Miranda, who had ventured to the edge where a cool spray from the river was flying up.

Without a comment, she returned to his side, pausing to reassure the restless Alfie. Of all the changes in Miranda this one worried Jamie the most, made him fear that her spirit had been crushed by the horror of the shootings—she had begun to obey his commands.

Chapter Twenty-Six

Each day, Miranda's mood sank deeper into gloom. Did she really want her marriage to Jamie to fade away? She had made her decision that she must give him up after her failure had nearly cost him his life but she had never expected it would be so easy to drift apart.

When they reached Flagstaff, Miranda sent another telegram to Charlotte and received a reply that her sister and her husband would meet them at the Imperial Hotel in Gold Crossing two days later. The trail became a bittersweet collection of lasts.

Last evening camp.

Last morning sunrise.

Last packing of the mules.

Last stop for coffee.

They drew up along the dusty thoroughfare through Gold Crossing at dusk. Startled, Miranda surveyed the town. It was nothing but a single street of ramshackle buildings, most of them boarded up. Farther away, she could see a small white church and another tiny building that might be a school.

Half a dozen children were racing up and down the rutted street, playing some kind of game with sticks and hoops. When Jamie and Miranda dismounted outside the building that bore a sign for the Imperial Hotel, a boy of around ten separated from the others and hurried over.

"Hey, mister, I'll watch your mules for two bits."

Jamie tossed the boy two quarters. "Watch the horses, too."

He'd be a good father. The thought flashed in Miranda's mind. Then she was up the steps and through the doors. A cozy, civilized scene met them inside the hotel. Two elderly matrons sat knitting at one of the tables, acting as chaperones for a couple taking tea at the next table. A tall man with neatly trimmed light brown hair played solitaire behind a reception counter in the corner.

"Captain Blue!" The joyous call came from near the window.

Miranda spun around. "Bosun Flint!"

The two sisters ran into each other's arms. "Where's Scrappy the Deckhand?" Miranda asked. The childhood nicknames emerged at times of high emotion. When other girls might have played with dolls, they had played pirates, with velvet patches over one eye and mustaches drawn on with charcoal and swords made from sticks of wood.

"Annabel hasn't arrived yet," Charlotte replied. She eased away and gave Miranda a thorough survey. "You look wonderful. I had a Pinkerton agent looking for you at every stop between Boston and Gold Crossing but you fooled him by going the wrong way. I hope Annabel has not done the same. And what was your strange message about Cousin Gareth?"

Pausing for breath, Charlotte turned to wave someone forward. A big man with a powerful body and hair as golden as a wheat field stepped forward.

"Meet my husband, Thomas Greenwood." Charlotte gestured between them, an introduction fitting for a Boston parlor. "Thomas, this is my sister Miranda, the beauty of the family."

"You're just as beautiful," the blond giant said, with an adoring look at Charlotte.

Miranda decided there and then that she liked her new brother-in-law. She glanced behind her. Jamie was standing to one side. Unlike the other men in the room, he hadn't removed his hat, as if to indicate he wouldn't be staying.

"This is James Blackburn," Miranda said. "My…"

Jamie stepped forward. "We signed a piece of paper to say we're married. Made it easier on the trail. Now that Miranda is safe with her family she can arrange an annulment."

Charlotte, the small and slight Charlotte with big hazel eyes and tumbling dark curls, had a way of surprising people by turning into a tiger when they had taken her for a mouse.

She lifted her chin. "I know my sister. She is wild and reckless, and there is absolutely no way I shall accept responsibility for keeping her safe. That will remain your task until you cease to be her legal husband, and after that she can terrorize the world on her own."

Oh, the surprise on Jamie's face! Miranda stifled a grin. For an instant, amusement lifted her spirits. Charlotte had done it again, shown her hidden claws. And now the eldest sister was directing her blunt, probing questions at Miranda.

"Are you married to this man or not?"

Miranda's response was a quick flicker of her eyes. *Not in front of the parents,* it had meant when Papa and Mama still lived. Now she hoped Charlotte would understand the new meaning. *Not in front of husbands.*

Charlotte gave a light nod. *I understand. Later.*

"I guess I'll be heading off," Jamie said.

"We booked a room for you," the blond giant said. "Only one room, though. We didn't know Miranda had a husband. I assume you were properly married, under your real names, so you will be man and wife until the annulment." His blue-green eyes twinkled at Charlotte.

Miranda's curiosity flared. It appeared that she was not the only sister whose matrimonial state wasn't quite straightforward.

"Mr. Langley, do you have a room for Mr. Blackburn?" Charlotte called out.

Miranda could see Jamie tense as he glanced over at the innkeeper, who kept turning his cards over on the reception counter. The tall man looked up. "I only one have one room, so the couple has to share. Just a warning, though, this place is run as an orphanage now. I guarantee no peace or quiet, but the room is clean and warm."

Jamie lifted his brows at Miranda. She nodded. With a bittersweet jolt she realized the art of wordless communication was no longer limited to sisters. She watched Jamie walk up to the counter, fill in a card to register. What would he write?

Mr. and Mrs. James Blackburn?

James and Miranda Blackburn?

Suddenly, it seemed important to know. She hurried up beside him, glanced at the card before he handed it back to the man behind the counter.

James and Miranda Blackburn.

Married…for just a little while longer.

Miranda sat on the floor in front of the small stove, drying her hair. She had bathed downstairs, and now Jamie was taking his turn. Instead of joining Charlotte and her husband for supper, Miranda had arranged for a tray to be brought up to the room.

The door swung open. Jamie walked in, soundless in

his bare feet, boots carried in one hand. He wore a clean shirt and trousers, the dirty ones slung over his arm. Miranda watched him as he crouched to pack his things in his saddlebags.

"There's cold chicken and bread and ham." She gestured at the tray set out on the small table beside her. "Shall I pour you a cup of coffee?"

Jamie glanced up. "We're not eating downstairs?"

Miranda shook her head. "It's too late."

And I wanted one more evening with you. Her gaze drifted around the room. Furnished with heavy pieces, the setting reminded her of the honeymoon suite in the railroad town after they left Devil's Hall. A painful mix of doubt and regret stirred inside her. What might have happened there if she hadn't been in such a hurry to get away from Cousin Gareth? And could she make it happen now?

Her fingers rose to the buttons at her neck. Why hadn't she put on her pale blue wool gown with a low neckline, instead of the shapeless dress made from an old shirt? How would Jamie react if she slowly pulled the garment over her head, baring herself in front of him?

Would he take what she offered?

Would he seal their marriage and be forced to stay?

"What's on your mind, Princess?"

"What makes you ask?"

"The expression on your face. You look ready to fight."

Fight? Perhaps it was the right word. Fight for the future, fight for what she wanted. For, despite her decision that she must give up Jamie, Miranda had never believed it would come to that. She had thought *he* would be the one to fight—fight to hold on to her, fight to remain her husband, but to the contrary, he seemed keen to be on his way.

"I'll leave the mules with you," Jamie said. "Your sister can use them on the farm. The livery stable has closed down but Art Langley lets people put their horses in the stalls, provided they do the cleaning. I've arranged for one of the orphanage boys, Timothy Perkins, to muck out after Alfie. He'll do it for two bits a day. I've paid him for the first month."

Tidying up loose ends. That's what he was doing. If it didn't hurt so much, it would have made Miranda laugh. How to get rid of an inconvenient wife while still doing the honorable thing and looking after her.

"I can muck out after Alfie," she told Jamie, an edge of bitterness creeping into her tone. "At least I now know how to do it. Something good has come out of this temporary marriage. I am no longer a spoiled Eastern princess."

"You never were." Jamie put down his packed saddlebags, then noticed her forlorn expression and took a step toward her. "Oh, Princess... Miranda. Don't..."

"It's all right." She spoke lightly, fighting back tears.

Jamie came over to her, sat on the floor beside her, long legs stretched out in front of him. Wrapping one arm around her, he pulled her against his side. Miranda had left the hatch open on the small, square stove, and the flames crackled and danced, like a campfire.

How many times had they sat like this?

How many opportunities had she had to tell him that she loved him?

"I'm sorry, Princess," Jamie said softly, as if reading her mind. "There is no other way. I should have known it from the start but I let myself dream. I should have known how hopeless it was when that woman chased us out of her hotel with a rifle. Because of me, you had to sleep in the hayloft. Because of me, you were put in danger, with a stranger grabbing at you in the darkness. Because of me, you witnessed death and bloodshed.

"I can't ask you to give up your safe, comfortable life.

I saw my mother and my sister give up everything for love, and they ended up alone, penniless, with children to support. I won't allow that to happen to you."

"You have it backward."

Puzzled, Jamie contemplated her. "Backward?"

Miranda studied his face, storing it in her memory. His hair was damp, framing his features that looked stark and fierce in the flickering firelight. She met his gaze, the deep, mysterious gaze in those clear gray eyes, and held it while she formulated her thoughts.

"It was not your mother, or your sister, who made the sacrifice. Your mother had already come out West to marry a soldier, even though she ended up marrying a different one. And your sister had already chosen to move to the reservation, to embrace the Indian ways. She merely reinforced that choice by marrying a man with Indian blood."

Miranda lifted one hand to emphasize the words that tumbled out as she finally understood the restless frustration that had been niggling inside her. The only way for them to stay together was for Jamie to give up bounty hunting, but she couldn't demand it, or seduce him so the choice would be forced upon him.

"Can't you see?" she went on. "It was your father who made the sacrifice. He married your mother, and as a result he lost his career as a soldier and suffered public disgrace. And it was not your sister but her husband who made the sacrifice. He wanted to hunt buffalo, but he had to take up the white man's ways, prospecting for gold, so he could support a wife and child. Just like it is with us…"

Just like how with us it is you who needs to make a sacrifice. Give up bounty hunting. That is the only solution. But I love you, and I can't ask you to give up the only life you know.

Jamie made no reply. Miranda felt his arm tighten

around her. He lifted his hand and stroked her hair. One more time, Miranda wanted him to kiss her. One more time, she wanted to feel his body pressed against hers.

She tilted up her face. Her eyes misted, making her vision blurred, but she refused to cry—refused to spoil their last moments together with a show of weakness—yet when she spoke her voice was thick with tears. "Do I always need to ask?"

Jamie would have never admitted to being a coward but he knew it to be true, for he wished he had ridden away instead of staying for the night. Why did saying goodbye have to be so hard?

"You don't have to ask," he replied to Miranda's question.

Adjusting his position on the hard floor, he leaned over her, cupped her face between his hands and lowered his mouth to hers. This time, the kiss was soft and tender, one of parting, a kiss that tasted of farewell and tears, of lost opportunities and sorrow.

Miranda understood it, too, for she made no effort to deepen the embrace. When Jamie lifted his head, he could feel her following him, trying to prolong the moment, trying to postpone the instant of parting.

He leaned back and let his gaze drift over her features, memorizing them. Already, the grief of loss ached in his chest. A part of him, the part of him that lacked chivalry, wished he'd bedded her, had not left her virginity for some other man to take.

He would have given anything to feel her naked skin against his, even if just once. To be inside her, just once. To make her his woman, in a way that could never be turned back, never be wiped away, never be forgotten or denied. But of course, it couldn't be.

"Don't be sad, Princess," he said. "It's for the best."

She blinked to stop the tears from falling. "I know."

He wished he had something to give her, some memento to remember him by. Something she could take out once in a while as the years passed and recall her youthful adventure with a bounty hunter.

But he had nothing to give her. All he had ever bought her was boy's clothing, a gun and a bedroll. Of those, only the gun would last through the years, leaving Miranda's only memento of him an instrument of killing. Perhaps that was fitting.

In the stove, a piece of timber collapsed, sending up a hiss of sparks. Heat enveloped them. From downstairs came the sound of a trumpet playing a mournful tune. Jamie pulled Miranda tighter against his side and resumed the slow, smooth stroking of her hair.

He wanted to tell her that he loved her, wanted the words said between them, just once, but he knew it was no use. Why deepen the wound? It was best for her to forget him, find someone else. A man who could keep her safe, give her the kind of life she deserved.

He could feel her body trembling against him, understood how hard she fought to keep the tears inside. He did not wish to drag out the parting. He had to leave her while he could summon up the strength to do the right thing.

"Sleep, Princess," he said softly. "I'll watch over you."

With a tired sigh, Miranda relaxed against him. Minutes passed. Jamie saw her eyelids flutter down, heard her breathing grow slow and even. Her head drooped to his shoulder. When he could be sure that Miranda slept, he eased their bodies apart.

Taking care not to wake her, Jamie got to his feet, leaned down to scoop her into his arms and carried her over to the bed. He lowered her down on the mattress, settling her beneath the covers and tucking them snugly around her.

Straightening, he watched her for a long moment. Her hair fanned over the pillow, like a web of gold. Her smooth complexion was tanned to honey. One of her fists was clenching and unclenching. She must be having a dream.

"Dream of me once in a while, Princess," he whispered.

Then he turned on silent boot heels and walked out of the room. Out of her life. Back to the lonely existence of a man who earned his living by hunting down other men. A man who had no home, no family, and whose only hope for the future was to meet a good death.

Chapter Twenty-Seven

Jamie lay flat on his belly at the top of the cliffs, surveying a narrow canyon and the path that came up from it. For a week, he'd been trailing Frank Floyd, a small, wiry outlaw known as Nine Lives Floyd. Wanted dead or alive, the man had robbed a bank in a mining town called Burnt Oak, killing a female customer who had panicked and started screaming.

Since the death of his sister, Jamie had been particularly eager to hunt men who robbed banks. And all through his years in the business he had detested outlaws who were prepared to kill a woman. In addition to the bounty of five hundred dollars, Frank Floyd gave him the satisfaction of ridding the world of a piece of scum who had done both.

The slow, steady clip of a horse's hooves against the stony ground alerted Jamie. He peered into the shadowed depths of the canyon. The midday sun burned against his back, coating his skin with sweat and parching his mouth with thirst, but he hadn't made a single move since he settled into his vantage point at the first glimmer of dawn.

At the bottom of the canyon, a lonely rider emerged between the rocks. Pinto pony. Thin, wiry man with two cartridge belts crossing his body, bandit style. Fancy black

Stetson, with concho beads of silver. Winchester rifle strapped to the saddle.

Jamie eased forward on top of the cliff. He moved with supreme care, not letting a single grain of sand ripple down into the canyon, where all sound would be magnified with an echo from the walls.

He waited for the outlaw, now hidden out of sight, to climb up the path. The moment the pinto emerged between the rocks, Jamie intended to call out a demand to surrender. He was not afraid of gunfire. A man with his six-shooter already drawn had an advantage against a man with his weapon still in a holster.

Wait for the best line of fire, about ten paces along. Nine. Eight. Seven. Six. Five. Four. Three. Two. Now!

Jamie lifted the revolver in his right hand and took aim. When he tried to cock the hammer, a sudden pain pierced his palm. His fingers refused to work. The sweat on Jamie's skin turned to ice. He barely managed to bite back the demand to surrender he'd been about to shout out.

At a steady clip, without a care in the world, Frank Nine Lives Floyd rode up the path from the canyon and vanished out of sight where the trail dipped down again. Jamie pushed up to his knees. He lowered the hammer on his gun, slid the weapon into the holster and took out his left-hand gun, just in case the outlaw had spotted him.

Baffled, Jamie inspected his right hand, slowly curling and uncurling his fingers. There was no pain, no stiffness. The puckered white scar in the middle of his palm seemed no different from before.

Dismissing the pain as a cramp that had passed, Jamie settled back down on his belly to wait. Two hours later, Frank Floyd returned, at the same leisurely pace of a man unaware of danger. From this direction, Jamie only had a clear firing line for a second. He lined up his revolver, waited for the right moment.

Use your left-hand gun, his mind whispered, but something held him back. In his head, he could hear the voice of his sister, telling him the scar in his palm would reveal his fate. He'd always refused to accept the Indian superstitions, but now he wanted to know. Wanted to understand what it all meant.

Cock the hammer. Now!

The pain came again, like a hot poker piercing the center of his palm. His fingers twitched, weak and without control. Jamie felt the gun slide from his grip. The long steel barrel hit the rock beneath him with a sharp clatter. If his hand hadn't suddenly come alive and darted out to snatch back the revolver as it skittered along the rock, it would have tumbled down into the canyon.

Holding his breath, Jamie craned forward to see the outlaw's reaction.

The man was riding along at an unhurried pace. The brim of his black Stetson tilted as he cocked his head to listen. He looked left and right, until he noticed the small flurry of grit and pebbles rattling down the canyon wall. Unperturbed, the outlaw rode on.

Jamie knew what Frank Floyd was thinking.

It was just a rabbit, or a bird, or a lizard. For if it had been a lawman or a bounty hunter, the last of his nine lives would be gone and he'd lay sprawled in a pool of blood on the ground, the echo of gunshots ricocheting from the canyon walls.

For three days, Jamie kept up his vigil. He lay flat on his belly at the top of the cliff, as unmoving as a corpse. Without food. Without water. Without fire. Without shelter. The way an Indian brave might do, when seeking a vision to reveal his fate. At night, the desert chill made him shiver. During the day, the sun intensified his thirst and fatigue.

But he endured, as was the Indian way. Four more times, Frank Floyd rode past him, the pinto pony's hooves clattering on the rocky path, as if mocking Jamie for his inability to complete the hunt. Thirst and starvation and exposure to the elements gave Jamie a narrow tunnel focus, the way a human mind does when stripped to the basic instinct for survival.

Finally Jamie understood the meaning of Louise's prophecy. It didn't mean that some infirmity from the old injury would cripple his fingers. It meant that his fingers would refuse to obey a command from his brain. The scar was merely a symbol, the pain a subconscious sign of the mental battle that would change the direction of his life.

He had lost the taste for killing.

Slowly, Jamie crawled back from the cliff edge. Only when he was safely away from the precipice did he scramble to his feet. Staggering, shuffling, he made his way across the rocky ground and tumbled down the slope, half skidding, half falling.

Stunted trees and vermilion stones and clouds of dust swirled in his vision as he forced his feet to move. His tongue felt thick and swollen in his mouth. He could feel his heartbeat all through his body, as weak and insubstantial as a tremor. A tune filled his ears, a feminine voice singing, with no words, merely a soft, mournful melody.

"Miranda," Jamie rasped through cracked lips. "Miranda."

He'd endured his quest to learn his fate, but if his endurance failed to carry him through alive, he wanted her name to be the last word he spoke. He stumbled, fell to his knees. His right hand slammed on an ocotillo branch. A spike pierced his palm in the center of the scar, as if reminding him what his subconscious had been telling him.

His life as a bounty hunter was over.

Jamie swayed upon his knees, pulled the cactus spike out of his palm. He could not feel anything. There was so little life left in him, his nerves couldn't spare the energy to signal the sensation of pain to his brain. He lifted his palm to his mouth, licked away the drops of blood.

It was as if that tiny bit of moisture gave him strength. He scrambled up to his feet and lurched along. A joyful neigh came from the small grassy valley, bisected by a creek, where he'd left Sirius grazing.

Clip-clop. Clip-clop. Clip-clop.

The brown shape of the bay gelding appeared on the edge of his blurred vision. Closer and closer it came, until Jamie could touch the shiny coat, could lean against the powerful flank. His hands reached up, fumbled for the leather canteen tied to the saddle horn. *Please, God, let my fingers work now,* he prayed as he struggled with the cap.

The canteen snapped open. Water spilled onto his shaking hands. Too thirsty to wait, Jamie didn't slosh around the first mouthful and spit out the desert grit and dust, but he drank it all, the grains of sand scraping his throat as he swallowed. Careful not to deliver a shock to his dehydrated body, he drank slowly, pausing to catch his breath between mouthfuls.

When he'd quenched his thirst, hunger made its demands. Jamie walked over to where his possessions lay hidden behind a thick juniper. He pulled out his saddlebags and settled to sit cross-legged on the ground beside Sirius. The gelding kept butting at his shoulders with his nose, blowing and sniffing, nuzzling him with what Jamie took for horse kisses.

He patted the animal, then searched for food in the saddlebags, tossing the rest of the contents aside. A book.

A thick white envelope. A small painting, wrapped in a green-and-brown neckerchief. Jamie uncovered the picture of a small girl and a fair-haired woman riding on a gray Appaloosa. He spent a moment studying the painting, then propped it against a stone, so he could look at it while he feasted on strips of jerky and kept sipping from the canteen.

Water. Food. Rest. The picture of Miranda and Nora on Alfie.

Revived, Jamie let his thoughts wander. *It was your father who made the sacrifice. And it was not your sister but her husband who made the sacrifice,* Miranda had told him.

He understood the message his subconscious was telling him. If he loved Miranda, he had to give up bounty hunting. But how could he support a family? He didn't have the money to buy a piece of land to raise horses. No peaceful business would employ a former bounty hunter. No store would employ a part-Indian clerk. He had an aversion to being underground, which ruled out mining.

Lawman?

Cow puncher?

Those seemed the only options. Jamie's gaze fell on the thick white envelope. The address had been written on a typewriter. "Mr. James Blackburn, Carousel Saloon, Devil's Hall, Wyoming Territory."

The two previous letters had been addressed by hand, jointly to him and Louise. They'd burned them unopened. It was Louise who had insisted they destroy the letters from their mother's family. She had claimed to sense evil when she stroked the envelope with her fingertips.

It had just been a mix of superstition and hate that cut too deep, Jamie suspected. Two years older, Louise had remembered their grandfather's rejection more vividly.

And unlike Jamie, who had gone on the road after their mother died, Louise had remained in town, suffering the sharp edge of prejudice as she tried to keep their mother's dressmaking business going.

Jamie picked up the envelope from the ground. This one was different. Official looking. And it didn't have Louise's name, so the choice was his. Quickly, not allowing the impulse to fade away, Jamie tore open the flap. Inside were several sheets of thick, expensive vellum, each covered with lines of neatly typed text.

Dear Mr. Blackburn,

Enclosed is the last will and testament of your grandfather, Eustace Wilkinson, who passed away in May of this year. As you will see, he has left the bulk of his estate to your cousin, Ethan Wilkinson.

However, there are some holdings in the western territories your grandfather has chosen to bequeath to you. The most important of these is a substantial block of stock in the Denver and Rio Grande Western Railroad, together with land holdings along the railroad tracks. The properties may have significant commercial potential, should the railroad and the towns near it grow and prosper. If not, the land will still have value for ranching use.

There are also significant stock holdings in the Atlantic and Pacific Railroad and Southern Pacific Railroad, as well as several smaller local railroad companies.

In order to claim your inheritance, you are required to contact my office within six months of the date of this letter and fulfill the following two conditions:

1. You will never use your middle name, Fast Elk.

2. You will marry a woman of European white origin.

I await your instructions.

Yours truly,

Lionel McLeod, Attorney at Law.

Jamie scanned the rest of the documents. Listings of land parcels, copies of stock certificates, an excerpt of the will. His fingers tightened around the papers as he recognized the moment of choice. Just like his father and his brother-in-law, he had to give up something for the woman he loved.

How much was he willing to give up for Miranda?

Both he and Louise had middle names, from their father's parents. Louise Katherine after a white captive who had lived the rest of her life as an Indian squaw. James Fast Elk after the Cheyenne brave who had loved his white wife.

Giving up the name meant nothing. Jamie groaned at his grandfather's ignorance. For many Indians, the name was sacred, never to be spoken out loud. When he'd called himself James Fast Elk Blackburn, he'd been using his middle name in the white man's way, mostly to annoy his grandfather.

No, his Indian heritage was not in a name. It was in the blood that flowed in his veins, in his physical features, in the color of his hair and his skin. It was a set of skills already learned, ancient beliefs he had always made an effort to ignore and an affinity with nature.

Anyway, he'd already dropped his middle name on the certificate recording his marriage to Miranda. And he'd already married a woman of European white origin. He had already fulfilled both conditions. Moreover, his subconscious had already told him he must give up bounty hunting. Surely there was nothing else he needed to give up?

Even as the thought formed in Jamie's mind, a cold, hard feeling settled in the pit of his belly. He'd have to give up the hate. The hate that had sustained him over the years, had given him the stiff pride to become a man at the age of twelve.

The childhood trip to Baltimore burned bitter in Jamie's memory. He thought of his mother's shaking fingers as she bundled him into his coat before they fled into the night. He had sworn never to ask for anything from her family again. To accept the legacy, he would have to forgive, for otherwise living on the wealth would tear him apart.

Jamie picked up the small oil painting from the ground. He touched Miranda's face. The longing was like an ache inside him, but the deep, lifelong resentment burned like bile in his gut. How could he forget? How could he forgive the rejection that had driven his mother to an early grave, had marred his childhood and that of his sister?

The hate seemed like a living thing that clung to him with sharp claws. As Jamie wrestled with the pain, he heard a bird sing. He raised his gaze from the painting. A skylark, a bird one normally only noticed in flight, had hopped down onto a rock. Head tilted, the bird studied him, then darted up and soared into the sky.

In that instant, Jamie opened his mind to the Indian superstitions he had always attempted to deny. The spirits of the dead walked among the living. His sister, in the form of the skylark, had just paid him a visit, perhaps to tell him the choice was his to make.

Jamie took a deep breath and closed his eyes, focusing on his inner feelings. On that rocky piece of land beside Sirius, the late-morning sun baking down on them, Jamie let go of the old resentments, let go of the bitterness, let go of the hate. He accepted the gesture of apology from his snobbish, intolerant grandparents and met it with forgiveness.

For a full hour, Jamie sat there, letting his mind purify itself. Finally, feeling oddly at peace, he gathered up the painting and the papers and got to his feet.

Six months, the letter had said. Jamie glanced at the top of the page. "April 11."

He ticked his fingers to count out the months. October. The deadline would be October 11.

His body stilled, then burst into frantic motion. He grabbed the newspaper that had been wrapped around the parcel of jerky and smoothed out the crumpled pages: "Friday, October 4."

He figured out the time backward, day by day. He'd bought the paper exactly a week ago. Today was Friday, October 11. The final day for him to claim his inheritance.

Jamie jumped up, packed away the painting and the rest of his belongings. Forgetting the need to rest and nourish his body, he vaulted into the saddle, dug his heels in the flanks of Sirius and shot down the trail.

Where was the nearest telegraph office? Would it be open when he got there? Would the lawyer accept his message if the office in Baltimore was already closed? When did the deadline end? At the end of business hours East Coast time? At midnight?

Jamie gave up thinking. He rode.

Chapter Twenty-Eight

~~~~~~~~~~~

Miranda pranced up and down on the stage at the Drunken Mule, wiggling her bottom as she sang about a sailor with a girl in every port. Before, she'd enjoyed performing to an audience of lonely, homesick men. How could she be so bored now? Where had her spirit of adventure gone? Why did everything seem so flat and meaningless?

"Take a break, Miss Randi," called out Manuel Chavez, the one-eyed cardsharp who ran the Drunken Mule for Art Langley, the owner. Art Langley owned most of Gold Crossing, but despite his valiant efforts for a revival, the played-out mining town was slowly sliding toward oblivion as an empty, forgotten ghost.

"It's all right, Manuel," Miranda called back. "There's nothing else to do."

The saloon only packed out on Thursday nights when the train came. During the rest of the week, Miranda filled the hours by reading or sewing, or she visited Charlotte and her husband, Thomas, on their farm. Miguel passed the time writing cowboy stories he was trying to sell as serials to magazines.

"A customer." Miguel tossed down his pencil, closed

the exercise book with his latest jottings and hurried to stand behind the counter. "What's your drink, stranger?"

"I'll just watch the show for now."

The deep, husky voice made Miranda's skin tingle. Was she going mad? She kept hearing Jamie's voice at night when she couldn't sleep, but her mind must be slipping if she heard it coming from a stranger dressed in a black broadcloth suit and a frilly white shirt and polished black shoes. She twirled the parasol over her shoulder, resumed her prancing and tried to put some effort into the song.

The batwing doors clattered again. Miranda peered over to the entrance. Two men walked in. One wore round spectacles. The other had a neatly trimmed moustache. Both were around forty, and possessed the self-important air of petty bureaucrats she had learned to distrust.

The stranger with Jamie's voice leaned against the counter and turned to look at the newcomers. He nodded a greeting to them, then darted a glance in her direction. The saloon doors were still swinging and the last rays of the setting sun spilled in through the gap, illuminating his sharply drawn features.

Miranda's heart seemed to leap out of her chest. The man in a frilly white shirt had not only Jamie's voice but his face. And he had Jamie's pale gray eyes. *Jamie!* The name formed on her lips. She was just about to whoop with joy and jump down from the stage and rush out to him when he pivoted on his shiny black shoes and set off up the stairs.

He was going up to the bedrooms! Miranda gripped the handle of the parasol almost hard enough to make it snap. How dare he? How dare he go looking for the favors of a saloon girl before their marriage had even been annulled! Before he had even asked her about the annulment papers! Before he had even acknowledged her presence.

It would serve him right to discover there were no saloon girls at the Drunken Mule. No demand existed for such services in a town which up to recently had only had eight permanent residents.

Miranda tried to keep up her singing but the lyrics muddled up and the notes fell into discord. A crash sounded from upstairs. She tripped on a rapid turn as she craned her neck, alerted by the thud of footsteps along the staircase.

What was Jamie hauling over his arm? It looked like a curtain pulled down from one of the bedrooms. He strode over to the stage, jumped up in a single agile leap and wrapped the dusty velvet fabric around her shoulders. "Haven't I told you not to parade half-naked in front of a saloon crowd?"

He was standing toe-to-toe with her, his hands beneath her chin, his face bent to hers. She could feel the heat of his body, could smell the familiar scents of leather and soap on him.

Miranda's heart was beating so fast it felt like the flutter of a hummingbird's wings. She saw laughter in the crystalline depths of Jamie's eyes, laughter and a promise that made a wild hope soar inside her, but she didn't dare to give in to it, so she kept aloof.

"There is no crowd in here," she replied.

"Five people are a crowd if one of them is my half-naked wife."

"I'm not half-naked. It is only a low neckline, no more revealing than a lady might wear to a ball."

Jamie wrapped his arms around her and lifted her down from the stage, setting her firmly on her feet. After making sure the curtain remained securely covering her, he jumped down to join her.

"Gentlemen, may I introduce my wife, Miranda Blackburn. She used to be Miranda Fairfax from Merlin's Leap, Boston, Massachusetts. She is white, educated to a high standard and brought up in a cultured home. In addition to belting out sea shanties she can sing Mozart and Puccini. Will she do?"

The two petty bureaucrats inspected her, as if she were once again a lottery prize on display. They put their heads together and held a whispered conference. Then the one with spectacles pulled out a piece of paper and held it up in front of her.

"Can you confirm that you are married to Mr. James Blackburn, as recorded on this marriage certificate?"

Miranda leaned forward, scanned the text. "Yes," she said. "But we—"

Jamie bent down to her and silenced her with a quick, hard kiss that made her knees go weak. He increased the pressure of his arm around her, steadying her. Then he flashed a conspiratorial smile at her, straightened and turned toward the two strangers.

"I apologize, gentlemen. I have been separated from my wife for too long. I had hoped to discuss the situation with her in private, but I understand the urgency as you need to continue your journey. Can you confirm you're satisfied?"

The two men nodded. The one with a moustache lifted his briefcase to the table, opened it, pulled out a document and handed it to Jamie. "Congratulations, Mr. Blackburn. Everything is in order. You can send this affidavit to your lawyer in Baltimore. I wish you every success in your new position."

The man closed his briefcase, and the pair of them turned about and walked out. As the doors swung wide, Miranda could see a horse and buggy waiting outside.

"Do you have the annulment papers?" Jamie asked when the buggy had rattled down the street.

Miranda spread her hands in a gesture of defeat. "You try to get them issued. There is no judge, or justice of the peace, only an ancient preacher who is going senile. When you explain what you need, Reverend Eldridge will nod at you, and then he'll pull out his ledger. He'll turn over a new page and smile at you and say, 'Welcome, welcome, dear. What is it I can do for you?' It'll drive you mad."

She didn't add that it could also fill a person with a secret satisfaction. She could honestly claim that she had tried to arrange an annulment, and yet her marriage remained as legal and binding as it had ever been.

"Good," Jamie said. "Simplifies things." He swept a glance around the quiet room and lifted his brows. "Why are you singing in an empty saloon?"

"I have to do something to occupy my time and make myself useful." Miranda patted the curtain that hung like a cloak around her shoulders and sneezed when a cloud of dust tickled her nose. She might as well let Jamie know the rest of her failures.

"I tried to teach school, but I lacked patience. I tried to help Doc Timmerman. He is almost eighty and has arthritis. It turned out that I swoon at the sight of blood."

She didn't mention it was only because every time she saw a bleeding wound she remembered the small round hole on Jamie's tan buckskin coat and the circle of blood spreading around it.

"I thought you would stay with your sister on the farm."

"I did but…" *But it was too painful to watch them so happy while I'm so miserable.* "We decided it is better if I stay in town, in case a telegram comes from my sister

Annabel or the Pinkerton detective who is trying to locate her. She is still missing."

"Are you interested in a new adventure, Princess?" Jamie leaned closer to her. She could feel the warm brush of his breath against her cheek as he bent to whisper into her ear, "How would you like to own trains instead of robbing them?"

Jamie tried to fix back up the curtain he'd torn down and at the same time listen to his wife interrogating him. It had started while he led her up the stairs, questions bombarding him like a swarm of buzzing bees. During the ride over, his thoughts had centered on bedding her, but it seemed he had to clear the hurdle of talking first.

"What are you doing here? Why are you dressed like a bank manager? Who were those two men? Why did they look at me like I'm livestock on an auction block? Why are you not wearing your guns? Have you given up bounty hunting? What did you mean about trains?"

The curtain crashed to the floor as Jamie abandoned the effort. The window faced the gravel back yard, with no buildings opposite. No one could see inside, and he liked the idea of awakening to the dawn light with his naked wife beside him.

He turned around. "I'm dressed as befits my new station in life. Those two men were a lawyer and his aide and they were studying you like a broodmare on an auction block because that's what you were to them. I'm wearing a gun under my coat. I've given up bounty hunting. And I'm here because…"

A twinge of irritation slowed him down. He'd already proposed to her once. Why did he have to do it again, particularly as they were already married? He spoke in a low voice. "A while ago, I asked you a question, Princess. You promised to think about it. And as to the trains…"

He crossed the room, wrapped one arm around Miranda's waist and hauled her close to him. "How would you like to be married to a railroad magnate, Princess? A man rich enough to buy you whatever you wish."

She gave him that look of hers, eyes round as blueberries. "Rich?"

Jamie sighed with frustration. There would be no way around the talking. He ushered Miranda to the small table by the window, settled her in one of the chairs, sat down opposite to her and explained it all to her—trailing the outlaw, the scar on his palm, his grandfather's will.

"You hated your grandfather."

Angry voices along the corridor disturbed the quiet. A child, arguing with an adult. The Imperial Hotel served as an orphanage now, Jamie recalled. A trace of amusement tugged at his lips at the thought that his grandfather had finally succeeded in sending him into one.

"Yes," he said. "I hated the old man. And you were right. I had to give up something for you. Not just bounty hunting. I had to give up the hate. It felt like tearing out something from inside me, but afterward I realized I'd torn out something poisonous. Something I'm better off without."

Miranda jumped to her feet and came to stand over him. Looking down at him, she raked her hands into his hair, stirring the neatly trimmed layers. "It doesn't matter to me if you're rich or poor. As long as I don't have to lie awake every night, worrying that you might be sprawled in the dust somewhere, an outlaw's bullet in you."

Jamie pulled her down to sit on his knee. "Was that a yes, Princess?" His tone was firm. "I want a definite answer. Three months is a long time for a man to wait for his wedding night."

"Three months is an equally long time for a woman."

Jamie leaned forward and rested his forehead against

hers, which also gave him a perfect view down the low neckline of her gown. The impatience that had simmered in him during the long ride over burst into flame. "Princess, can I just have a simple *yes*?"

Miranda tugged at his hair, forcing him to look up at her. Her eyes met his, solemn and without guile. "Yes."

Jamie fought the urgency that seized him. If a man ever needed restraint, it was on his wedding night. He traced one fingertip along the pale upper slopes of Miranda's breasts, letting the sense of anticipation build within him.

"Princess, could you do something for me?"

"What is it, bounty hunter?"

"Do you still have the dress you used to wear, made from an old shirt?"

"I sleep in it every night."

He eased her up from his knee and settled her on her feet. "Go put it on."

Miranda gave him a startled look. Then understanding flickered across her features. She spun around and hurried to the big oak armoire along the wall.

"Close your eyes," she ordered.

"Why? We're married."

"I don't want you to see me fumbling with buttons and hooks and petticoats. Not today. It's not romantic."

Jamie closed his eyes. He had never realized how erotic it could be, listening to a woman undress without being able to see her. The swish of fabric. Dainty footsteps. A rattle on the floor—perhaps a scattered button— and a whispered swearword.

He smiled. "You've come a long way from 'oaf,' Princess."

"So have you," Miranda replied.

Sharp mind she had, his little Eastern princess. Jamie listened, his senses alert. Outside, a horse trotted up. The saloon doors swung and the barkeep called out a greeting. Cooking smells drifted up from the kitchen. It was close to supper time.

"You can look now."

He opened his eyes. Miranda stood a few paces away from him, dressed in the baggy garment that covered her from neck to toe. She had let her hair down, and the thick strands cascaded like a golden cloak over her shoulders. Twilight was falling outside, filling the room with shadows, making her appear as ethereal as a dream.

His heart pounding in his chest, Jamie rose from the chair. He took a step toward Miranda, reached out one arm to touch her, then came to an abrupt halt. It wasn't enough to put his hands on her. He wanted to feel her naked skin against his.

Quickly, Jamie shrugged out of his tailored wool coat and white linen shirt. A man who lived on the road learned to be meticulously tidy, each item in its place, but now he merely tossed the garments aside.

With two determined strides, he closed the distance between them. Fisting his hands in Miranda's golden tresses, he tipped back her head. For a moment he waited, letting the need build up within him until there was no room in his mind for anything else.

Then he settled his mouth upon hers. Rising on tiptoe, Miranda wrapped her arms around his neck and clung to him. Her scent filled his breath. He could feel her feminine curves against him, could feel his arousal fit snugly at the juncture of her thighs.

And yet he refused to hurry. He kept the kiss soft and tender, only slowly letting Miranda taste his hunger. A promise and a demand at the same time. A pledge and a claim. Seconds ticked by. Emotion soared within Jamie. How could he ever have thought he could live without her? He broke the kiss and lifted his head.

"I missed you, Princess."

Her eyes were bright. "I missed you, too."

With unsteady fingers, Jamie eased open the first two buttons on Miranda's dress and slipped one hand inside to cup her breast. He could feel her trembling beneath his touch. His blood was pulsing through his veins, swift and hot, but even then he kept the pace slow.

"Are you hungry, Princess? Do you need to eat supper first?" He glanced over to the bed. "Once I get you in there, it will be a long time before I let you go."

"I'm not hungry."

"Afraid?"

She shook her head. "I know you won't hurt me any more than is necessary."

"I'll do my best." Jamie bunched the worn cotton in his hands and slowly eased the dress up over her head. Miranda helped by lifting her arms, and he pulled the garment away. Taking a step back, Jamie dropped the bundle of fabric to the ground and let his gaze drift over his naked wife.

She was shapelier than he'd expected from having seen her fully clothed, her breasts fuller, her hips more rounded. Her skin glowed pale in the shadows, making her look like a marble statue of a Greek goddess.

"You're too beautiful for words, Princess."

She reached down to his waist. "My turn to see the rest of you."

With fumbling hands, she unfastened his trousers. Jamie sucked in a sharp breath. Was he dreaming? Then a fingernail scraped his skin and the flash of sensation drew a smile to his lips. It was no dream.

Miranda tugged his trousers downward, her fascinated gaze lingering on his erection. Encouraged by her boldness, Jamie lifted up his feet, one at a time, and kicked away the last of his clothing.

Bending down, he scooped Miranda into his arms and carried her over to the big oak bed. Twilight, so brief in the desert, was already giving way to darkness. Jamie straightened by the bedside and surveyed Miranda as she lay naked on top of the covers.

"Shall I light the lamps, Princess? Or would you prefer the room dark?"

"I'd like some light."

Jamie moved around, lit the lamp on the table and two more in wall brackets. The golden glow bathed him as he went about the task. He could feel Miranda watching him.

"I hope you like what you see, Princess."

"I like it exceedingly well."

Jamie had never given much thought to his looks, apart from how they reflected his Indian heritage, but now it pleased him to know his wife found him an appealing sight. He returned to the bed stretched out next to Miranda. "I've dreamed about doing this until I thought I was going mad."

Gentle and reverent, he set out to possess her body, his lips and hands tracing the smooth, fragrant skin. He kissed the side of her neck, the edge of her shoulder, the hollow between her collarbones, slowly making his way down toward her breasts.

When his mouth closed over one puckered nipple, Miranda let out a husky moan. Guided by her response, Jamie sought out the spots on her body that gave her the most pleasure, keeping up the quest until he felt her hips undulate against him in a restless rhythm, asking for more.

He settled over Miranda, his legs sliding between hers. For a moment, Jamie stilled, their gazes locked. He had expected to give her the words later, as they lay side by side, sated and complete, but something compelled him to say them now.

"I love you, Princess. Have from the beginning. Maybe from the first moment I saw you in that saloon, sitting in a rocking chair, looking like an angel."

Miranda reached up and traced his features with her fingertips. "I love you, too, bounty hunter. Maybe not right from the start, but when I saw how deeply you cared for Nora. When you held me through my grief. When you kept me safe on the trail."

Not taking his eyes from hers, Jamie eased inside his wife. Hot and tight and slick, she closed around him, making him quiver with a mix of pleasure and restraint. When the pain came upon her, he could feel her flinch, but she made no sound.

He lowered his head for a gentle kiss. "My brave wife."

Jamie waited until he could feel her relax again, and then he rocked his hips in a smooth, controlled motion. After a while, Miranda wrapped her legs around his waist, anchoring him close, and tentatively she began to meet his movements.

Slowly, Jamie let the tension build between them, holding back until he could tell Miranda was with him. Only when she was writhing beneath him, her hips rising and falling, her body restless with the need for completion, did Jamie increase his pace and force.

Arching beneath him, Miranda cried out, her eyes closed, her body pulsing around him, and Jamie took his own release, burying himself deep inside her. As the waves of pleasure rolled over him, he thought his heart might shatter. He pitied any man who had only known the tawdry imitation of love bought from a saloon girl.

Later, as they lay together, their breathing gradually slowing, the trembling in their bodies subsiding, Jamie braced up on one elbow. Twirling his wife's golden tresses in his fingers, he studied her flushed face. "Sometime soon, I want to take you shopping in San Francisco."

"You don't have to buy me things."

"I'd like to. My mother and my sister lived in poverty and I can't help them anymore. Let me spoil you. To start with, I have a very special wedding present for you."

He handed Miranda a small velvet pouch. Curious, she loosened the drawstring at the top of the pouch and shook the object inside onto her palm. Jamie watched her eyes widen as she inspected the ruby-and-diamond-studded jewel.

"Mama's brooch." She breathed out the words, then glanced up at him. "How did you get it back?"

"I made inquiries with the railroad company. It seems the conductor who arrested you on the train was a stickler for rules. He recorded the woman's details."

Jamie gave a teasing tug to the strand of golden hair he'd wrapped around his finger. "At first, I considered buying the jewel back for you, but it occurred to me you might resent paying for what was rightfully yours. So I went to San Francisco and showed the woman our marriage certificate with the name Fairfax on it and told her the brooch belonged to my wife. She could either hand it over or accompany me to the nearest law office and explain how she got it."

"And she handed it over?"

"With such haste she pricked her skin when pulling the brooch from her chest. I left her sucking at the bleeding finger, looking sour, as if it was lemon juice running through her veins."

Miranda hooted with delight. "Oh, Jamie, you're wonderful. The best husband a girl could have."

She scrambled to lie on top of him, gave him a big smacking kiss on the lips and wriggled downward along his body. She scattered kisses on his chest, then moved lower still, her mouth burning a trail on his belly. Jamie held his breath. The lust that had a moment ago seemed spent surged to life again.

His voice was rough. "Miranda, what are you doing?"

His innocent virgin wife craned her neck to look at him. A wicked smile flashed across her patrician features. "The saloon girls told me there is one thing men ask for more than anything else."

And she lowered her mouth to him and completed her kissing journey. Jamie closed his eyes. His breathing grew ragged. A harsh sound tore from his throat as his wife once again proved her wild, reckless streak. It was a glorious, decadent thing for a gently bred woman to do, and Jamie knew the moment would remain in his memory forever.

Afterward, as they lay in each other's arms, Jamie thought he might never have the strength to move again. Outside, the night had thickened. One of the lamps had guttered out, but he felt too lazy to get up and deal with it.

They talked. To Jamie's surprise, the words came easily now. Perhaps talking was like shooting or riding— with practice you became better at it.

As they shared confidences in the shadowed room, their passions ignited all over again. When the dawn painted the sky pink, Jamie did not awaken beside his naked wife. Instead, he drifted off to sleep, exhausted and languid, his wife tucked into the curve of his body, his arm anchoring her close, one hand cupping her bare breast.

Miranda yawned and stretched beneath the covers on the big bed in their private railroad car, listening to the noises outside. Hooves clattered on timber as the horses came down from the freight car. Metal clunked as the coupling fell down. The iron wheels churned and the engine pulled the rest of the train away, leaving the private car on the side spur.

And finally, footsteps thudded up and the door opened and closed, and Jamie strode in. She never got tired of looking at him. He wore tall boots in polished black leather, fawn riding breeches, and a white shirt hanging loose. He was wiping his hands on a rag. He never let anyone else deal with the horses or the mechanics of their private railroad car.

"What does the town look like?" Miranda asked.

"Like all of them. Has a post office, though."

"It is wonderful to go from place to place and still have your home comforts," Miranda remarked with another luxurious yawn. They had been traveling along the railroad from Denver toward Salt Lake City, exploring the towns along the line.

"I don't know," Jamie said, deadpan. "I was kind of used to the oilcloth lean-to."

Miranda laughed. She swept her gaze around the mahogany-paneled walls and red velvet sofas and brass fittings and the fully equipped kitchen and the door that led to the bathing room. She gave a lazy wave to encompass it all and Jamie within it.

"You fit in here. You look like a Spanish grandee. Or an Italian prince. Or a French count. Or an English duke with a dash of exotic blood in him."

"How about a part-Cheyenne former bounty hunter?"

"That, too." She fell silent, then mouthed *I love you.*

"Doesn't work." Jamie walked over to the bed, bent down to kiss her. "You have to wait until I'm ready."

The night when he came to find her at the Drunken Mule, the night they finally made their marriage complete, had been the first time he'd told her that he loved her. Since then, he had told her again twice, at random moments.

Once, he'd greeted her with the words as she woke. Another time, he'd scraped them in the sand while they sat out having lunch. She had become greedy and impatient, trying to tease the declaration out of him by telling him every day, as if she could make the words echo back from him. But Jamie could not be shaken out of his reticence.

"Did you stop by the post office?" she asked.

Jamie nodded. "No telegrams for you. Sorry."

Miranda bit her lip. She tried not to worry. The Pinkerton detectives still hadn't located Annabel. They were looking for Cousin Gareth, too. Miranda couldn't help thinking there might be a connection, that somehow Cousin Gareth might be to blame for Annabel going missing. She wished now that she had told him the truth, had helped him to recover his memory.

Her attention scattered as Jamie stripped out of his shirt to change into a fresh one. Lean muscles rippled on his belly. Heat suffused Miranda as she thought of how at night she ran her hands along his skin, and how he did the same to her.

Would she ever get used to him? Would she always feel breathless and quivery at the sight of him? Would his touch always make her ache with desire?

Miranda recalled her parents, how they had remained besotted with each other even after gray streaked her father's temples and crow's-feet surrounded her mother's eyes. Would it be the same for her and Jamie? Would the magic between them last?

"Will you still love me when I'm old and gray?" Her question was only half in jest.

Jamie came back to the bedside and smiled down at her. "Of course I will. You are a good investment, and good investments grow and multiply with age."

She sent him a puzzled frown. "I am an investment?"

Jamie bent to press his mouth to her ear, the way he liked to do when he wanted to tease her. "Princess, you were a bargain," he told her. "The best ten dollars I ever spent."

* * * * *

If you enjoyed this story, make sure you check out the first book in Tatiana March's
THE FAIRFAX BRIDES *trilogy*
HIS MAIL-ORDER BRIDE

And don't miss these short sexy reads by Tatiana March
THE VIRGIN'S DEBT
SUBMIT TO THE WARRIOR
SURRENDER TO THE KNIGHT
THE DRIFTER'S BRIDE

COMING NEXT MONTH FROM
HARLEQUIN®

HISTORICAL

Available June 20, 2017

All available in print and ebook via Reader Service and online

FROM RUNAWAY TO PREGNANT BRIDE (Western)
The Fairfax Brides • by Tatiana March

On the run, disguised heiress Annabel Fairfax shares one stolen night with Clay Collier. He knows his dangerous world means they can't wed...but Clay's forbidden bride-to-be is already pregnant with his child!

RUINED BY THE RECKLESS VISCOUNT (Regency)
by Sophia James

Viscount Winterton unintentionally ruins Florentia Hale-Burton's reputation when he abducts her to protect her from harm! Now, years later, Florentia must face the kidnapper who still haunts her fantasies...

CINDERELLA AND THE DUKE (Regency)
The Beauchamp Betrothals • by Janice Preston

Rosalind Allen long ago gave up her marriage prospects—but when she encounters the Duke of Cheriton, he's determined to persuade this wary Cinderella to trust him with her heart!

FORBIDDEN NIGHT WITH THE WARRIOR (Medieval)
Warriors of the Night • by Michelle Willingham

Commanded by her dying husband to provide him with an heir, Rosamund de Courcy must spend one sinful night with Warrick de Laurent... the man she's always loved!

THE FOUNDLING BRIDE (Georgian)
by Helen Dickson

Marcus Carberry is captivated by his family's orphaned servant Lowena Trevanion. But can the returned soldier overcome the difference in their stations to give Lowena the happy-ever-after she deserves?

A WARRINER TO RESCUE HER (Regency)
The Wild Warriners • by Virginia Heath

Jamie Warriner rescues Cassie Reeves only to find himself drawn into working on her storybook. Soon he longs to rescue the lonely vicar's daughter all over again...by making her his wife!

YOU CAN FIND MORE INFORMATION ON UPCOMING HARLEQUIN® TITLES, FREE EXCERPTS AND MORE AT WWW.HARLEQUIN.COM.

HHCNM0617

SPECIAL EXCERPT FROM

⬧HARLEQUIN

✦ISTORICAL

*Desperation forces Georgiana Wickford to propose to
her estranged childhood friend. The Earl of Ashenden
swore he'd never wed, but the unconventional debutante
soon tempts him in ways he never expected!*

Read on for a sneak preview of
THE DEBUTANTE'S DARING PROPOSAL
by **Annie Burrows**.

Georgiana couldn't really believe that his attitude could
still hurt so much. Not after all the times he'd pretended
he couldn't even see her, when she'd been standing
practically under his nose. She really ought to be immune
to his disdain by now.

"Did you have something in particular to ask me,"
Edmund asked in a bored tone, "or should I take my dog
and return to Fontenay Court?"

"You know very well I have something of great
importance to ask you," she retorted, finally reaching the
end of her tether as she straightened up, "or I wouldn't
have sent you that note."

"And are you going to tell me what it is anytime soon?"
He pulled his watch from his waistcoat pocket and looked
down at it. "Only, I have a great many pressing matters
to attend to."

She sucked in a deep breath. "I do beg your pardon, my lord," she said, dipping into the best curtsy she could manage with a dog squirming around her ankles and her riding habit still looped over one arm. "Thank you so much for sparing me a few minutes of your valuable time," she added through gritted teeth.

"Not at all." He made one of those graceful, languid gestures with his hand that indicated *noblesse oblige*. "Though I would, of course, appreciate it if you would make it quick."

Make it quick? Make it quick! Four days she'd been waiting for him to show up, four days he'd kept her in an agony of suspense, and now that he was here, he was making it clear he wanted the meeting to be as brief as possible so he could get back to where he belonged. In his stuffy house, with his stuffy servants and his stuffy lifestyle.

Just once, she'd like to shake him out of that horrid, contemptuous, self-satisfied attitude toward the rest of the world. And make him experience a genuine human emotion. No matter what.

"Very well." She'd say what she'd come to say without preamble. Which would at least give her the pleasure of shocking him almost as much as if she really was to throw her boot at him.

"If you must know, I want you to marry me."

Don't miss THE DEBUTANTE'S DARING PROPOSAL by Annie Burrows, available June 2017 wherever Harlequin® Historical books and ebooks are sold.

www.Harlequin.com

HARLEQUIN®

A Romance FOR EVERY MOOD™

Love the Harlequin book you just read?

Your opinion matters.

Review this book on your favorite book site, review site, blog or your own social media properties and share your opinion with other readers!

Be sure to connect with us at:
Harlequin.com/Newsletters
Facebook.com/HarlequinBooks
Twitter.com/HarlequinBooks